Dear Reader,

One of my earliest memories is going to a bookstore on Cape Cod. My parents vacationed there before I was even born, and after my brother and I came along, they continued to take us there every summer until we moved to the Midwest, where East Coast vacations became a tricky proposition for a young family.

One of my favorite places on the Cape was a bookstore that overlooked the water, and it was a place I returned to often in my memory. So when I heard about the series Secrets of Mary's Bookshop, I was intrigued, and once I started writing I was hooked. Unlike other books I worked on, I didn't have to do a lot of research to learn what the Cape was like. I already knew all about it: the sleepy roads, the pine trees, the quiet bay, the rolling ocean, and the warm freshwater lakes that dot the curve of land in between.

Usually I get to learn all about a new world when I work on a new book. But with this series, returning in fiction to the Cape Cod I'd known as a child felt even better. It felt like coming home.

I hope Mary's world in Ivy Bay will feel that way for you, and that whether or not you've ever been to Cape Cod, this book will make you feel at home, not just in Mary's Bookshop, but also amidst the beauty of the coastal villages of the Cape.

Fondly,
Vera Dodge

Rewriting History

SECRETS *of* MARY'S
BOOKSHOP

Rewriting History

Vera Dodge

Guideposts
New York, New York

Secrets of Mary's Bookshop is a trademark of Guideposts.

Published by Guideposts
16 E. 34th St.
New York, NY 10016
Guideposts.org

Acknowledgments

Every attempt has been made to credit the sources of copyrighted material used in this book. If any such acknowledgment has been inadvertently omitted or miscredited, receipt of such information would be appreciated.

"From the Guideposts Archives" originally appeared in *Guideposts*. Copyright © 2004 by Guideposts. All rights reserved.

Cover and interior design by Müllerhaus
Typeset by Aptara

Printed and bound in the United States of America
10 9 8 7 6 5 4 3 2 1

ONE

Mary stood in the doorway of her bookshop, gazing at the street corner in the twilight. From behind her in the shop came the hum of dozens of voices, punctuated occasionally by peals of laughter and the unmistakable ring of the old-fashioned cash register. Mary had discovered the till, with its heavy drawer and gorgeous brass scrollwork, in an antique store just weeks before she opened the shop. The clunky register might not have been the most practical purchase in the world, but it reminded her of the days she'd spent as a girl in Ivy Bay, decades ago, and the old-fashioned feel and slow pace of life that had drawn her back to town to open the bookshop after she lost John. As soon as she'd seen the old register, she'd marched up to the counter at the antique store and slapped her brand-new business credit card down without hesitation. Then the next day, she sent back the fancy new electronic register she'd already purchased. Of course, she wasn't living in the past as far as business was concerned—she did have an up-to-date computerized system to keep track of accounts and ordering.

And right now, for the first time, somebody else was running the cash register: Rebecca Mason, Mary's very first employee. Or perhaps, Mary thought with a wry smile, Rebecca's seven-year-old daughter Ashley had taken over management of the old cash register.

When Mary first opened the shop, the idea of spending all her days among the books had seemed like a dream come true. But she quickly discovered that, despite her love for the shop, it just wasn't practical for her to try to run it all by herself. The ad she ran in the local paper had brought a flurry of applications, but Rebecca's had stood out among the rest. Rebecca had worked in bookstores in college, was an avid reader, and was a writer as well. She had even attached a page of her publications to her résumé, listing all the little magazines and contests she'd placed in. Mary had been ready to hire her on the spot, but when she called Rebecca for an interview, Rebecca had asked immediately whether Mary would mind if she brought her daughter with her.

"She's seven," Rebecca had told her. "During the school year, she'll be in class during the days, but for the summer months, while her dad is out on the fishing boat, she's with me. She's just great. I think you'll love her."

Mary hadn't been so sure about that. And she hadn't been so sure about the professionalism of a woman asking to bring her child along with her to a business interview. In fact, Mary had started to rifle through the other applications on her desk while she was still on the phone with Rebecca, wondering if someone else might be a better fit. When she ended the call, she told herself that even if the little girl managed to behave herself at the interview, she'd have to be clear with Rebecca that she'd need to find some other place for Ashley during the days, so that Rebecca could concentrate on her work at the shop.

But as soon as Ashley swept into the shop, in a pale blue gingham shirt under a pair of sturdy overalls and her ash-blonde hair in a pair of pigtails, Mary had been undone. And for all her girlish charm, Ashley had comported herself very much like a young lady. She read quietly in the corner while Mary and her mother talked, and then she gave Mary a quite serious review on the strengths and weaknesses of Mary's children's section. And Rebecca herself had done a wonderful job in the interview. She was smart but didn't show off, was confident but not brassy, and had a warmth and quick enthusiasm that Mary knew would be perfect with customers in the shop. Half an hour after Rebecca arrived, Mary had offered her the job, and the interview had changed to a training session. Ashley had padded over to join them, and she caught onto Mary's directions for operating the old cash register before her mother, who was used to the computerized versions she'd used at the bookstore where she'd worked in the past.

"Wait," Rebecca had said after Mary's first explanation. "Do I press this button?" The one she chose was on the opposite side of the real drawer release, but before Mary could correct her, Ashley jumped in.

"No, Mom!" she said and reached unerringly for the right button. At the touch of her small finger, the drawer sprang open, and she regarded Mary and Rebecca with a beatific smile. "See?" she said.

"I don't know," Rebecca had joked. "Maybe you should give the job to her."

Mary had laughed and never did give the speech she'd planned, about how Rebecca should leave Ashley home. For the last several days, since Rebecca started, Ashley and Rebecca had both been a welcome presence in the shop. Rebecca had quickly picked up on Mary's systems for organizing and ordering stock, and she had done a great job connecting with customers and suggesting titles that Mary wasn't even familiar with. And Ashley spent most of her time curled up in the rocking chair in the children's section, reading Nancy Drew and Encyclopedia Brown titles.

"She's such a good reader," Mary had told Rebecca.

Rebecca had sighed. "I know," she said. "I can barely get her to do anything else."

The three of them had established a comfortable rhythm in the shop. Mary had even left Rebecca alone in the shop yesterday afternoon for the first time, while she ran some of the much-needed errands she'd been neglecting since the store opened. But tonight was the big test, not just for Rebecca, but for Mary herself.

Mary glanced down at the cell phone in her hand. There were no new messages or texts. The last call she'd received from Addison Hartley's publicist was to let her know that the famous mystery writer was only a few minutes away.

The publicist's name was Janine Briarwood, and she always spoke in a clipped rush, as if she were trying to spit out the last set of orders before the ship she was on sank. Mary had given her the number at the bookshop half a dozen times, but she persisted in calling Mary's personal phone and calling it at any hour of the day or night. "If you wouldn't mind just meeting us outside," she'd said this time. "We just like to have someone escort us in. Otherwise, you never know what might happen."

Mary's lips had curled into a smile at this. She wondered what sort of danger, exactly, Janine thought the crowd of book lovers waiting inside might pose to Addison Hartley in a safe little town like Ivy Bay, other than a repetitive-motion injury from demanding too many autographs. But she'd gone outside to wait anyway. Addison Hartley wasn't somebody Mary was in a position to refuse. He'd topped the mystery best-seller lists for the better part of two decades, and his books weren't just pulp titles that people cycled through and then tossed away. Each one of them built on the previous, creating a wide, vivid world with seemingly endless detail and backstory. His readers were devoted and passionate, and the Internet was full of message boards where people compared notes on the world he'd created, identifying gaps, guessing at what he might do next—even working up recipes based on meals he'd mentioned in his stories. The president had been photographed last year on Air Force One while reading one of Addison Hartley's books.

He was one of Mary's favorite authors too. In fact, he'd been on the top of the wish list Mary had scrawled for author events when she began to dream about opening the shop. She didn't think he'd really come, but she was dreaming at the time, so why not dream big? And then, after the shop opened and she came across the list again, she thought, why not? She sent an e-mail off to his publicist, inviting Hartley to an author event at the shop, promising that the whole town of Ivy Bay would turn out for it—which they pretty much had.

She hadn't been able to believe her good fortune when Janine wrote back with a handful of potential dates. And she still couldn't really believe that he was about to drive up any minute.

"Should I look for anything in particular?" Mary had asked Janine when they spoke a few minutes ago.

"It's nothing special," Janine had told her. "Just a standard limo."

Mary shook her head. It seemed that Addison Hartley lived in a completely different world than she did. Janine's request for an escort might seem over the top to Mary, but Mary had no idea what he'd had to deal with in the past. She'd never had a crowd of people fighting to meet her or get her autograph. And as far as she knew, nothing she had ever written had been read by the president.

Still, when the limo finally turned onto her street, she had to suppress a smile. Parts of Cape Cod were undeniably high-end, with lavish mansions crowded along the coast and fancy cars clogging the streets. But Ivy Bay had always been a more laid-back community. It was a true fishing village and was out of the way enough that it hadn't been completely overrun by tourists, although more and more of them were drawn these days by Ivy Bay's unspoiled charm. The sight of the limousine nosing its way between Ivy Bay's neat but humble downtown storefronts was just so out of place that she couldn't help but laugh. At the same time, a thrill ran through her. The limousine among the wind-ravaged Cape buildings, the twilight all around, and the fact that Addison Hartley was about to walk into Mary's very own bookstore all had an air of unreality. Still, the little scene on the street continued to play out. The limousine rolled smoothly past the other stores before coming to a stop outside the bookshop.

Mary gave a little wave to let them know they were in the right place and smiled, her eyes darting over the tinted glass of the limousine, looking for any human face that might smile back. The limousine purred at the curb, but no one got out.

Mary's smile faded. She folded her arms, not sure what to do next. Should she wait for them to come to her? They didn't expect her to go down and knock on a window, did they?

As she was wondering, one of the doors of the limousine finally swung open, and a thin, birdlike woman in a black suit got out. Her face was young, but her suit was severe, and her straight black hair was cut in a blunt wedge that fell just to her jaw. She strode across the sidewalk to Mary, stuck her hand out, and gave her a brilliant smile. "I'm Janine," the woman said. "You must be Mary."

Mary smiled and pressed Janine's hand in return. "Welcome to Ivy Bay," she said. "We are just so honored that Mr. Hartley—"

As quickly as it had appeared, Janine's smile vanished, replaced by an expression of intense urgency. "Now, are we all ready in there?" she asked.

Mary tried to give a nod that would give Janine confidence. "I think so," she said. "I think Mr. Hartley will be very pleased. This is one of the biggest turnouts we've ever had at the store."

Mary gave a proud little glance into the store as she said this. The crowd completely engulfed the two comfortable chairs in the reading area in the back of the shop. Mary and Rebecca had brought up chairs from the basement to hold the overflow, but even those were taken now, and many people were standing at the back and even between the shelves. It was a mixed crowd too, because Addison Hartley's fan base was so broad: older men and women Mary knew from church; high school students; a few young couples including the Courts, who owned Meeting House Grocers; and Susan Crosby of Sweet Susan's Bakery. She also saw Leroy Steckler, a man who had known Mary's great uncle George, as well as Tabitha Krause, Mary's mother's childhood best friend. Mary wasn't surprised to see the elderly woman there; when Mary had recently visited the woman's Ivy Bay home, she noticed a Hartley hardcover on the coffee table. And, of course, there was Betty, her sister, who had arrived an hour early to make sure she got her seat in the front row.

Janine frowned in what might have been confusion. "But," she said, "you haven't been open very long, have you? I checked the business history. It's only been a short while."

"Well, yes," Mary said, descending into confusion in her own turn. "But we have had a few events, and—"

"Nothing like this, I'm sure," Janine interrupted her.

"Well, no," Mary had to agree.

"When we bring Mr. Hartley in," Janine said, "we want to start the event immediately. No mingling with fans beforehand. They're welcome to ask questions during the Q and A and have their books signed afterward, but once the line dies down, we'll be leaving. You may need to make some apologies for us. You understand."

Mary nodded, but she was nodding at Janine's back. Janine had turned to the limo again and was opening the back door. A moment later, Addison Hartley himself stepped out onto the sidewalk.

Mary's face broke into a smile. He was a little bit older and a little bit pudgier, but the familiar face that had graced the back of so many of her favorite books was unmistakable. "Mr. Hartley," she said, "we are just so delighted to have you here in Ivy Bay."

As Addison Hartley shook her hand, she noticed another difference between him and his author photo. In the author photos, he always looked straight into the camera, his eyes so piercing, even from the page, that she felt he might be searching out one of her own secrets. But in person, he could barely seem to meet her gaze.

"Please," he said, glancing away, "call me Addison."

He looked into the glowing windows of the shop at the people milling about inside, with something of a haunted expression. But Janine touched his elbow, and he squared his shoulders.

"Everyone's so excited to meet you," Mary said. "Nobody's talked about anything else in the shop for weeks. Or in the town either, really."

"Well," Addison Hartley said, still looking through the shopwindows, "shall we?"

Mary swung the door of the shop open and gestured for him to enter, but he insisted she go first. When she walked into the store, followed by Addison Hartley, with Janine on his heels, the voices rose suddenly in surprise and exclamation and then hushed as the little procession reached the small podium where Mary had set up a microphone and a glass of water for Addison.

She stopped beside it. "Are you ready?" she asked, her voice low. "I'll just introduce you, and then you'll be up."

Addison nodded.

Mary stepped to the microphone and cleared her throat. She glanced over the crowd, taking in the faces of a few old friends and new customers. Her sister Betty gave her a wink from the front row, where she was seated next to her sister-in-law Eleanor. "I'm so glad to see so many of you here tonight," Mary said. "And I'd like to ask you to join me in giving a very special Ivy Bay welcome to Mr. Addison Hartley."

The room broke into applause, and there was even a whoop of enthusiasm from the back.

"Mr. Hartley hardly needs my introduction," Mary said. "Many of you may know him better than you know me."

Laughter rippled through the room.

"He's been on the *New York Times* best-seller list fifteen times since his debut novel *Stones Speak* twenty years ago. He's won Edgar Book, Agatha, and Hammett Awards. But the highest praise I can actually give to him as a bookstore owner is the response his books get from my customers. Some authors write books that people just read to pass the time. But Addison Hartley creates a world where people want to live. His readers love his books. They still remember stories he wrote many years ago, and they can't wait for the next one to come out. To me, that matters more than any best-seller list or award. Ladies and gentlemen, Addison Hartley."

Mary circled back behind the counter as Addison stepped up to the podium. From his basket below the counter, her cat Gus looked up at her balefully, as if asking why exactly she had let all these strangers into their perfectly nice, quiet little store. She bent down and scratched his head. Pretty soon they'd all be gone, and he'd be able to roam the stacks and shelves the way he usually did, curling up on an Agatha Christie omnibus or sprawling out on a stack of the newest arrivals.

To her surprise, Addison Hartley didn't make any of the opening comments that she'd often seen authors give at other events she'd attended, explaining the background of the story or the research he'd done while writing it. Instead, he just cracked open a copy of his latest book and began to read.

Once he started reading, though, nobody seemed to notice the lack of introduction. The story was immediately absorbing: a mystery set in a small coastal town, with lots of touchstones to draw in an audience like Ivy Bay's. Everyone in the shop listened raptly, until he stopped reading about ten minutes later. Then the hands began to go up around the room. Addison chose one and pointed.

When the other hands went down around the room, Mary could see it was Rebecca who had the question. "I'm a writer," Rebecca said, blushing. "And I'm just wondering if you can tell me where you get your ideas? You've written so many books over the years. Where do all the ideas come from?"

Addison Hartley seemed to dodge Rebecca's gaze, Mary noticed, just the way he'd dodged her own. Mary looked at him with sympathy. It seemed like almost every reading opened with this question. She could understand why he might be tired of answering it. "Well," he said, looking up at the ceiling, as if for some kind of help. "I guess you're never really sure where the next idea might come from. You're just glad when it does." Then he added, "But it can be hard."

Around the room, heads nodded.

"Well, you make it look easy," Rebecca said.

He nodded at a middle-aged man in a green-and-blue plaid shirt. The man smiled somewhat nervously. "I'm always impressed with the research that goes into your books," he said. "Can you tell us a bit about that process?"

Addison raised his eyebrows. "Research is just as important as pure imagination to me," he said. "You've heard the sayings, 'You can't make this stuff up' or 'Truth is stranger than fiction.' I find it to be true. A lot of the things that seem strange in my books are actually drawn from real life."

The man in the plaid shirt nodded. "Thank you," he said.

Like everyone else, Mary glanced away from the man in the plaid shirt and looked around again as hands began to go up around him. But then a woman, who stood beside Rebecca near the back, caught her eye. There was nothing flashy about her—she was about Mary's age, with short, well-styled graying-blonde hair, and she wore a conservative collared shirt with white polka dots on navy. She was intensely familiar. Mary had the sense that she'd known her and known her well. But Mary couldn't remember where. Was it college? One of the libraries she'd worked at? Or even further back, from her high school days in Boston?

Then the crowd broke into laughter over Addison's next answer, and the woman smiled as well. As she did, forty years fell away in an instant, and Mary knew exactly who she was: Claire Wilkes, her summertime best friend from Ivy Bay. She'd had no reason to expect Claire to be there—Claire's family had moved away years ago, and by then, she and Mary weren't on speaking terms. But when Mary saw Claire's familiar face now, all the old affection from previous years rushed back to her. She'd always felt bad about how things had ended between them. But before that, Claire had shared years of girlish secrets with Mary, and she and Mary had spent some golden times together. Maybe Claire's appearance now was a chance to patch things up and make them right, after all these years.

Addison Hartley and Claire Wilkes on the same night. Lord, You certainly know how to surprise a woman.

She glanced at Betty, to see if her sister had caught sight of Claire. Betty would be just as surprised to see her as Mary was. But Betty was totally absorbed in Addison Hartley's next answer.

Mary looked back at her old friend. As she watched, Rebecca leaned over and whispered something to Claire. Claire nodded and said something in return. Mary slipped out from behind the counter and began to make her way through the crowd toward them. As she did, Claire glanced up. When the pair locked eyes, Mary smiled and gave a small wave, but Claire immediately turned her head. Then, trying to stay unobtrusive, Mary ducked behind a shelf, still making her way through the crowd.

But when she emerged, Claire was gone.

Mary scanned the crowd, but Claire was nowhere to be found. Then her eye caught a slight motion at the door as it swung shut, and a shadow passed by the window in the night outside. Had Claire left before the book signing was even over? With the woman gone, Mary's certainty fled. What were the chances that Claire would come to her bookstore after all these years? Especially on a night like tonight. Could she just have been mistaken in the excitement of the event? Had it really been Claire?

Mary had been waiting for weeks to meet Addison Hartley, but she could barely pay attention to any of his question-and-answer session. Memories of Claire, the Ivy Bay of her youth, John, and everything that had gone on between all of them swirled in her mind. After about a dozen questions, Addison glanced at Janine, and she took the microphone, thanked everyone, and then began to hustle the crowd into a line of autograph seekers. The bookstore erupted into a happy buzz.

"Rebecca," Mary said, finding her in the crowd. "The woman you were talking to. Where did she go?"

"Who?" Rebecca said, puzzled.

"You were standing beside her, during the Q and A," Mary insisted.

Rebecca's brow furrowed.

"Her name is Claire," Mary told her. "Claire Wilkes." Was Claire's name still Wilkes? Mary wondered. Had it even been Claire whom she'd seen?

Rebecca spent a moment in thought. Then she shook her head decisively. "No," she said. "I don't think I met a Claire."

"Are you sure?" Mary pressed.

Rebecca shook her head, somewhat helplessly. "I've met so many people tonight," she began, glancing toward the counter. "Oh my gosh!" she said. "Look at that!"

Mary followed her gaze. Behind the counter, seated on the high stool, Ashley was calmly taking a pair of bills from the first customer in a long line that had formed there.

"I'd better—" Rebecca began.

"Go," Mary finished.

She made her own way to the signing table, where Janine was briskly opening books, placing them before Addison, then shuffling the fans off so the next one could take their place. She nodded at Mary with what might have been an expression of approval. Mary gave her a tentative smile.

True to her word, when the last book was signed, Addison got to his feet and Janine bustled him out the door. Mary followed them out onto the street.

"I can't thank you enough," she said. "I hope you enjoyed the event. We're just so grateful you took the time to visit with us."

Addison Hartley shook her extended hand without meeting her eyes at all and disappeared into the limousine.

"Great event," Janine said briskly, switching her brilliant smile on, then back off again before she followed him into the car.

The big black car pulled away from the curb and disappeared into the night, and the famous author was gone, leaving Mary alone on the street as the customers began to trickle out of her store.

But despite all the excitement leading up to the event, it wasn't the famous author who stayed on Mary's mind. Instead, she looked around the darkened street wondering about her old friend. Had that really been Claire? Where had she been all these years? What did she think about what had happened between them so long ago? And where had she gone?

TWO

◆◆◆

Mary poured a last dollop of pancake batter into the sizzling pan. Then she set the mixing bowl on the counter beside her and picked up the colander of blueberries and raspberries she'd rinsed a few minutes earlier. Carefully, she began to settle them into the half-cooked batter, first the raspberries, then the blueberries. Raspberries were a decadent thing to put in pancakes, but she'd gotten a good price on several boxes of them down at the farmer's market the day she'd left Rebecca to manage the store—and Mary was in a mood to celebrate the previous evening's event.

As she set the last blueberry into the final pancake, the batter began to bubble, a sure sign that they were cooked through and ready to be turned. Mary flipped the first pancake, taking care not to let the berries roll.

"Well, well, well," Betty said, shuffling into the kitchen. Mary could tell from her voice that her spirits were high, but no matter how high they were, Betty never moved very fast anymore due to her rheumatoid arthritis—especially in the morning, when her joints were stiff from the long rest overnight. "I guess I'll be having breakfast this morning with a very successful bookstore owner."

Mary turned away from the stove, and Betty peered into the pan. "What's this?" she said. "Blueberries *and* raspberries? What would Grandma Franklin say?"

Their beloved Grandma Franklin had migrated from Ireland during some very hard times and lived the rest of her life a little bit suspicious of any extravagance. When the two sisters had shown off new dresses or dolls to their grandmother as girls, she was just as likely to warn them not to get too used to fancy things as she was to give them a compliment. But the hardship she'd been through had given her a rare ability to appreciate good things, whether they were simple or extravagant. Nobody else's eyes ever seemed to glow quite as bright at the sight of a beautiful flower or the taste of a simple sweet as Grandma Franklin's.

"She'd be shocked," Mary said. "And then she'd eat a whole plate."

Betty laughed and sat down at the place Mary had already set for her. Mary flipped the last several pancakes and waited as the berries, now facedown, hissed on the hot metal.

"So, what was it like hosting a famous author?" Betty asked. "Were you scared at all, to get up in front of so many people? If you were, I couldn't tell. You did a great job."

"It was good," Mary said. She began to scoop pancakes out of the pan onto the pair of plates she'd laid out on the counter. Then she settled a pat of butter on each and spooned powdered sugar over it all. She carried them to the little kitchen table where she and Betty ate each morning and set one down at each of their places.

"Just good?" Betty said.

Mary nodded. "Do you want to say grace?" she asked.

Betty took Mary's hand, and the two sisters bowed their heads. "Lord, thanks for this new day," Betty said. "Thanks for famous authors and berry pancakes. We give it all to You and ask that You'll lead us through it. Amen."

"Amen," Mary said and cut into her pancakes. They were delicious, just as she'd hoped—fluffy and gooey and sweet. As they ate, Betty told Mary that her son Evan had stopped by to borrow their hedge trimmer, and she relayed a story about her granddaughters Betsy and Allison that Evan had told her.

When silence settled between them, Betty asked, "Did everything go the way you'd hoped yesterday?"

Mary's mind flashed back to the image of the woman in the back of the shop who'd looked so much like Claire. Seeing her had left Mary with a strange feeling—a combination of excitement and nostalgia at the prospect of talking with Claire again and the old feeling of betrayal and loss she'd felt when their friendship first foundered. It left her with the nagging feeling she got when she couldn't remember something or when something was lost. She'd hoped it would fade with a good night's sleep, but it was even stronger this morning.

"Did you see anyone unusual in the crowd last night?" Mary asked.

Betty laughed. "Besides everyone in town?" But when Mary's expression stayed serious, her own became serious as well. "I can't say I did," she said. "Really, there were so many people there. And I was sitting right there in the front, so I had my back to most of them. Why do you ask?"

Mary hesitated. At the prospect of putting it all into words, the idea just seemed so outlandish. Why would

Claire even come back to Ivy Bay, and if she did, what were the chances that she'd wind up at Mary's store? It was much more likely that Mary had just noticed a stranger who resembled Claire. But then why would a stranger hurry out before the event was even over?

"I thought I saw Claire Wilkes last night," Mary told her.

Betty's eyes widened.

"Claire?" she repeated.

Mary nodded. Betty and Mary may have their differences sometimes, but in moments like this, Mary was incredibly grateful for her friendship with her sister. Unlike Claire, Betty had never failed her. And even with all the years of history since then, she could see that Betty knew how much Mary's friendship with Claire had meant once and what a shock it must have been for Mary to see Claire after all these years.

"Are you sure?" Betty asked.

Mary shook her head. "I'm not," she said. "That's why I was asking you. The woman I saw was so much older…"

"Well, it's been over forty years," Betty said.

Mary nodded again. "Yes," she said. "And her hair was different. But there was one moment when she still looked so much like Claire that I would have sworn it was her."

"Did you talk to her?"

"I tried," Mary said. "That was the other strange thing. As soon as I saw her, I waved and started over to her, but while I was working my way through the room, she disappeared. I think she actually left when she saw me."

"Before the event was over?" Betty asked.

"Right in the middle of it," Mary said.

"Did she recognize you?" Betty asked.

"I don't know," Mary said. "I think so. It all happened so fast. But whoever it was, why would she leave in the middle of the event?"

Betty frowned. "That's really strange," she said.

"That's what I thought," Mary agreed.

"How do you feel?" Betty asked her.

Mary gave her sister a grateful smile. "I'm fine," she said.

"I just know that was such a hard time for you," Betty said.

Mary nodded. "It was a long time ago," she said. "I don't feel the same way I did when I was seventeen. It was funny; I really just wanted to connect with her again. I'm not upset. But I guess I'm just...curious."

"Uh-oh," Betty said, the corners of her mouth turning up in a smile.

Mary grinned. "There's nothing wrong with being curious," she said.

"Famous last words," said Betty.

Mary stood and collected her own plate and her sister's.

"That was absolutely delicious," Betty told Mary as she set the plates in the sink and turned on the hot water. "Thank you." Betty pushed her chair away from the table. "I think I'm just going to wander out and see what's happening in the garden."

"In case the morning glories have decamped since last night?"

"You never know," Betty said. "They do have minds of their own."

Mary rinsed the plates as her sister shuffled out, then watched through the back window as Betty crossed the yard and began her morning investigation of her beloved garden.

Then she sat back down at the kitchen table, as she often did in the morning, to spend a bit of quiet time before the day began.

Lord, she prayed as she took her seat, *thank You for this home and for Betty. Thank You for the store and for the event last night. Thank You for that glimpse of Claire or whoever that was. Please be with her, wherever she is. I just wish I'd gotten to talk with her. It would be so nice to sort things out between us after all these years, now that we're not still seventeen.*

She hadn't thought about Claire in years, but ever since last night, the memories had been flooding back to her. She and Claire had first met when they were both seven and Mary's family had come to stay with Gram and Gramps for the summer. Claire had lived just three houses down. She was an Ivy Bay native, and Mary spent most of the year in Boston, but over the course of the long summers Mary spent in Ivy Bay, she and Claire became playmates and then best friends. In some ways, the distance might have helped solidify their friendship. Because they were separated by so many miles, they didn't get into the little conflicts that shattered so many youthful friendships. Instead, they poured out their hearts to each other in long letters. In many ways, they became each other's diaries through those years of letters. If something went wrong at school, if they were confused or scared or up-set, they could go to their rooms and confide everything by mail to the one friend they believed understood them perfect-ly. Maybe the letters had given them a false sense of closeness, Mary mused now. After all, when one of them was writing a letter, the other one couldn't interrupt or ask a foolish ques-tion or go on and on about themselves.

But, she thought, the times they'd spent together had been genuinely wonderful as well. Maybe that was just because they only got to see each other in the summers, amid the dazzling Cape waters, when neither of them had any responsibilities or troubles to speak of—no school, no jobs, not even any winter coats. But as Mary thought back over it, she remembered moments that still seemed special to her, even in the light of what had happened—staying up all night to watch a meteor shower over the water, the way they'd traded hopes and dreams and encouraged each other in them, and their shared passion for books.

Both of them had always loved to read, and they talked about books in their correspondence and when they saw each other—at least as much as they talked about dresses or dances or boys. It had been Claire, in fact, who first told Mary that she thought Mary would be a perfect librarian.

"Oh, because I wear wire glasses and put my hair in a bun?" Mary had joked, pretending to be insulted.

"No!" Claire had told her. "Because I don't know anyone else who talks about books the way you do. You can make them sound fascinating to anybody. You almost got me to read a book on cranberry bogs last week. That's practically a miracle."

For her part, Claire loved books too, but she didn't have any illusions about devoting her life to them. She had always been dead set on getting a practical college degree. Her father had passed away before Mary even met her, and Claire had seen how her mother struggled to take care of her. She had it all planned out. She would get some kind of useful degree to become a teacher or a nurse—but she'd take all the English classes she could along the way.

Had all of that, their whole friendship, been nothing more than a girlhood phase? Mary didn't think so, even after all these years. Growing up, Claire had been one of the most important people in the world to her. She remembered telling Claire that they'd be friends no matter what and that nobody mattered more to her besides her own family.

In some ways, that was what had happened. Claire had forced Mary to make a choice between Claire and her own family, although neither of them had been certain at the time that John would one day become Mary's family. Mary had had her suspicions when she met him—or maybe just her hopes. She'd seen him around school for years—a handsome basketball player who never seemed to like to talk to any of the girls who swarmed around him. It wasn't until Mary was partnered with him in chemistry during her junior year that she realized that he wasn't stuck up, just shy. And that once he got over his bashfulness, he was also funny and smart. By that summer, the two of them were inseparable. For the first time in her life, the prospect of going to the Cape for the summer was not appealing. She felt sorrow over being separated from John rather than excitement at the promise of seeing Claire, whom she'd kept up to date about all the development with John in long letters. She and John had been overjoyed when their parents agreed that he could come to visit her for the last few weeks in August, and she and Claire had planned for those few weeks all summer. While Mary read Claire little pieces of the letters John now wrote her every day, Claire would give her advice on just what phrase to use when she wrote back.

At first, when John arrived, everything had seemed idyllic. Mary had been delighted by how well her best friend and her boyfriend got along. They seemed to slip into conversation together almost as easily as she did with both of them. And that made sense—after all, she and Claire had not just a long history but all kinds of shared interests, and John was a good listener and an avid reader himself. Together, Mary and Claire had taken John all over the Cape, swimming and boating by day, going to clambakes and dances by night. The one place John and Mary hadn't invited Claire was their own secret overlook on a bluff outside town, looking down at the lights of the harbor. John had actually found it a few days after he arrived.

"Come on," he told her as they walked home along the coast from some dance in the bright moonlight that reflected off the wide sea.

"Where are we going?" Mary had asked him. "You don't know your way around here."

"You've been showing me your special spots ever since I got here," he'd told her. "But I wanted us to have one of our own." By then, he was leading her through a small stand of pine trees. "I found this place when I went for a walk this morning, before everyone got up. Do you like it?"

He led her out onto a sandy slip of land, high above the water but sheltered by the arching branches of hundred-year-old pines. Mary had loved it, and from then on, they'd stopped there often on the way home and found their way back every time they'd returned to the Cape, until he passed away last year. Sometimes she still went there now. She didn't exactly talk to him while she was there, but she liked the feeling that he was somehow near.

The whole visit—John getting to see the summer place that had meant so much to Mary; Claire getting to meet

John, and John getting to meet Claire; and the golden hours spent with all of them—seemed like a dream come true to Mary until a few days before John was supposed to leave.

That's when Claire had walked down the coast to Mary's family's house, as she had so many times before, and made her announcement. "I'm in love with John," she said. "And I believe John's in love with me."

Mary hadn't been able to believe what she was hearing. The thought that John might betray her had never crossed her mind, but now a shadow fell across all the hours the three of them had spent together, all the connections she'd been so happy to see Claire and John make.

"He wouldn't say anything," Claire told Mary. "He's too much of a gentleman, and he would never want to hurt you. But he'll be happier with me."

Mary had only been able to listen to so much of this before she'd had to ask Claire to leave. Then she'd fled to John and poured everything out to him. Of course, he'd insisted none of it was true, that Claire had gotten the wrong idea from his friendliness, and that he'd never really been able to talk to girls and was sorry if he'd done anything wrong. Mary had listened to all this gratefully. He'd given her no reason to doubt him, and even Claire admitted that nothing had happened between them except conversation.

But when she had tried to talk with Claire again, Claire was even more adamant. "John and I have a connection you can't understand," she said. "Maybe it's because I'm more emotional and you're more of a librarian. Maybe I just feel things deeper. But if you don't let him go now, he'll always regret it. He'll remember me. He won't be able to forget it."

Mary and John hadn't seen Claire again before he left. Before Mary went home herself, she'd tried to talk it out with Claire, but Claire was unmovable. Their letters had stopped that fall, for the first time in ten years. The sweet whirlwind of her budding romance with John had helped drive the sorrow from Mary's mind.

Mary made only one visit to Ivy Bay during her college years, and she had walked down the shore to Claire's small cottage. However, while she was standing there, wondering whether or not she wanted to knock on her door and greet her old friend, a strange woman had come out and asked what Mary was doing on the property.

"I'm sorry," Mary had stammered. "I was looking for my friend."

The woman had softened then and told Mary that Claire and her mother had both moved away the summer after Mary's senior year in high school. She didn't know where they had gone.

And that was the last Mary had heard of Claire, till now.

THREE

The bell over the shop door dinged. Tucked into a shelfful of Victorian crime novels, Gus lifted his head to observe the new visitor, his blue eyes alert and his soft gray ears pricked with curiosity. When he recognized Pastor Miles, Mary's pastor at Grace Church, he hopped to the floor and padded quickly over to the door to greet him. But as the pastor's eight-year-old grandson Trevor barreled through the door behind him, Gus hesitated, gazing at Trevor with open suspicion. Trevor tended to express his affection for Gus by pulling Gus's ears and yanking his tail, which hadn't exactly endeared the boy to the cat.

Mary turned back from reorganizing one of the shelves that had been reshuffled last night by the large number of browsers. She smiled at Pastor Miles and smiled even wider at Trevor. "What do we have here?" she asked. "Hello, Trevor!"

Trevor rewarded her with a wide smile of his own, then broke away from his grandfather and made a beeline for the children's section. He knew it well. Since the shop opened, Pastor Miles had often brought him in and let him pick out any one book he wanted. Mary was touched by her pastor's support of her new shop and by his evident love for his grandson.

With Trevor well out of reach, Gus judged the coast clear. He darted in and wound himself around Pastor Miles's ankles, purring audibly. Pastor Miles gave Gus a gentle scratch on the head and patted Gus's substantial gray belly.

"Rebecca," Mary said. Rebecca smiled brightly from behind the counter, where she'd been checking over the substantial receipts from the previous evening. "This is Pastor Miles. Pastor Miles, Rebecca."

Pastor Miles strode across the shop and gave Rebecca a warm handshake. As he did, Ashley popped her head out from behind the counter where she'd propped up one of the pillows from the children's nook and curled up with a new mystery.

"And this is Ashley," Rebecca said.

Ashley gave Pastor Miles a curt nod, then craned her neck to look down the aisle at the new boy in the children's section.

"That's Trevor," Mary explained. "Pastor Miles is his grandfather."

"Does he know about all the books down there?" Ashley asked with a serious expression.

"I don't know," Mary said. "Would you like to go ask him?"

Ashley sighed. "I think I better," she said and started down the row to join him.

Mary smiled, but with a certain amount of trepidation, as Ashley went. Trevor was a sweet boy, but he wasn't just like the other kids. He'd been diagnosed with autism as a toddler, and as he'd grown older, the differences between him and the other children had become more and more pronounced. Pastor Miles wasn't ashamed of his grandson—in fact, he talked frequently about how much he enjoyed getting to hear Trevor's sometimes unique take on the world. But even good kids like Ashley could be unintentionally cruel when they noticed something that seemed out of place to them, and she was too observant a child not to notice the differences between Trevor and other children. As unobtrusively as possible, Mary followed Ashley through the shelves, Pastor Miles behind her.

When they reached the picket gate at the children's section, Ashley was already deeply engrossed in the sales process.

"Well, do you like chapter books or picture books?" she asked.

Trevor gazed at her with his searching and somehow tender eyes. "A boat!" he exclaimed.

"We went on a boat ride this weekend," Pastor Miles explained to Mary in a low voice. "I don't think I've ever seen him so excited about anything before. Now I can't get him to talk about anything else."

Ashley scanned the shelves with a professional's eye. "Like a rowboat?" she said. "Or a tugboat?"

"A boat!" Trevor repeated happily. His ability to concentrate on one thing was far beyond that of most children. Pastor Miles sometimes said he wished he could get as much enjoyment out of a single book or toy as Trevor seemed to. But this kind of single-minded focus was one of the things that set him apart from the other kids. Mary watched Ashley closely, to see how she'd react.

Ashley didn't blink. She just pulled a bright picture book down from a shelf slightly above her head, opened it, and put it in Trevor's hands. A gorgeous painting of a three-masted schooner spread out across the page, with a watercolor sunset in the background. Trevor's face was suffused with delight. He gazed at the picture for one rapturous moment, then slammed it shut and looked around for his grandfather. When he caught sight of Pastor Miles smiling down at him, Trevor clutched the book to his chest. "This one!" he said.

"Well, all right," Pastor Miles said. "If you're sure about that."

"A boat!" Trevor explained.

"You liked that boat, didn't you?" Pastor Miles said.

"That's one of our best books about boats," Ashley assured Pastor Miles, ever the saleswoman.

"Why don't you give it to Ms. Mary?" Pastor Miles asked. "And she can ring it up for us."

The sight of Mary interrupted the train of Trevor's thought with another of his favorite things. "You make ice cream," he said, looking up at Mary without relinquishing the book.

"That's right, I do," Mary said. For years, she'd been something of an ice-cream hobbyist in Boston, dreaming up all kinds of variations with a stainless steel ice-cream maker: salt maple, peach blueberry, strawberry mint. When she first moved to Ivy Bay, she'd struck up a conversation with Tess Bailey at the ice-cream shop, and Tess had been so impressed with Mary's experiments that she asked Mary to create a new flavor for the shop each month. Mary's first concoction, named Caramelized Banana Walnut, had been one of Trevor's all-time favorites, and when Pastor Miles informed him that Mary was its inventor, she had taken on a special new status in Trevor's eyes.

"What kind is next?" he asked.

"I'm not sure," Mary said. "I was thinking chocolate with caramel and chocolate-covered pretzels. How does that sound to you?"

Trevor's eyes widened. He nodded.

"Trevor," Pastor Miles said, holding out his hand. "Why don't you give me the book, and we'll take it up to the register?"

Still unwilling to hand over his prize, Trevor compromised by scampering down the long aisle, back to the register where Rebecca still sat watching all the action. When he reached it, he looked up at her doubtfully, as if uncertain whether she could be trusted with such a prize. Gus, who had been lingering around the front of the register in hopes of another pat from Pastor Miles, darted quickly around the back.

"I hear you've found a good mystery about boats," Rebecca said.

Trevor nodded.

"Could I see it?" Rebecca asked.

Trevor couldn't resist this appeal to his generous nature. Carefully, he handed the book over. Rebecca scanned it quickly, then admired the schooner under a night sky that graced the cover. "This is wonderful," she said. "I bet you're going to love it." Trevor nodded politely, but his eagerness to reclaim the book was palpable. Rebecca handed it back to him with a smile.

Pastor Miles tousled his grandson's hair as he and Mary and Ashley gathered around the register. "I wish I'd known how much he loved boats before this," he told Mary as he took his wallet out. "We sure have enough of them around here."

Rebecca took the money. "Thank you," she said.

"What does he like best?" Mary asked.

"I'm not sure," Pastor Miles told her. "If I let him, he'd just sit in the bay for hours and watch them just bob at anchor. And then Henry took us out on the *Misty Horizon* this weekend, and you'd have thought he died and went to heaven. I don't think he stopped smiling the entire time."

Rebecca made the change and handed it back.

"Thanks," Pastor Miles said and pocketed it. Then he grinned at Ashley, who had retreated behind the counter and taken up a post beside her mother. "And thank *you*," he said. "You're a very helpful young lady."

Ashley nodded with dignity, as if he wasn't telling her anything she didn't already know.

"Thanks for coming in," Mary said.

"Oh, we'll be back!" Pastor Miles assured her. At the door, he swung it open for Trevor. "You want to go look at some real boats, buddy?" he asked.

Trevor nodded vigorously and scooted out the door.

"Bye!" Mary and Rebecca chorused after them.

The bell chimed again, and the door swung shut.

"You did a very nice job," Mary told Ashley.

Ashley nodded politely, taking this compliment in stride as she collected her book and settled into her reading nook again.

"Thank you so much for having her here," Rebecca said as Mary circled back.

"I think she's a better salesperson than either of us," Mary said.

Rebecca smiled gratefully. Then she turned the computer screen so Mary could see it. "We did really well last night," she told Mary. "We sold more than two hundred copies."

"Two hundred copies?" Mary said. "I wouldn't have guessed we had two hundred people here."

"I don't think we did," Rebecca said. "A lot of people bought two. Some even bought three."

Mary did a quick calculation. A night of sales that good could make up most of their receipts for the week.

Rebecca clicked down to the bottom of the screen to show her the total. "You can look for yourself," she said. "I'm going to straighten out those front shelves. I could see people putting things in upside down and backward all night last night. Or not putting them back at all."

"Thanks so much," Mary said and sat down at the computer. She looked over the numbers, then sat looking at the healthy balance in her account with a feeling of satisfaction. She'd have to send Addison Hartley a special gift in thanks. Of course, it was good for him to connect with his readers, but when a writer of that stature visited a store like hers, it seemed that the store benefited even more than he did. Maybe she could find him some kind of interesting gift—perhaps one of the intriguing rare editions of classic Agatha Christie books.

She shut down the accounting program, revealing the search engine she'd set as her Internet start-up page on the screen behind it. At the same time, the glimpse she'd gotten of the mysterious blonde woman rose up again in her mind. It must have been Claire, Mary thought again. She'd known her so well, for so long… How could she mistake someone else for her? Then again, it had been over forty years. Who knew what tricks her memory might play on her after all those years?

She found her fingers moving across the keys, typing in Claire's name. As she did, she realized it was Claire's maiden name. If she had any presence on the Internet these days, Mary thought, it would likely be under her married name, if Claire had married, which she almost certainly had. Probably this was a fool's errand, she told herself as she pressed Enter.

But to her surprise, several pages came up under the search for "Claire Wilkes."

Mary felt a little rush of excitement along with the tug of fear and sadness at the list of links. It had been so long since she had seen that name in print.

She hesitated for a moment, then clicked on the first link. It opened the Facebook page of a fifty-five-year-old account manager in Texas. That was a little younger than Claire should be, but Claire might not have divulged her actual age online… And for all Mary knew, she could be anywhere in the world. But when the picture came up, Mary shook her head. The woman had sparkling brown eyes, a round face, and a fall of shiny brown hair—nothing like Claire's paler, familiar features.

Mary worked her way down the page. A cheerleader in Kentucky, a paralegal in Miami, an assistant at an art gallery in New York City. None of them looked a thing like the Claire who Mary remembered or the woman she'd seen the night before.

Mary sighed. She probably wasn't even searching under the right name. And if she searched for "Claire Wilkes" and "Ivy Bay," what could she expect to find? Well, it was worth a try.

To her surprise, the search did come up with a hit: Ivy Bay High School. Claire's name appeared in a long list of other names as part of the index, some of the names familiar to Mary from her youthful summers.

Mary clicked on the link, but nothing in the yearbooks had been scanned and put online—just the index of students featured in each edition. But she remembered poring over the yearbooks with Claire each summer, reading the things Claire's friends and crushes had scrawled in the margins and trying to squeeze a hint of romance or longing into the clumsy lettering of a varsity ballplayer's, "I'll see you in September!"

They'd spent most of their time reading the handwritten messages, but Mary had flipped through the books a few times, especially after her junior year, when Claire and a few other girls had surprised Mary with a special addition to the yearbook. They'd taken a school picture Mary had sent to Claire that year and included Mary as an "honorary Ivy Bay High School" class member, because of all the years Mary had spent with Claire and her classmates during their summers. The gesture had brought tears to Mary's eyes.

"Why are you crying?" Claire had asked her, laughing. "This was supposed to make you happy!"

"I am happy!" Mary had insisted, smiling through her tears. But the way Ivy Bay had embraced her always brought on the same reaction. Her place in the Ivy Bay yearbook had been a source of comfort to her the following year, whenever she felt out of place or left out at her own school. And it might even have given her the courage she needed to begin to come into her own there and to do things like taking a chance

on talking to the handsome basketball star who had been as-
signed as her chemistry lab partner.

But if she remembered correctly, the Ivy Bay yearbooks
usually contained a section where the seniors listed their plans
for the future. Claire's family had moved out of town just
after her graduation, but maybe Claire had left some clue behind in the yearbook about where she'd gone next.

Gus leapt up on the counter beside her and peered into
the depths of the computer screen.

"What do you think, Gus?" Mary asked. "You think it's
time for a little trip to the high school?"

Mary wasn't sure if it was real feline behavior or just wish-
ful thinking on her own part, but sometimes she could almost
swear that Gus nodded. And what was the point of hiring a
new staff member if Mary couldn't get out of the store once
in a while during business hours?

"That's what I thought," she said. "Rebecca?"

Rebecca poked her head up from the front stacks. "Yes?"

"I'm going to run a quick errand," Mary said. "Will you
be all right here on your own for a little while?"

"Sure!" Rebecca said, but Mary saw a touch of worry on
her face. "Do you know when you might be back?"

Mary checked the clock. The high school was nearby. It
wouldn't take her that long to find what she was looking for,
as long as someone was there to let her in. "I'd say about half
an hour," she said.

Rebecca looked relieved. "Oh," she said, "that would be
great. I was just going to take Ashley over to a playdate on
my break."

"When do you need to leave for that?" Mary asked.

"About eleven thirty," Rebecca said.

Mary checked her watch again.

"Let me just check on something," she said.

She picked up her cell phone and dialed her neighbor Sherry Walinski, who was the high school secretary. Since it was summertime, Sherry wasn't always at the school, but Mary knew that Sherry still spent a lot of time there, since the administrative duties at the school never really ended, even when class wasn't in session.

To her relief, Sherry answered on the second ring. "Mary," she said, sounding pleased to hear from her. "How are you doing?"

"Great," said Mary. "And you?"

"I'm just up at the school," Sherry told her. "Trying to make these class schedules work."

"Actually," Mary said, "that's what I was calling about. I have an old friend I'd like to look up in one of the Ivy Bay yearbooks. Would you mind if I stopped by?"

"Mind?" Sherry said. "I'd love it. You don't know how quiet it can be over here without the kids."

"Great," Mary said. "I'll see you soon." She ended the call and collected her keys. "I'm just going out for a few minutes," she told Rebecca. "I'll be back by eleven thirty."

Sherry greeted her with a smile when Mary bustled into the high school office just minutes later. She was a tall, slender woman with green eyes and red hair styled in a pixie cut. "Hi, neighbor," she said.

"Great event last night," Sherry said as Mary came up to the desk. "I just wish I could have gotten that kind of turnout for the summer reading series the school did on *War and Peace*. Victoria kept telling people it's really just a gossipy historical romance, but she couldn't seem to get them to believe it." Victoria Pickerton was the Ivy Bay librarian and waged a constant and only sometimes successful battle to introduce the residents of Ivy Bay to the classics of world literature.

"So they probably wouldn't believe her if she told them how funny it is either," Mary said.

"Definitely not," Sherry agreed with another smile. "So you said you want to look through the yearbooks? Be my guest; you know where they are."

"Perfect. Thanks!" Mary headed out of the office and down the hall to the school library. It was hushed and empty, waiting for the students to return. She headed over to the shelf of yearbooks. She quickly recognized the spine of the yearbook that included her picture but let her hand drift past it to the following year, when she and Claire had both graduated.

Mary set the yearbook on a nearby card catalog and opened it to the back. Sure enough, it fell open to the section of senior photographs. As she'd remembered, under each photo, the student's achievements and a quote of their choosing was listed as well as their postgraduation plans—farming, fishing, nursing school, military academy. She flipped quickly through the Ns, Os, Ts—to the Ws. At the sight of Claire's senior picture, she had the same mixture of happy recognition and betrayal that she'd felt at the sight of the results to her Internet search. She knew all the details of Claire's activities—how she'd struggled and struggled to learn the complex dives as a member of the diving team, her hilarious mimicry of the Key Club faculty adviser, how proud she'd been when she was elected president of the literary society. Even Claire's senior quote was familiar, her favorite line from Emily Dickinson. But under it all, there was a new piece of information, Claire's chosen university: California State University.

Mary gazed down at the crisp black-and-white image of her old friend. Then she let the yearbook fall closed, got up, and replaced it on the shelf.

A few minutes later, she greeted Rebecca back at the shop. "You're right on time!" Rebecca said.

"I do my best," Mary said with a wink, then took her seat behind the counter at the computer, brought up a search engine, and hit a few keys. A moment later, she was dialing the alumni office of California State University on her cell phone.

"Hello," she told the man who answered. "I'm trying to locate an old friend who's an alumni of yours. I wonder if you might be able to give me any information about where she went after graduating. Her name was Claire Wilkes."

"I can't promise anything, but I'll be glad to take a look," the man said. "What's the graduation year?"

Mary did some quick math and told him her best guess.

"Hold on," he said. The line filled with classical music.

As the tinny violins swelled on her cell phone, Rebecca waved from the door, leading Ashley out. Mary nodded back.

The man came back on the line as the door swung shut behind Rebecca. "No Claire Wilkes," he said. "I'm sorry. I checked a few years around it too." Well, maybe she had changed her mind after the yearbook was printed, Mary thought. After all, some big change must have happened in the family for Claire and her mother to leave Ivy Bay where they'd lived for most of Claire's life.

"We've quite a few Wilkeses, but no Claire," the man added.

That lit an idea in Mary's mind. She'd received years of Claire's letters, always from Wilkes but with a long parade of different names: Clare, Clayre, Clarice—even variations on Claire's unusual middle name, Verlaine. "What about Claire Verlaine?" Mary tried. "Is there anything like that?"

"Verlaine?" the man said in a why-didn't-you-tell-me-this-in-the-first-place? tone of voice. "Yeah, I remember one of those. Weird name." From way out in California, Mary could hear the papers shuffling on his desk. "Yep, right year and everything. You think that's your friend?"

"I don't know," Mary said. "Would you have any information about her plans after graduation?"

"Chicago," the man said.

"I'm sorry?" she asked.

"That's where your friend went," the man said. "Looks like she wanted an advanced degree. She went to Chicago. Graduate School of Business."

"You've been very helpful. Thank you," Mary said.

"You might try giving them a call," the man suggested.

"I might do that," Mary told him and ended the call.

She shook her head, squinting against the glare from the window on her computer. Business? Claire had talked a lot about a practical degree with Mary but never about business. Was it possible she had changed so much in the few years since Mary had known her? Or was this Claire Verlaine even the same person? Yet what were the chances of another student named Claire Verlaine showing up the same year as Claire at California State University?

FOUR

Tuesday morning, Mary padded down the quiet hall of the church to the prayer chapel, carrying a pan of fresh-baked brownies, her own special recipe, which just included a boxed mix and a bag of chocolate chips. It was simple, but she always got rave reviews on them.

She was early for this first meeting of the women's prayer group she was trying to start in Ivy Bay. Back in Boston, she'd been part of a prayer group for almost two decades. Those women had turned into some of her closest friends, and over the years, they'd prayed not just for their own hopes and worries, but also for the whole life of the church and sometimes the world too—troubled teenagers, ailing older members, new marriages under stress, sister churches in other countries, tragedies and changes they read about in the press. God didn't always answer every prayer the way they expected, but she'd seen enough to believe that He did hear the prayers she and her friends had prayed so faithfully. And she recognized the changes the prayers had made in her own life over the years: how she'd learned how to give things into God's hand instead of holding on to and worrying over them herself, and how He often seemed to answer her with His peace when she brought her cares to Him, even if she didn't understand or see how a situation would work out. She'd also learned that what she asked for often didn't turn out to be the best answer or even what she really wanted. Over and over, when she was frustrated with what He seemed to be keeping from her, she'd look back years later to thank Him for not answering her prayers—and for the way He seemed to keep working in her life even though she wasn't always wise enough to know what to ask.

When she moved to Ivy Bay and started attending Grace Church with Betty, she'd asked Pastor Miles about joining a women's prayer group the first week.

"Well," the pastor said, "we don't actually have one of those right now."

"Oh," Mary said, feeling a little sheepish. She didn't want her new pastor to think she had just breezed in from out of town with all kinds of new ideas about how he should change his church around. "All right."

Betty had elbowed her. "Mary could start one!" she volunteered.

"Well, I wasn't trying to say—" Mary had protested.

"That would be wonderful," Pastor Miles had said warmly. "I've been trying to get one started for years, but we just never seem to find the right leader."

"Mary was in one for years," Betty said. "In Boston. They were always praying for me about everything. I guess I must have seemed like I needed it."

"Would you be interested in starting a group?" Pastor Miles asked. He had spoken a bit tentatively, as if he didn't want to scare off his new member with too much responsibility right away.

But Mary was delighted. "If you really think—" she said.

"I do," Pastor Miles said decisively. "You're welcome to meet in the prayer chapel any time you'd like."

"We used to meet in one another's homes too," Mary told him. "Sometimes it's cozier that way."

"That would be fine too," Pastor Miles had told her. "But please consider the prayer chapel at your disposal. And have you met Dorothy Johnson yet?"

Mary could feel Betty stiffen a bit at her side, but she didn't quite know why. "I don't think I have," she said.

"Dorothy's just wonderful," he told her. "I think you should get to know her. She's into just about everything around here, and it sounds like you're the same kind of person, with your bookshop, and your prayer group. I'm sure the two of you will get along."

That Monday, Pastor Miles had given her a call at the bookshop, and together, they'd worked up a small announcement to put in the church bulletin. He had also suggested the names of several other women he thought might be special additions to the group, and over the course of the next few weeks, Mary had called them and answered the e-mails and calls from the announcement, planning toward this first meeting of the group.

Because of Pastor Miles's high praise, she'd been especially excited to talk with Dorothy, but when she did, the conversation hadn't gone as she'd imagined. Dorothy hadn't exactly come right out and asked why Pastor Miles would put a newcomer like Mary in charge of the group, but she did ask a lot of questions about how short a time Mary had been in town and what her experience with prayer groups was, exactly. When Mary let Dorothy know that she'd been part of a decades-long group in Boston, Dorothy couldn't seem to think of much to say, but when Mary tried to assure her that she had deep roots in Ivy Bay, because of the summers she'd spent there as a child, Dorothy had had a few choice words to say. "Oh, summer people," she said. "You all love to think you're from Ivy Bay, don't you?"

Those words had stung, but Mary tried to tell herself that maybe Dorothy had a point. After all, she hadn't spent her life in Ivy Bay like Dorothy apparently had. Maybe it wasn't fair for her to pretend she had. But she'd had to put her foot down over Dorothy's attempts to commandeer the group. "If you'd like," she offered, "I can talk to Brita over at the office and reserve the room. I'm there almost every day."

"I actually already have it on the calendar," Mary said.

"Well, do you think it will always be on Tuesdays?" Dorothy said. "I mean, I'm just not sure that that will always be a good day. In the summer, it might be fine, but in the fall, there's bell practice, and several of the women might like an evening meeting instead. I can look at the church calendar, if you'd like, and let you know some times that might work better."

"Pastor Miles and I just thought this might be a good time to start. We can talk with the whole group and see what they think. In Boston, we just scheduled each week according to what worked for everybody. We actually moved from home to home each week too. That seemed to work well, because then one person didn't get tired out from having to host all the time."

"Well, I always like to have a plan myself," Dorothy said. "But just let me know if there's anything at all I can do to help. Speaking of which, would it help you if I led the first meeting? I know you won't know anybody there, and it might be a bit of a whirlwind trying to learn everyone's names. I know everyone, so it wouldn't be anything for me just to get us started, until you really get into the swing of things."

Mary had raised her eyebrows, despite the fact that she was on the phone. Gus had looked up at her in surprise, his tail twitching. "That's very nice of you," Mary had said, trying to keep the annoyance out of her voice. "But I find I learn things best if I just jump right in."

"Well, if you seem to be missing anything, I'll be sure to let you know," Dorothy said.

"Thank you," Mary had managed before she hung up.

When she'd relayed the conversation to Betty to get her perspective, Betty had just nodded knowingly. "That's Dorothy," she said.

"But Pastor Miles seems to like her so much," Mary said.

"Of course he does," Betty said. "From his point of view, she runs half the church. She just looks a little different if you have to work with her."

"Well, I'm not sure I have much choice now," Mary said.

"Oh, you don't," Betty assured her.

Lord, Mary prayed as she walked down the hall now, *please be with us today. Please show us what You'd like this group to be. And please help me get along with Dorothy.*

She checked her watch. It was about five minutes before the meeting was supposed to begin, just as she'd planned. At least she'd have a bit of time to settle in and collect her thoughts.

But when she opened the door to the chapel, Dorothy greeted her with a tight smile. "Mary," she said. "I was wondering when you'd make it."

Make it? Mary repeated in her head. *She makes it sound like I'm five minutes late, not five minutes early.* But she forced herself to smile.

"I've already got all the chairs set up," Dorothy said, gesturing to a circle of about twenty folding chairs she'd set up in the center of the room.

Mary looked longingly at the little nook of comfy stuffed furniture in the corner, but she didn't want to directly contradict Dorothy if she didn't have to. "That's great," she said. "I'm not sure we'll need all those, though."

"Well, why don't we wait and see?" Dorothy said with a somewhat steely smile.

Mary let her purse slide off her shoulder. *She hasn't actually gone and invited people without asking me, has she?* she wondered.

"Is this the prayer meeting?" a new voice asked.

Mary recognized it from the phone. "Bernice?" she said.

Bernice Foster had short gray curls and was wearing a velour tracksuit, and she broke into a wide grin. "That's me!" she said and made a beeline for the little cluster of comfy sofas in the corner.

"I have these set up over here," Dorothy said, her voice light but pointed.

Bernice settled into an overstuffed pink couch and waved her hand dismissively. "Those?" she said, looking at the flimsy folding chairs. "They're as bad as sitting on pews."

"Well, when everyone arrives—" Dorothy protested.

"Actually, I think this should be fine," Mary said. "We're only expecting six people."

"Six?" Dorothy repeated with an air of disbelief. "You mean—including you and me?"

Mary took a seat next to Bernice on the pink couch and nodded.

Before Dorothy could really come to terms with the fact that the prayer meeting would only be comprised of six women, another one of them arrived: Jill Sanderson, a young blonde in a neat blue oxford cloth shirt. "Well, I am delighted to be here," she said. "I think this is the most quiet I've heard all week." Her two towheaded sons, Luman and Benjamin, ages eight and ten, were favorites in the church but a handful for their mother.

Mary rose to greet her.

"You must be Mary," Jill said. "Thanks so much for inviting me."

Reluctantly, Dorothy settled into an armchair as Jill took the last seat on the couch.

The last two members of the group arrived together: Lynn Teagarden and Amy Stebble. Both of them were in their forties, Lynn tall and thin, and Amy plump and glowing. Pastor Miles had told Mary that they had been best friends since anyone in Ivy Bay could remember and that they were as opposite as you could imagine, with the exception of the deep faith that both of them shared.

"We're not late, are we?" Lynn asked, looking worried.

"They weren't going to start without us, though," Amy said with a dazzling smile. "Were you?"

"Thanks so much for coming," Mary said as they settled in to the last few seats. "I'm so glad all of you took the time to be here."

"Well," Bernice said, "I figured if everyone in the church needs as much prayer as I do, then we better get praying."

Everyone laughed but Dorothy, who shifted in her seat. "I'd just love to know what we're going to be *doing*," she said.

"Well, I just thought we'd pray," Mary said simply. "Pastor Miles has passed on a few requests to me that came in to the church office. Aaron Sharp is in the hospital with kidney problems, and Matilda Bressie would like us to pray for her grandson. He's been having trouble getting along with the other kids at school since his dad has been overseas."

Heads nodded around the room. "And I thought we also could pray for one another or for needs we know about," Mary said. "Maybe we can just go around the room and share a bit."

One by one, the women in the room talked a bit about what was happening in their world. Jill's husband was opening up a new business, and she was excited but apprehensive about taking the risk in the current business climate, and with two young kids still to take care of. Bernice was planning a big trip across the country to see her daughter in Arizona. She hated flying, but nothing was going to stand between her and her grandkids. Without giving a name, she mentioned another older woman who had just lost her husband and was struggling with loneliness and depression. Amy volunteered to pray for her and shared that she had been struggling for a long time to have a good attitude at her job as the elementary school secretary. She worked for several different administrators, and they all had different ideas about how she ought to do her job. "I love working with the kids," she said. "That's the highlight of my day. But I'm having a lot of trouble with the stress." Lynn asked for prayer for insomnia. She'd always had trouble sleeping, and it had been especially bad recently.

"Is there anything we can pray for you?" Mary asked when the circle came around to Dorothy.

"Well," Dorothy said, looking uncomfortable, "I guess I didn't know we were supposed to have requests."

"Only if you want to," Mary said, trying to give her a graceful way out.

"Oh, I can make a request," Dorothy said, as if Mary had challenged her to some kind of contest. "Annabelle Travers just came home from the hospital with a broken hip. I was over there visiting her yesterday, and she's feeling pretty down over it all. I think it would be good if we prayed for her."

Mary didn't point out that this wasn't exactly a request for Dorothy. "We'll do that," she said. "And for me, I'd like to offer a praise. It hasn't been exactly easy getting the bookstore up and running, but we had a great event the other evening. I really feel like we're on our way. But we could keep praying for that, because it's touch and go every week with a new business. And also"—she hesitated, but if she wasn't willing to be vulnerable with the other women in the room, how could she ask them to be?—"I'm still making friends in Ivy Bay. I'd just love to get to feel more at home here and less like a visitor."

Beside her, Bernice reached over and squeezed her hand. "We'll see what we can do about that," she said.

"Would it make you feel more at home if I asked you to babysit?" Jill joked.

"Do they like to read?" Mary said. "You can send them over to the bookstore."

As the laughter died down, Mary leaned forward. "Let's pray," she said. "For today, we can just pray for one another and the requests we've heard as we feel led. And is anyone willing to close for us?"

Lynn nodded.

"Thanks, Lynn," Mary said.

Around the circle, the women bowed their heads. They prayed for one another, for the concerns they'd mentioned, and for things that came to mind in the moment. Sometimes several women would pray for the same request, and sometimes the prayers flowed easily from one request to the next. A feeling of warmth and peace came over Mary. Ivy Bay had always felt familiar to her. But since she'd returned to open the bookshop, this was one of the first times it had felt like home.

It wasn't until Lynn gave the brief closing prayer, thanking God for hearing everything they'd said and asking Him to guide them forward as a group, that Mary realized she didn't remember Dorothy adding anything.

After the chorus of "amens," the women broke into friendly chatter. Something about seeing Amy and Lynn's close friendship, and the new ones budding around the room, made Mary think of Claire. This was a small town, she realized. And she'd never really asked around about where Claire had been or if anyone had seen her. Maybe now was a good time.

"I actually think I might have seen an old friend at the event the other night," she told the group after a lull in the conversation. "But it had been so long, I could hardly believe it. And I didn't get a chance to talk to her to see."

"Who was it?" Amy asked.

"Claire Wilkes?" Mary tried. "She was my very best friend in high school."

Amy just looked confused. That made sense, Mary guessed. After all, Amy was a good twenty years younger than Mary. If Claire had moved out of town after their senior year, there was no reason someone Amy's age should remember her. But beside Mary, Bernice shifted on the couch. "I remember her," Bernice said. "She was a few years ahead of me in school. Blonde girl. Real pretty."

"That's her," Mary said, smiling.

"They moved out of town when I was a sophomore," Bernice said.

"Have you seen her around town since?" Mary asked. "I wasn't even sure it was her, but the woman just looked so much like Claire did. It made me curious if anyone else had seen her around."

Bernice shook her head. "I can't say that I have," she said. "In fact, I haven't heard her name mentioned around here since high school."

"Well, it sounds like most of us never knew her name at all," Dorothy said, with the strong implication that the conversation had taken a turn that many of them didn't find interesting.

"I guess not," Mary said, trying to keep the tone light. "I just thought it might be worth it to ask."

The conversation swept on around her, but as Dorothy asked Lynn about some detail of the upcoming spaghetti dinner, Bernice turned to Mary.

"I haven't seen Claire around," she said again. "But I'm a little surprised that you'd want to see her again. I mean, after everything that happened with her and your boyfriend."

"John?" Mary said with a smile. "You mean my husband."

Bernice's eyes grew wide. Was it Mary's imagination, or did Bernice's expression seem more alarmed than a high school misunderstanding warranted? "Oh!" Bernice said. "Oh, you *married* him."

Mary's smile faded. What kind of stories had Claire been telling about Mary and John? And how far had they traveled? She'd never met Bernice before. How did Bernice seem to know so much about it?

"Were you friends, then?" Mary asked. "With Claire?"

Bernice dropped her eyes and shook her head. "I wouldn't say that. I knew her to speak to, but friends, no."

So some sort of story had been circulating through Ivy Bay about Claire and John, Mary thought. But what sort of story was it?

"What do you mean by 'everything that happened'?" Mary asked.

"What?" Bernice said, evidently uneasy.

"You said, everything that happened with Claire and John," Mary said. "What did you mean?"

"Oh, I don't really know," Bernice said and tried to laugh. "I'm sure you know all that much better than I do."

"Because nothing happened, really," Mary said, not certain if she was trying to convince Bernice or herself. "It was all just a misunderstanding."

"I'm sure it was," Bernice said in a tone of voice that said she wasn't sure at all. She seemed to be sure about the fact that she couldn't wait to leave, though. She was already on her feet, swinging her quilted purse up onto her shoulder. "This was so lovely, Mary. Thanks so much for putting it together." With that, she turned and headed for the door.

Mary watched her go, her mind suddenly racing. Her memories of Claire had already been stirred up and confused by the sighting of the mysterious woman at her bookshop. Now her memories of John rose up too—sweet and painful from his recent loss but now unstable and confused too, because of Bernice's discomfort.

Clearly, Bernice thought that whatever happened between Claire and John that long-ago summer had been more than a simple misunderstanding. What stories had Claire been telling around town after Mary returned to Boston, Mary wondered? And then, unbidden, Mary wondered something else: Were any of them true?

FIVE

•──◆◆◆──•

On the drive home, Mary felt a strange sensation as she nosed the car down the streets she'd known all her life. Everything was just where it had always been, but at the same time, she felt as if it almost ought to be different.

So maybe Claire told a few stories around town, Mary thought. *It was such a long time ago. Why should I be bothered?*

Still, she couldn't shake the sense of uneasiness that Bernice's comments—or lack of them—had given her. She hated the idea that Claire had told stories about her and John behind Mary's back, and that, decades later, those stories still had a life of their own in the town Mary had always considered her second home. She was embarrassed and curious. Maybe it wouldn't have helped if Bernice had told her exactly what she'd heard about Claire and John all those years ago, but Mary couldn't stop wondering. Had Claire told everybody that John had feelings for her and not Mary? But Bernice's reaction seemed to hint at even more than that. Had Claire told them even more—that John had confessed his own love for Claire? That they had been in some kind of relationship? Mary suspected some of these thoughts had drifted into the irrational, but it was hard for her to tell which ones, and when. The whole idea that stories about Claire and John and her were still remembered from decades ago was so unlikely that it made everything else seem strange and uncertain as well.

These questions stirred up all of the old feelings she'd had when Claire first confessed her feelings for John—shock, betrayal. And they sent her mind racing back over the same paths they'd gone then. Claire had been such a good friend to her. Until the situation with John, she'd always been loyal and understanding. Had there been clues along the way that she didn't see? Mary wondered now, as she had then. As a teenager, she'd gone over and over the events of her friendship with Claire, wondering if there had been signs earlier that Claire couldn't be trusted, signs that she'd missed. After all, they spent most of their time apart and communicated mostly through letters. And Claire was a great writer even then, able to build up stories and call whole worlds into existence with just a handful of words. Had she always been pretending to be something she wasn't? Had Mary been fooled by her because she was so young and inexperienced? If she looked back on their friendship now, with all the wisdom of her years, what would she see?

But it was almost impossible for her to answer these questions. Everything had happened so long ago, and even with all the experience she'd had between then and now, she couldn't tell which memories were accurate and which were just symptoms of her youth at the time. In retrospect, she wasn't even sure of her own take on Claire. Had their friendship been a true one? Had Claire falling for John been a onetime mistake, the kind of thing that could happen to anyone, especially as a teenager? Or did the fact that Claire had tried to steal Mary's boyfriend prove that she had never been a good friend to begin with? Nevertheless, Mary could hardly blame Claire for developing feelings for John. Mary had always found John pretty irresistible herself. What would Mary have done if she had been in the same situation? Had the friendship Mary had counted on for all those years been real or just a mirage?

There was no way to tell now. And her questions about Claire, Mary realized as she pulled up to the house, weren't really what was bothering her the most. It was her questions about John.

Whatever had happened between Claire and John all those years ago, John had been a good husband to Mary. They'd shared the ups and downs of life, the small triumphs and the hard moments. They'd raised wonderful children, who sometimes looked more like Mary and sometimes looked more like John, depending on their ages and moods. They'd shared some dreams that had come true, like seeing John become partner at his law office, and others that hadn't, like the trip to Europe they'd always meant to take but hadn't and then it was too late. But there had always been a part of John that Mary didn't quite feel she could get to. On good days, she chalked it up to his shyness. Before meeting her, he'd told her, he had never shared his thoughts and feelings with anybody, and even with her, he said, it was sometimes hard for him to put into words the things he wanted to say. For Mary, who loved words in every form—filling the pages of books or used in long conversations between good friends—this was hard to understand, although she tried. On her bad days, though, sometimes it just felt like John was keeping things from her, like he might have a whole secret world that he never let her in on and that she would never know. And a few times, Claire's words when she'd insisted that John would be happier with her came into Mary's mind to haunt her: *If you don't let him go now, he'll always regret it. He'll remember me. He won't be able to forget it.*

Mary had never taken those doubts very seriously, in part because she never felt that John had ever given her a reason to. He wasn't the sort of man who looked at other women when they were out or who got involved in long conversations with pretty strangers at parties. Maybe that was part of why the old story with Claire still bothered Mary. John wasn't the kind to have his head turned by a pretty face. But ironically, it was because she believed in the goodness of his heart that Claire's long-ago comments had worried her. John wasn't the type to change his feelings on a dime. If he really had felt something for Claire that summer, Mary couldn't tell how long those feelings might have lasted. It was hard to get close to John, but once you connected with him, that connection lasted.

Each thought of John, as these thoughts rushed through Mary's mind, hit her with a new shock. He'd been gone a little over a year, but the loss still felt fresh and raw. He'd been the foundation of her life, and Mary didn't really know how to deal with it when he passed away. Friends had told her that she needed to do all kinds of things: cry, visit the grave, make memory boards, put away reminders of him or take them all out. Mary hadn't really made a choice to do or not do any of these. The only way she'd known to carry on was just to keep putting one foot in front of the other, day after day. She knew she needed hope to keep going, so she'd decided to follow her dream of opening the bookstore in Ivy Bay. She'd cried a little, visited his grave before she left, and packed up all his things that she didn't give away to bring them with her to Ivy Bay. She'd done a pretty good job of accepting the fact that he was gone.

But she didn't know how to deal with her memories of him or the deep ache that rose up when they came. What good were they, anyway, if all they did was cause her pain? So she'd gotten pretty good at just shooing them away. Unless someone else brought John up, like Bernice had today, Mary just kept on moving forward in her life, full speed ahead, keeping her memories of John and the sadness they caused in a well-sealed box in her heart.

When Mary came in, Betty was in the living room, sitting on the corner of a giant swath of white tulle. An assortment of quite realistic silk flowers, clipped from their stems, were jumbled in the center.

"Decorating?" Mary asked with a faint smile.

Betty nodded, clipped the head of a silk daisy from its plastic stem, and tossed it lightly into the pile. "This is actually a ceiling drape," she said. "I'm going to put it over one of the guest beds. Just four thumbtacks, boom, boom, boom. The tulle is as light as air. And then you can see the flowers through the net."

Mary's spirits lifted slightly with Betty's excitement, but her worry didn't really fade. "That's going to be beautiful," Mary said. She tried to keep her voice natural as she answered, but something in it must have given her away. Her sister looked up at her closely.

"Are you all right?" she asked.

Mary nodded.

"You sure?" Betty asked.

Mary set her purse on the nearby table. She wasn't ready to put her thoughts into words yet. In fact, she wasn't even sure what her thoughts were. Sometimes it helped to share things with others, but occasionally that was the moment it became real. And she wasn't sure she wanted whatever Bernice had been hinting at during the prayer meeting to become any more real than it already seemed to her. "I've just got a lot on my mind," she said.

"Do I need to go egg anybody's windows?" Betty asked, her brows drawing together in a mock glare.

Mary smiled. The two of them had never actually egged anybody's windows, but Betty still loved to threaten it, even though they were decades too old for that kind of girlish prank. It was one of the ways she had of saying, "I'm on your side. Anyone who messes with you better watch out for your sister too."

"Not yet," Mary said. "I'll let you know."

"You do that," Betty said. "I just bought a dozen of them this afternoon."

Mary smiled.

Betty paused what she was doing and looked up at her, a red silk gerbera daisy in her hand. "When was the last time you read something?" she asked. "You love reading so much, but since you opened that bookstore, you've barely had time to do any of it. Have you finished Addison Hartley's new book yet?"

"I haven't even started it," Mary said. She'd set aside a copy for herself when the big shipment came in, meaning to get to it before Addison read, but the preparations for the event had taken so much time that she'd never gotten to it.

"Well, there you go," Betty said. "Why don't you curl up with it now? Everything will look different after a few hours with your nose in a book."

"Maybe you're right," Mary said.

She went back to her room, where the copy of Addison Hartley's new title lay on the little stand beside her bed. As she picked it up, she could feel her fears fade as the familiar excitement of holding a new title by a favorite author rose. She carried it downstairs to her favorite reading nook—a sunroom overlooking Betty's beautiful back garden. The room had an upholstered reading bench long enough to stretch her legs and deep enough to curl them up under her. The bench was decorated with brocade pillows and draped with the Victorian crazy quilt their mother's mother had pieced together to celebrate a long-ago Christmas. Betty, ever the decorator, loved the dazzling blend of silks and velvets their grandmother had used to piece the bright surface together, but Mary had always loved the playful figures embroidered on the various patches: a sunflower, a man holding his arms out toward the sky, a pert girl holding a giant umbrella, a horse and buggy, a tree with spreading branches. Since she was a girl, they'd all combined and recombined as new and different characters hundreds of times, lighting a new story in her mind every time. Until their mother passed away, neither she nor Betty had ever seen it in anything more than glimpses, stolen when they threw open their mother's cedar chest and ran their fingers over the beautiful fabric. But as Betty was helping Mary unpack the things she'd brought from Boston with her, she had pulled the quilt out and spread it on Mary's new bed.

"I think we ought to put this out," she said.

"But it's so old," Mary had protested. "What if something happens to it?"

"I can't think of a worse fate than being locked up in some box," Betty said. "Grandma didn't make this for us to hide it away. She meant for it to be seen. And besides, it's not like we have a lot of toddlers over these days, brandishing their juice cups and popsicles. And if we do, we'll just put it up for the day."

Mary hadn't wanted to contradict Betty at that moment— her head was still reeling from the move, and she felt a deep debt of gratitude to Betty for welcoming her into her home. So she'd gone along with the idea, despite her reservations. But now, several months later, they'd all faded. Curling up under the blanket seemed to have some kind of magic. It made her feel connected with the generations that came before her and reminded her of the little girl she once was—and the beauty and the details of the quilt still charmed her even as a grown woman.

Now, as she settled in among the pillows, the new book on her lap, a feeling of peace and excitement came over her. *Thank You for books*, she prayed, and she flipped past the title and dedication pages to the first line.

Like all Addison Hartley's books, this one was instantly engaging. His detective's travels had brought him to the East

Coast, to a seaside village very much like Ivy Bay, to investigate another piece of the great mystery that he had been unraveling over the past volumes of the series. The description of the town made Mary smile—maybe all seaside towns were alike, she thought. As she read on, the familiarity with coastal life that Hartley had shown in the brief snippet he recited at the reading became almost eerie. Like Ivy Bay, his fictional town was right on the bay and populated with a combination of fishing folk and shop owners. Like Ivy Bay, the townsfolk had always struggled a bit to decide where they stood in relation to the summer people who came to town each year. The townsfolk knew they needed their business to survive, and sometimes real friendships grew up between them—but the summer people didn't weather the harsh Atlantic winters in the town and didn't have to earn their living at the mercy of the sea.

All this might just have been good research on Hartley's part, but when Mary reached the description of the downtown, her eyebrows drew together in surprise. It was strangely identical to Ivy Bay, with a half-moon bay and nearby lakes. The fictional village even had an ice-cream store right next to the souvenir shop, just like in Ivy Bay. But, Mary told herself, most of the towns up and down the Cape boasted an ice-cream store and a souvenir shop. And a lot of them, she might guess, must stand side to side. But he also mentioned a diner on the other side of the souvenir store, exactly where the Black & White Diner stood.

Just out of curiosity, she pulled the biographical information on Addison Hartley, which the publishing company had included with the book, out of the back cover, where she'd tucked it. A quick skim through showed no personal connection between him and the East Coast. It mentioned childhood stints in Texas and Kentucky, and his current residence, in the hills outside Los Angeles. However, as far as she could tell, he'd never spent much time in this area.

She shook her head, flipped back to her place in the novel, and began to read again. The next chapter introduced a subplot—the detective befriended a local girl in the small town. She pestered him until he allowed her to come with him on some of his investigations. After about a chapter of sleuthing, the detective realized the girl had some secrets of her own; she was in love with her best friend's boyfriend.

Mary sped through the next several chapters, skimming the larger elements of the mystery the girl and the detective uncovered, and pored over the details of the subplot. Some of the details had been changed—the hair color of the girls, the names of the towns they were from. But much of it tracked Mary's experience with John and Claire all those summers ago. The boyfriend was from out of town, shy, sensitive and a basketball player. His girlfriend was petite and had been friends with her competition since both of them were only seven years old. They lived just a few houses away from each other, on the banks of an inland lake. But even though the details lined up with the story Mary knew, the sense of it didn't. The girl the detective had befriended painted herself as a victim. She hadn't meant for anything to happen between her and the boyfriend. In fact, she was heartbroken over the idea of hurting her friend. But the way the story was told made it clear that the connection between the girl and the boyfriend was unique and undeniable, and it painted his current girlfriend as sweet but clueless.

All of this was told in Addison Hartley's signature prose, so riveting and well drawn that the scenes sprang to life immediately in Mary's mind, competing with her own memories of the time. Coupled with the experience she'd just had with Bernice at the church, the effect was overwhelming, especially a scene where the boyfriend confessed his love to the other girl and told her that he just couldn't find the words to break up with his current girlfriend.

When that chapter ended, Mary closed the book, her heart pounding. Her first thought was to go find Betty and tell her what had happened, but even as she thought about trying to explain the situation to her sister, common sense began to kick in. How in the world would Addison Hartley have learned about the little drama that had played out between her and Claire and John all those years ago? And if he had known about it, why on earth would he ever have agreed to do a reading at her shop, of all places?

No, she told herself. There must be some other explanation. After all, she and John and Claire weren't the only teenagers who had ever been involved in a love triangle. The details were spookily similar, but simple chance might account for that. How often had she heard her customers or readers at libraries tell her that they'd read a book that seemed like it was about their own life? Well, now it was happening to her.

Still, she couldn't quite bring herself to pick up the book again. Instead, she walked to the living room and pulled down the memoir Addison Hartley had published a few years ago. Was there any chance these details came from Hartley's own life or the life of someone he knew? She scanned through the index, looking for any references to Cape Cod, Boston, or even the Atlantic Seaboard. Nothing. Then she skimmed through the first few chapters, looking for any reference to love triangles in his own history, but he spent several paragraphs explaining that he was a late bloomer in love and never managed to work up the nerve to ask a girl out until his first book became a best seller. Mary wasn't exactly impressed by his definition of love after that point either, which seemed to be a string of broken marriages, punctuated by romances with starlets. She put the book back on the shelf.

Claire, John, Mary, Addison Hartley. As the names and memories swirled in her head, one of them became more and more prominent—the woman who looked so much like Claire at Addison's reading. That was the only connection Mary could make between her story and Addison Hartley. But the woman had given no indication that she knew Hartley. Mary had met him on the street, and the woman had fled before Addison was done speaking. But that didn't change the fact that Claire and Addison might have been in the same place, right under Mary's own roof. Had they ever crossed paths before? Had Addison somehow learned Claire's version of the story from her or someone who had heard it from her years ago?

Mary picked up her laptop, which she'd left sitting on the coffee table the last time she'd used it, and ran a series of Internet searches. Searching Addison Hartley's bio just brought up the same canned language, mirrored over and over again on different sites. Refining the search with "Cape Cod" brought up hits referring to her own bookshop and not much else. She took a deep breath, then tried searching Hartley's name with

Claire's. Apparently Hartley had done an event once at the Wilkes Botanical Gardens in Florida, but nothing actually connected with Claire came up.

Mary could feel her blood pressure rising as each fruitless search came up. Finally she closed the computer, set the book aside, and bowed her head. *Lord,* she prayed, *I don't know if I'll like it or not, but I want to know the truth.*

SIX

The woman who answered the phone at the alumni department of the University of Chicago had quite a different tenor than the easygoing man Mary had spoken to at California State University.

"I'm sorry," the woman said after Mary gave her little spiel, saying she was looking for an old friend. "Who did you say you were?"

"Mary Fisher," Mary answered, a little unnerved. She was sitting at the counter of the bookshop, which she'd just opened. It was empty except for the morning light that poured through the front windows and her and Gus, who sat next to her on the counter and observed her seriously, as if he were just as interested in the results of this conversation as she was. When he heard the stress in her voice, he butted her shoulder gently with his head. She scratched between his ears.

"And you're a relative of this student?"

"No," Mary said. "Just an old friend."

"Well, I'm sorry," the woman said crisply. "But we're not in the habit of giving out personal information on our students under these sorts of circumstances."

"Oh," Mary said, surprised. "I wasn't trying—I mean, I just had been wondering how she was, and I thought perhaps I'd try to get in touch with her. This university was the last place I knew she'd been, so I thought I'd start here."

Something in Mary's tone seemed to soften the woman's attitude. "Well," she said, "for some of our students, we do have current information. I couldn't give it to you, but I might be able to send a message to them."

Mary hesitated. This wasn't quite how she'd imagined re-connecting with Claire. She'd pictured a phone conversation or sending a letter of her own. How would Claire respond to getting a message from her old university, saying that Mary was trying to get in touch with her? Mary had just been fol-lowing her curiosity up to this point, but getting in touch this way felt awkward. And she didn't know if it would even work. If that had really been Claire in her store the other night, she hadn't seemed to want to talk to Mary face-to-face. But perhaps there was some other reason Claire had bolted, something that had nothing to do with Mary. The fact was that Mary didn't have any idea how Claire would respond if Mary reached out to her. But at this point, what other leads did she have?

She glanced at Addison Hartley's newest book beside her on the counter, the bookmark showing she was halfway through. Whatever had gone on between her and Claire, it wasn't just between the two of them, it seemed. She had too many questions to back off now.

"Okay," she said slowly.

There was a blaze of typing from the other end of the line. "*Hmm*," the woman said.

Mary resisted asking her what the woman had discovered. Gus flopped over on the counter. She rubbed his soft belly.

Another ferocious burst of typing. "*Mm-hmm,*" the woman said. "Well."

"Yes?" Mary said.

"I'm sorry," the woman said. "Your friend hasn't exactly been an active alumna. I was looking for a recent e-mail or mailing address, but the only thing I have here is—" Another flare of clicking. "Her first employer, from the 1970s."

"Well," Mary said, "perhaps I could get in touch with them, and—"

"This is a firm that went belly-up in the early eighties," the woman told her. "It's been decades."

"Oh," Mary said. "And there's nothing else?"

"I'm afraid not," the woman said and managed to sound at least slightly sorry about it.

"Well," Mary said, "thank you."

She hung up the phone and scratched Gus's belly again. He caught her hand in both paws and chewed idly on a finger. Then the bell over the door rang: Rebecca coming in with Ashley, the tempting fragrance of Sweet Susan's Bakery sweeping in along with them. Instantly, Gus was on his feet. He leapt from the counter to the floor and observed the intruders from behind the shelter of one of the long shelves.

"Good morning!" Rebecca said.

"Good morning!" Mary replied.

Ashley wandered down the aisle to investigate the children's section while Rebecca slipped behind the desk and stowed her purse in the cubby Mary had given her.

Gus's departure had left the Hartley book as the only item on the counter. Mary looked at it with a mixture of curiosity and dread. The similarities between her story and the one the book told were eerie, but part of her couldn't wait to see how they played out. On the other side of the cash register sat the folder where she'd kept all the details of Addison Hartley's visit. She opened it idly. On the top sheet of paper was a Post-it that Janine, Hartley's publicist, had attached to one of her countless notes and addendums. It had just her name and cell phone, written in her bold hand and underlined three times.

As Rebecca scurried to begin the day by making sure everything was in order in the shop, Mary picked up the phone. To her mild surprise, Janine actually answered after a few rings. Well, if she had expected Mary to answer at all hours, at least it was fair that she pick up her own calls.

"Mary," Janine said with the breathless urgency Mary had gotten used to during their dealings before the reading. Mary was slightly amused to hear she used the same tone even when it was Mary who was doing the calling. Janine couldn't have any way yet of knowing whether what Mary was calling about was urgent or not. "How are you doing? What a great event. What can I do for you?"

What is she calling about anyway? Mary wondered. She knew what her questions were. She just wasn't sure how to phrase them. "It was so wonderful," Mary agreed. "I just wanted to call to thank you and Mr. Hartley again. I hope he enjoyed it as much as we did. People are still talking about it around here."

"That's great," Janine said. Mary could hear the faint impatience and also the question in her voice. For once, she sympathized. If Mary was just calling to say thank you, she could have just sent a note. She'd need to come up with something else to make the call worthwhile—both for Janine and herself.

"You know, it's interesting," Mary went on. "Some of our local readers had felt that they've found some very distinct flashes of local color in the book."

Was it her imagination or did Janine suddenly seem guarded? "Well, it is set on the coast," Janine joked. "I guess there must be some similarities any time you mix people and boats."

"Of course," Mary said. "But these similarities are a little more...pronounced. The layout of the town is very much like Ivy Bay, down to the location of the shops on the street. The lakes and the bay are in basically the same orientation. And some of the local history seems remarkably similar to events in the book. We were just curious if Mr. Hartley might have had some history with the town that we weren't aware of. My readers would be so interested to know if there was a deeper local connection."

Mary's heart was in her throat. She didn't know what she'd do if Janine questioned her about exactly *what* history Addison Hartley seemed to know about in Ivy Bay. But the question was a reasonable one, she told herself. Just the kind of thing a responsible bookstore owner might ask a publicist about, even if that bookstore owner didn't have any personal history involved.

"No, I don't think so," Janine said abruptly. "Mr. Hartley's visited most of the world in the course of promoting his books, and he always does meticulous research. I think you'll agree that all his books have an authentic ring, even though he never, for instance, worked as a lion tamer like the characters in *Roaring Thunder*. But he doesn't have any connection with Ivy Bay."

How can Janine be so sure? Mary wondered. She was only Addison Hartley's publicist, after all. Why should she know his whole history?

"Well, these similarities are really striking," Mary insisted. "I just can't quite believe they're coincidence. Is it something you'd mind asking him about for me? We'd be so grateful, and we had such a good time hosting him."

"Mr. Hartley is in Europe," Janine said. "He's very strict about his vacations. None of us here have any of his information while he's traveling. He won't be available for several more weeks."

"Well, maybe you could make a note for when he returns," Mary tried.

"I'm just about to go into a meeting," Janine said. "In fact, I was on my way in when I picked up this call. I'm sorry, but I really can't keep them waiting any longer. If you'll excuse me."

"Oh. Good-bye," Mary said as the line went dead.

She gave the receiver a long, strange look. Then she set it back in its cradle.

Rebecca came up, carrying a stack of Agatha Christie reissues. "I got so excited putting these out last night that I forgot to put price tags on them," she said. "I'm just going to print them all up now."

She glanced at the phone. "Is everything okay? Who was that?" she asked.

Ashley padded up from the children's section, carrying a long-suffering Gus. Her arms were crossed under his front paws, which reached to the sky in an unmistakable gesture of alarm. His light gray belly was exposed to the world, and his hind legs and tail dragged along the ground. Mary suppressed a smile. This was true love. Gus wouldn't accept this kind of handling from anyone else, not even her, but Ashley had absolutely charmed him over the past few weeks, to the point that he was willing to tolerate the indignity of being treated like the little girl's favorite doll.

"Oh, just Janine," Mary said.

Rebecca looked quizzical.

"She's the publicist," Mary said. "For Addison Hartley."

"Oh," Rebecca said. "Do we usually do post-event calls with the publicists, then?"

Mary hesitated. Maybe post-event calls would be a good idea, but the truth was that they weren't really a store policy. She didn't want to mislead Rebecca any more than she had to, but she also didn't want to invent a new company policy right there on the spot, without giving it some thought.

Ashley actually saved her from having to answer. "Addison!" she said with an expression of rapture. "He's my favorite. He's so nice to me."

Rebecca looked down at her fondly.

But something about the way Ashley was talking about Addison didn't sit right with Mary. Ashley talked about Addison as if he was some kind of old friend. Had she seen Addison Hartley before?

"I love Addison," Ashley burbled on. "When do we get to see him again?"

"I don't know, sweetie," Rebecca said, mussing her hair.

"Do you know Addison Hartley?" Mary asked, surprised.

Rebecca looked up. "No, no," she said, then glanced down again. The way Rebecca broke Mary's gaze didn't sit right with Mary either. If Rebecca was telling the truth, why would she be so quick to look away?

Ashley looked almost offended. "Yes, you do, Mommy!" She stared up at Mary, her blue eyes wide. "Are you his friend too?" she asked.

Mary smiled to avoid upsetting the little girl, but inside her stomach was tight. "I don't know that I'd say that, exactly," she said.

"He's *my* friend," Ashley said, as if she were standing up for the character of another child in a school-yard argument.

Mary was doing her best to hide her discomfort, but apparently Rebecca could see some of it on her face. "Come on, honey," she said. "Want to help me dust the hardcovers?"

"Yes!" Ashley crowed and trundled off down the aisle, Rebecca behind her.

For the rest of the morning, as she placed orders, looked through catalogs, made plans for placing stock, and helped the customers who came and went, Mary's mind circled the question of Rebecca's strange answers. They weren't the first ones she'd gotten from Rebecca. She'd almost forgotten the fact that Rebecca claimed not to have spoken to the woman who looked so much like Claire in the crowd at the reading, but her suspicions now called upon the faint suspicion she'd felt then. Alone, those two incidents might seem to have simple explanations. But side by side, combined with Rebecca avoiding her gaze and breaking off the conversation with Ashley, they raised uncomfortable questions in Mary's mind about Rebecca's honesty.

The suggestion that Ashley, and therefore Rebecca, might be more friendly with Addison Hartley than Rebecca had let on also raised a new possibility. Mary already knew that stories about Claire and John had circulated through Ivy Bay after Mary had left for the summer. Bernice hadn't been willing to tell her what they were, but if she had to guess, it might be something like the story Addison Hartley was telling in his most recent blockbuster, with the Claire character as a hero and the character based on Mary as clueless and manipulative. But until now, she hadn't been able to make any connection between Addison Hartley, Claire, and Ivy Bay.

Now it seemed like the connection might actually be standing in her shop. Rebecca could have heard the story any number of ways. Tales had a long life span in small towns, Mary knew. Rebecca could have heard Claire's stories second- or third- or even fourthhand. But maybe she hadn't, Mary reminded herself. After all, Mary had seen the woman who looked like Claire sharing some kind of comment with Rebecca at the reading. It was possible Rebecca had been in touch with Claire directly and heard the story right from her. Mary had been looking for a connection between Claire and Hartley, but maybe the connection was between Hartley and Rebecca.

In any case, Mary realized, the one person she could be sure knew the truth about the connection between Addison Hartley's blockbuster novel and Mary's own life was Hartley himself. She tried to get at the answer by asking Janine and tracking down Claire. And she still didn't understand how Rebecca was connected with Hartley. But what if she just asked Hartley himself?

Quickly, she opened her e-mail. Janine had handled most of the arrangements for the event at the bookshop, but Mary thought she remembered Janine copying Hartley on some of those e-mails—and Hartley even responding to a few of them. Mary clicked to sort the e-mails alphabetically, then scrolled through the Hs. There, about halfway down, were three messages from Addison Hartley.

Mary clicked on one, read quickly through Hartley's terse confirmation of the event's start time, and hit Reply.

When the blank e-mail turned up on the screen, she stared at it. But she couldn't find a way to bring up the questions she wanted to ask. Everything she tried made her feel like a slightly unhinged fan. "Did you write this book about my life story?" "How did you know so much about my life?"

After a few fruitless attempts, she remembered the thankyou gift she'd thought of sending him. She wasn't sure yet what it might be, but perhaps mentioning that would be a good way to break the ice. That idea flowed more easily. She typed a few grateful lines, thanking him for joining her event and letting him know she'd like to send him a small gift to express her gratitude. She knew he was traveling and that he spent his time between homes. Could he direct her where to send it? Then she hit Enter and started a new paragraph. A few of her readers had had questions about his book after the event, she told him. Would he be willing to field a few of them by e-mail?

When she was finished, she read it over. Despite everything that had happened since the event, she still felt a little charge of anxiety at the prospect of sending a message to such a famous author. For a long moment after, she assured herself that everything in the letter was correct, but her hand still hovered over the Send button.

Then she clicked it.

SEVEN

"Daddy, Daddy, Daddy!" Ashley shouted, flying across the store to greet her father, a gruff fisherman in a denim shirt and a battered ball cap.

He knelt down and scooped her up in a big bear hug as Rebecca joined them. "How's my best girl?" he asked. He handed Rebecca a brown paper bag, and she took it and walked behind the counter and tucked it in her purse.

"I'm good," Ashley said. "We saw Addison Hartley this week!"

"You did?" her father said, then gave Rebecca a wink.

Mary's ears pricked. He didn't seem surprised at all by this news.

"I miss him," Ashley said with a hint of drama and buried her face in her father's neck.

"Ah, sugar plum," Russell said.

Was Mary imagining things, or did Rebecca give him a warning look? In any case, Rebecca didn't let this conversation run on, any more than she had let Ashley run on about Addison Hartley earlier.

"Russell," she said, "I don't think you've met Mrs. Fisher yet."

Russell turned to Mary with a big smile. "I just feel like I have," he said. "I've heard so much about you."

Mary smiled and slipped out from behind the counter to shake his hand. "Just Mary is fine," she told him. "I hope the things you've heard have been good."

Russell's grin widened. "Oh, you should hear her talk about this place at home," he said. "You'd think someone had given her a job inside the gates of heaven."

"Well, I certainly hope there are books up there," Rebecca said.

Russell raised his eyebrows at Mary. "You see?" he said.

Mary smiled while Rebecca dismissed him with a quick kiss.

"I'll be done at five," she said. "And dinner's at six."

"Right," Russell said.

Ashley popped up from his shoulder and flung both arms out, pointing toward the door. "Let's *go!*" she cried.

Her father laughed and carried her out the door.

Rebecca came back to the counter and circled around it. "Would now be a good time for me to go out and get some lunch?" she asked.

Mary checked the clock. There wasn't usually a big rush at noon, and she wouldn't mind some time alone to think things through. "Go ahead," she said.

"Thanks," Rebecca said. "I'm going to the Tea Shoppe for a bite." She collected her purse from the cubby, gave Mary a cheery smile, then made a beeline for the front door.

Mary watched her, confused. Hadn't Russell just brought her lunch? The bell clanged overhead as she stepped outside.

Mary felt another wave of mistrust wash over her. Mary stepped toward the door and watched her walk down the street, past the Tea Shoppe, toward Route 6A. Mary stood still for a moment. Maybe Rebecca was just going out to the main road for some reason and would come back in a moment. But the moment passed, and Rebecca didn't reappear.

Mary had now completely lost her own appetite. This was the third time Rebecca's truthfulness had been in question in as many days. Mary had been so confident when she hired her. Now she began to wonder: Had she made a mistake?

Slowly, she went back to the counter and sat down at the computer. Maybe she had trusted her own instincts too much. Perhaps she should have done a more thorough search on Rebecca before hiring her. What would she have found?

She typed Rebecca's name into the search engine and began to sift through the items that popped up. Much of it she already knew. Rebecca had been born and raised in Ivy Bay, so she'd had years for the false story about Claire and John to reach her. She'd attended a nearby college. Her Facebook page was public and filled with friends from Ivy Bay and a few from farther-flung areas—but none of them seemed to be Addison Hartley, even though Mary scanned through all two hundred and fifty of her friends' profile photographs, on the hunch that Addison Hartley, if he did have a Facebook account, might not keep it under his exact name.

There were several records of writers' conferences and gatherings that Rebecca had attended. Some of them had high-profile headliners, but as far as Mary could tell, Addison Hartley hadn't attended any of them—and the attendees of a conference weren't ever guaranteed the chance to talk with the big-name writers who made the keynote speeches anyway.

On the second and third pages of the search, Rebecca's own stories began to show up, in some lesser-known online literary magazines. Mary clicked through a few of them, not sure what she was looking for—some link to Addison Hartley? Some proof of the many little deceptions Mary suspected? Some reference to the story about Claire and John that had cropped up so unexpectedly in Addison Hartley's work?

But Rebecca's stories didn't give Mary any hints beyond those she already had. If anything, they made everything even more confusing. The stories weren't in big publications, but they were funny, tender, and well observed. Mary felt more like she was enjoying getting to know a new favorite writer than trying to solve a worrisome mystery. This was how she'd felt about Rebecca when she first hired her—that she'd just found a gem and a kindred spirit who would be a perfect fit with the store. But how could she make these stories match with all the evasion and deception Rebecca had shown her over the past few days?

Lord, what is going on here? Mary asked. *You know each sparrow who falls, so You must know the answers behind all this. Help me find them too.*

The bell over the door clanged. Mary looked up.

Rebecca came in, her smile bright as she bustled over to the counter. "Afternoon!" she said. "What are you up to here?"

Before Mary thought to close the browser, Rebecca was behind the counter and glanced at the screen.

"Oh my goodness!" she said. "I can't believe you found that! What on earth possessed you to look up that old story?"

The story Mary had open, a lovely short story about a young mother who planted a dogwood when her daughter was born, and the way the tree and the girl had grown up together, was actually excellent. Mary's librarian's instinct rose up in her; she needed to call a good story when she saw one. "It's wonderful work," Mary told her.

Rebecca tried to hide a smile. "Oh!" she said. "Well, I'm just grateful you spent your time reading it, instead of any of these." She gestured around the store.

"Well, it holds its own," Mary told her.

Now Rebecca's smile broke out in full. "Thank you," she said. "You didn't have to say that."

"I wouldn't, if it wasn't true," Mary said.

Rebecca dropped her eyes, bashful. When she broke Mary's gaze, all of Mary's doubts and questions about Rebecca swept back into her mind.

"How was lunch?" Mary asked, trying to keep her voice casual.

"Just fine," Rebecca said. "I just went out and had a little something."

Immediately, all the warmth Mary had felt from reading Rebecca's stories and their conversation vanished.

So where, Mary wondered, as she turned back to the story wavering on her computer screen, had Rebecca really gone?

EIGHT

——◆◆◆——

I don't know," the woman said to Mary the next day, flipping idly through the pages of one of the books on the
front display, without really looking at them. "What do you
think?" She was obviously a visitor to town, her wardrobe just
a little too carefully casual to really be a native Ivy Bayer. Boat
shoes, for one thing, were meant to be worn on the boats
themselves. That was the whole point of them—to keep the
dirt and grit of shore from leaving dull scratches that dulled
the high sheen of the varnished or fiberglass surfaces of the
boats. On land, actual sailors and fishermen were much more
likely to go around in sneakers or boots. Still, any customer
was a good customer, and Mary was grateful for the vacation
trade and that so many people still loved to read a good book
just as much as they enjoyed swimming or lying down on the
beach. The bump in business Ivy Bay saw each summer had
been a welcome cushion for her as she opened the business. It
meant that she was already beating her own budget, although
the true test of whether the business was a go or not would be
whether it was still open *next* summer.

"Well, tell me a bit about what you like," Rebecca said
with a smile.

Mary watched her from behind the counter. Just as Rebecca always did, she'd gone right up and greeted the woman as soon as she came in. But this time, Mary's doubts about Rebecca's truthfulness gave her a sick feeling, even as Rebecca did her usual beautiful job at customer service.

"Something good," the woman said. "I like stories that move along, but nothing too dark. Mysteries are great, but some of them are so gory these days. You don't have any romances, do you?"

"Well, sometimes there's a bit of romance mixed up in the mystery," Rebecca said.

One of the things Mary had wanted to do when she opened up the shop was broaden the definition of mystery. She loved the classic genre and all the great names who had written in it, but in her very first order of stock for the shop, she'd also included titles that weren't quite classic mysteries. Her librarian's instinct hoped that maybe helping people branch out would introduce them to whole new worlds they might not have discovered on their own.

Rebecca was holding up one of those titles. "This is a great one," she said. "It's a literary thriller based around a woman's quest to find her soldier sweetheart in the year after World War II ended. She gets a letter at the beginning that says he was killed in action, but the things his commander returns to her aren't his. She can't do anything about that until the war ends, but then she'd be free to go looking for him. A little mystery; a little romance."

The woman put down the other book she'd been flipping through. Her face showed interest for the first time. "That sounds good," she said, taking it from Rebecca's hands. "Do you have anything else like that?"

"Well, let's see," Rebecca said and led her down an aisle.

Mary watched them go, her uneasiness over Rebecca struggling against her admiration for Rebecca's sales skills.

A few minutes later, the woman walked up to the counter and plunked down four hardcover books. Whatever else Mary might think about Rebecca, her results were hard to argue with.

"Did you find everything you wanted?" Mary asked, ringing up the books.

"I found things I didn't even know I wanted," the woman said. "That girl is really good. I'm going to spend my whole vacation with my nose in a book."

"That sounds like the perfect vacation to me," Mary said.

The woman considered this for a moment, then smiled. "Maybe you're right," she said.

Mary packed the books into a bag and pushed them back across the counter. "Enjoy," she said.

"You bet I will," the woman told her.

The bell dinged over the front door, and the shop was quiet except for the sound of Ashley's foot thumping idly against the side of the bathtub where she sometimes liked to sit.

Rebecca hummed in the front of the store, shelving some of the new stock that had come in that week.

Only Gus seemed to notice Mary's subdued mood. Often he was off on his own prowls around the store, investigating all the interesting nooks and crannies. But today, for whatever reason, he stuck close by her, slinking between her legs and butting her gently with his head.

Now he took up a post beside her on the counter, watching her closely.

"Oh, Gus," Mary said and sighed. She scratched between his ears, and he stretched out on the counter, his paws landing on the cover of Addison Hartley's newest book. Mary's bookmark hadn't moved since the first night she started reading it, when she'd begun to recognize the weird parallels between her own story and the one Hartley told in his book. It was easier for her to pretend that maybe she'd been wrong about the resemblances if she didn't read anymore. And part of her was afraid of what she might find if she read on.

But now Gus patted his gray paws on the cover and gave a long, meaningful meow.

"You think so?" Mary said. "Are you sure?"

Gus began to purr like a well-oiled machine.

Mary rubbed his belly and pulled the book across the counter to her. "Maybe you're right," she said.

She began to lift the front cover, then hesitated. Wasn't there something else she needed to do instead? Ordering or receipts or a customer to deal with?

But try as she might, she couldn't think of another excuse to avoid finishing the story. The books, the ordering, and even her e-mail were up to date. And the store was empty except for her, Rebecca, and Ashley.

She lifted her chin and turned to the bookmark. Maybe she had been wrong, after all, she told herself. Maybe if she read on, the similarities between her story and the book's would become so small it would be clear the resemblance had been nothing more than a coincidence. In any case, she told herself, it was better to know the truth than to let her imagination run wild. *You will know the truth, and the truth will set you free,* she reminded herself. That was one of her favorite of Jesus' sayings from the Gospels, and it had always held true for her. Even if she didn't like the truth, facing it always turned out better than taking refuge in a lie. And the sooner she faced things, she'd learned, the better.

She opened the book and began to read.

As always, Addison Hartley's crisp, vivid prose pulled her through page after page. The mystery his detective was solving was engrossing; a complicated, multigenerational plot, with secrets that extended over several continents, all linked to one family home overlooking the coast, and the sailors and, later, shipping magnates who lived there. For a few chapters, as the detective tracked those clues everywhere from the local library to the Vatican records, Mary lost herself in the story. When she did remember her worries about the local romance subplot, she actually felt a little foolish. After all, how in the world would Addison Hartley have heard her story? And why would he include it in his book, of all the other stories in the world?

But all the explanations she'd built up in her head crumbled the instant she began the next chapter in which the subplot reappeared. Mary had been hoping the similarities would fade. If anything, they were even more stark, to the point that they seemed almost ridiculous. Even if Addison Hartley had known all the details, she thought, why wouldn't he have at least gone to the trouble to change them a little bit? But there were these little bits of her life story, down to the last detail. The character based on John wore a class ring that was set with an emerald, just like John had. That was a detail Mary would never have forgotten, since she'd actually worn the ring longer than John ever had—from about a week after it was shipped to him, to the day he replaced it with the engagement ring he'd bought her during their senior year of college. And just like John, Hartley's character had a high school letter jacket with patches for both swimming and basketball, an unusual combination. And he said the same thing in the book that John always said—that he worked ten times harder as a swimmer than he did on the basketball court, even though the whole school came out to see the basketball games.

In fact, the book seemed to have details in it that Mary herself hadn't even remembered, like the night she and Claire and John had gotten ice cream downtown, then walked down to the water and all sat on the end of a pier, watching the sun go down. Now that she read it, Mary could remember the strawberry ice cream she'd had that night—and that John had ordered rum raisin, in a departure from his usual order of plain vanilla, something she'd teased him gently about. But although the details were recorded with eerie accuracy, the book's interpretation of the events veered more and more sharply from Mary's memory of how things had happened. With the ice cream, for instance, her gentle teasing was transformed into something almost shrewish—proof her character didn't understand or appreciate the character who seemed to be based on John. In the book version, the John character and the Claire character shared a secret, knowing glance just after the exchange, with the John character wounded and mournful, the Claire character indignant on his behalf. And John's on-a-whim order of rum raisin was transformed into a metaphor for his choice between a rich and exciting life with the Claire character—rum raisin—and the safe but boring life he'd have with the character based on Mary, who was supposed to be like vanilla.

By this time, Mary couldn't have stopped reading the book even if she'd wanted to. The combination of the momentum of Addison Hartley's always-powerful prose and her own indignation and curiosity was irresistible. It was a good thing that everything was already in order in the shop when she picked it up, because for the rest of the day, with a few small interruptions to check out various customers, she did nothing but read. During the last hundred pages, she even retreated to one of the stuffed chairs at the back of the shop so she could read without interruption, leaving the shop entirely in Rebecca's hands, as her doubts about Rebecca faded in the light of the story that leapt out at her from the pages.

As the novel unfolded, the details continued with their eerie resemblance to Mary's own life, with just a few minor exceptions.... When the John and Mary characters slipped away together, Hartley had those conversations occur on the beach, rather than from the overlook John had actually found for her. For some reason, Mary found the fact that Hartley had changed that bit comforting—her times spent with John among the pines at the beginning of their courtship were among her most precious memories, and she wasn't sure she could have handled one of Addison Hartley's well-drawn but skewed scenes competing with her own private history.

But as the book drew to a close, Hartley added more and more scenes that Mary didn't want to believe could ever have happened. While the Mary character napped, the John character went for a walk and ran into the Claire character. Their clear connection resulted in an intense conversation in which John revealed his deep hopes and dreams to Claire and his questions about whether he could ever really pursue them if he chose to marry Mary and start a family. The two of them began to dream about just going off together and starting a carefree existence together. Over the next chapters, that conversation led to more clandestine meetings, until one starry night after Mary had gone to bed, John snuck out to meet Claire, and they both confessed their love to each other, sealing their promises with a kiss.

The scene was so well written that it was almost impossible to believe it was only a bit of fiction. Mary fought as she tore through the pages to keep Hartley's story straight from her own. *This didn't really happen,* she told herself over and over. *John would never have done this to me. He never talked about this again in all the years I knew him. Even the story Claire told me wasn't like this. She didn't say anything about these secret conversations—or a kiss.*

But thinking this was easier than believing it as the story continued to roll out in Addison Hartley's compelling prose.

The light in the shop shifted from the east to the west while she read. Around six o'clock, Rebecca stuck her head in. "Everything okay?" she asked. "I was just going to close up and take Ashley home."

"Sure, sure," Mary said, barely looking up from the page.

At that point, she was only a few chapters from the end. She flew through the smart, tense denouement of the central mystery of the book, then slowed down, her heart pounding as Hartley circled back to give the readers one more scene between the John character and the Claire character. While the Mary character was upstairs, obliviously packing for her return home with the John character, the John and Claire characters met together one last time. In a passionate, tearful good-bye, the John character tells the Claire character that he just can't bring himself to break the Mary character's heart and run away with Claire. As the Mary character began to call from an upstairs window, wondering where he was, the John character started to walk away. But after a few steps, he returned to the Claire character, swept her up in an embrace, and gave her a passionate kiss. "I can't lose you," he told her, burying his face in her hair. "I'll find a way for us to be together. I promise."

The book ended with the detective and the Claire character both sitting on the end of the wharf together, pondering the past events of the book and wondering about the future.

Mary closed the cover and pushed the book off her lap. She'd never felt this way when she finished a book before. She had an almost physical reaction to the sight of the book, the same kind of feeling of fear and hurt she might have had if she ran into someone who had been nasty to her the last time they met.

She stood up, shook her head, and shrugged her shoulders, but the feeling didn't leave her.

Gus, who had sat curled up at her side for most of the afternoon, circled around her feet and gave a tentative meow.

Mary looked around at the shadows gathering in her shop. Whatever she did, she couldn't stay here.

"Come on, Gus," she said, scooping him up. A moment later, she deposited him in his carrying case, collected both him and her purse, and shut off the last lights that Rebecca had left on. Outside the door, she checked to make sure the lock was secure, then got in the car.

She wasn't sure quite where she was going as she pulled away from the curb. However, after a few automatic turns, she realized that she was headed almost by instinct in the direction of the overlook where she and John had spent so many happy hours together, both in the beginning of their courtship and on return visits over the years that followed. Something was pulling her back there—a desire to talk to John, or simply the desire to replace some of Addison Hartley's disturbing images by reinforcing her own memories through the familiar scene. Whatever it was, she was in no shape to resist it. A few minutes later, along the narrow, twisting Cape roads, she'd reached the little pine rise, and she pulled over.

"I'll be right back," she promised Gus, then cracked the windows and locked the doors.

The spot she'd shared with John was perfectly invisible from the road, but it took her only a few steps to break through the screen of pines into the chapel-like silence below the trees. They'd grown since she and John were young. When they'd first visited, John had had to duck to avoid hitting his head on the lower branches, but now the lowest branches towered high above Mary's head, and the trees themselves were almost double the size they had once been. But the water was the same as it always was—the long comforting line of the horizon, the familiar blue of the waves, the hush and roar of the water as it rolled over itself and sizzled down among the sand and rocks below.

She hadn't been here since John died. In fact, she hadn't done much of anything that had to do with John since he passed away, except for those things that absolutely had to be done, including making the funeral arrangements, sending out his obituary, packing up all his things into boxes as part of her own move away from the house they had shared for decades. She'd cried a few times, of course, but mostly she'd just tried to press on. That's what John would have wanted, she told herself, and she knew that was true. He hated it when she cried or seemed down at all. He'd always gone to all kinds of lengths to lift her spirits when she was down, bringing her little presents or flowers when he came home from work, making all kinds of ridiculous jokes that became even more ridiculous as he grew from a high school ballplayer, to a serious undergraduate, to a well-respected lawyer.

But despite the truth of the fact that she knew John wouldn't have wanted her to sit around unhappy over him, some part of her knew there was something else to it. She missed him so much that she could barely stand to think about him, and so she did her best not to think about him at all. Until today, that had been easier than any alternative she could think of. But now, suddenly, she saw the problem with it. She hadn't let herself think about how much she missed John. But in the process, she'd shut away all her good memories of him too.

And now, in the face of Addison Hartley's strange version of their courtship story, she needed her own memories of John more than ever.

As she stepped through the pines to the edge of the bluff, those memories came flooding back to her—how he'd always taken her arm once they got into the pines, ostensibly to help her keep her balance, but really because he liked having his arm around her; how he'd brought her here years later and opened a dazzling diamond that sparkled like the glints on the waves below; how they'd come there together years later, on visits to see Betty, and enjoyed sitting side by side, enjoying the silence together, all their secrets already shared.

At least, that's what Mary had thought then. But had there been more secrets than she'd understood? Was there any grain of truth in Addison Hartley's story?

Mary had never been in the habit of talking to John since he died. But something about this place, and the day, brought words to her lips. "Sweetheart," she said, "I don't know if you can hear me. I don't know if it matters. But I miss you." Her voice broke, and warm tears rolled down her face. Her heart twisted in her chest for a long moment, and then it released. Despite everything, some part of her felt lighter than it had since she lost John.

Lord, she prayed, *You know I miss him. But I know that You don't leave us or forsake us. Thank You that You're always with us, even if we lose our loved ones or they lose us.*

She opened her eyes and looked out over the water.

It had felt good to talk to John, whether he could hear her or not. But she had to face the facts. She'd never be able to ask him any of the questions she had about Addison Hartley's book. Somehow, she'd have to find those answers out for herself.

NINE

All the lights in the house were out as Mary fit her key into the front door.

Usually Mary looked forward to seeing her sister when she got home. Not only had Betty always been one of her favorite people, but in her first days in Ivy Bay, Mary had also been incredibly grateful to be sharing her home with another person again after the long months spent alone in Boston, coping with the details surrounding John's death. Gus had been her faithful companion through those days, always running to the door and purring when she returned, but no matter how beloved Gus was, greeting him wasn't the same as greeting someone with whom you could really talk.

But tonight Mary found herself slightly relieved to see that Betty was out. It wasn't that she didn't want to talk to her. Mary didn't really want to talk to anybody, except, perhaps, the two people with whom she couldn't talk: Claire and John. But mostly, she didn't really want to talk at all. So many things had happened to her in the last few days, and so many words had washed over her, that she wanted a bit of peace and quiet, to let things settle into their right place and get to a point where she could hear both her own internal voice and God's quiet promptings again. She felt a bit like Moses, hidden in the rock, waiting to meet with God. The last days had been full of storms that didn't really seem to carry much truth with them. Maybe a few hours alone in the quiet would give the "still small voice" of God a chance to speak to her and to set things right in her heart.

Inside the door, she set Gus's carrying case down and opened the door. Gus flitted out like a soft gray shadow and disappeared into the shadows of the dark house, on patrol to make sure everything was just as he left it. Mary returned the carrying case to its usual storage place, then went to the kitchen. She'd been so carried away by Addison Hartley's story that she'd forgotten to eat lunch, she realized, but she still wasn't very hungry. The stress and the worry of the last few days had hardened into a knot in her belly, and the last thing she wanted to do was eat. Still, she knew she had to eat something.

She took a few things out of the refrigerator and half-heartedly made herself a toasted peanut butter and honey sandwich, slicing a tart green apple for herself while the bread was toasting. She ate it standing at the counter, looking out through the kitchen window at the dark shapes of Betty's garden in the twilight. Everything stood just where it always had, the hibiscus on the left, the stands of lilies and hostas, the plum tree, the borders of bright annuals. But in the darkness, they all looked incredibly strange, even spooky. If she squinted closely, she could make out what each of the shadows was and remember how it usually looked by daylight. But the darkness of night had transformed the familiar garden into a foreign landscape.

That was how Addison Hartley's book had made her feel about her own life. All the familiar events had been there in his story. But they'd been covered with some kind of shadow, so that the shapes were familiar, but they still seemed unrecognizably strange. And try as she might to shake it off, his writing was too powerful. Just like any good book, the scenes he'd written worked just like memories in her mind and the characters he'd created seemed like real people. They jostled in her mind with her own memories, elbowing them aside, blending with them, creating strange new combinations.

Mary put her plate in the sink and shook her head. She couldn't let Addison Hartley's version of the events, however well he'd written them, interfere with her own memories of the most precious events of her life. Somehow, she'd have to fight back. And somehow she had a sense that she'd need to begin to reclaim those memories she had hidden away from fear of the pain they might cause her after John died.

Gus slipped into the warmly lit kitchen and wound himself around Mary's legs. Mary knelt and scratched his head. "Hello, there," she said, stroking his long, silky back. Gus purred happily, then darted off again.

Mary headed to her room, but when she reached it, she didn't settle in as she usually did. Instead, she walked over to the closet where she had stored her mementos of John. In fact, she herself hadn't even really stored them. She'd simply directed the movers to carry each box that contained anything of John's into the closet and stack them all there. And since then, she hadn't opened any of them.

She couldn't be sure how long she stood there in front of the closet door, breathing quietly in the low light. She stared down at the pearl ring he had given her for their tenth anniversary. Eventually, she put out her hand and opened it.

Inside were half a dozen stacks of boxes, most of them book sized, all as tall as her or taller. Her heart seemed to tug and jump at the same time. Part of her felt the little warm shock she'd felt all her life when she thought about John. It was schoolgirls' stuff, but for Mary, it had lasted all her life. But another part of her wanted to draw back from all the sorrow and loss she'd felt when he passed away. That part of her shrank away like a hand from a hot stove. But for the first time since she'd lost him, she steeled herself against it. Before she could lose her nerve, she picked up the nearest box and set it down on the ottoman of her big stuffed chair in the corner, then picked up a sharp-pointed nail file from her dresser and used it to split the strips of clear packing tape that held the boxes together. At the time she'd packed them, she hadn't had the wherewithal to do an exhaustive inventory of each box. She'd just put as many things of his as she could in each and labeled them all "John." So as she set aside the nail file and flipped open the cardboard flaps, she had no idea what she'd find.

When she opened the box, the familiar smell of John was overwhelming. Cedar, from the cedar hangers Mary kept in his part of the closet, to preserve his good suits from moths and mildew. His cologne, an old-fashioned brand his father had used before him. And the faint scent of something that was just him. It all breathed from one of the only pieces of clothing Mary hadn't quite been able to throw away— his black cashmere overcoat, which she'd saved and saved to buy him as a graduation present from law school. He'd been freezing all the previous winter in a ski jacket that dated back to his college days, and his buddies in law school, who were already beginning to mimic the posh wardrobes of the lawyers they'd one day be, had mocked him for it mercilessly. John had had less money than the other guys in law school because he wasn't just living the student life—he had a wife and a young child to take care of at home. He'd shrugged off all the ribbing good-naturedly, but it had stung Mary because she knew that, in a way, he was wearing the disreputable old coat because of her. She'd wanted him to have something just as good as the other guys—in fact, even better. So she'd taken on a few freelance writing projects to earn the money to get him a proper coat. While he pored over his books each night, she'd retreat to her own room and wrote.

When she presented him with the new coat, the mockery of his friends had turned to hushed envy, and from that day on, he'd refused any other winter coat, even long after they could have afforded much nicer ones. He'd worn the lining to shreds at least three times, and each time, he'd insisted that Mary take it to a tailor to be repaired rather than replacing it. She'd even gone so far as to just buy him a brand-new coat the year he made partner at his firm, but he'd simply ignored it, pulling his old favorite from the closet each morning. "It reminds me of a lot of things I like to remember," he told her, when she'd complained about it. "Most of all, you."

Mary had found that hard to argue with. And she'd found it hard to part with the coat, even when she called a charity to come pick up most of his other things. Now, as she pulled it out of the box and folded it on her lap, tears sprang to her eyes. She'd hung this coat up so many times and been enfolded in it frequently by John's hugs when he swept in the door from work.

She had never really given into her tears since John died. Of course, she hadn't been able to resist crying at times. But she'd always fought the feeling, wiped the tears away, and carried on. Part of her might have even been afraid that if she started to cry, she wouldn't be able to stop.

But now she let herself go, her shoulders shaking as tears rolled down her face and dropped onto the soft fabric. To her surprise, they didn't hurt the way she had been afraid they were going to. In fact, they were a relief. Something like the way it felt to finally blurt out the way you really felt, even if everything in you wished you didn't feel that way. And to her surprise, they didn't last very long. They came and went like a summer storm, washing the heat from the air and watering the roots in the ground, and then moving on. When the tears stopped, Mary released her hold on the soft fabric and looked up. She wouldn't have believed it, but she felt as if the tears had carried away a weight with them that she didn't even know she had been carrying. And she also felt closer to John than she had since he had passed away—not as if he were right there in the room with her, but as if someone had led her to a door in the wall she'd built around her memories of him and opened it.

Then she set the coat aside and looked inside the box to see what she had packed under it. For the next couple of hours, she pulled the physical objects that had supported and surrounded her life with John from the boxes, padding back and forth from the closet to retrieve another when each one was emptied, and strewing the contents around her room. His coat was thrown over the back of her overstuffed chair, his books were spread across her bedspread, and his cuff links and coin collection were laid out in a clumsy circle on the floor. Tears flowed down her face again when she found the first valentine she'd ever given him tucked into the front of the organizer he carried with him to work every day and also when she turned over a sheaf of unassuming financial documents and saw his familiar handwriting on the signature lines. But mostly, she was overrun by good memories. She had found the cards their children had written for him when they were just eager toddlers, when they gained more control of their crayons and pencils as they entered school, and when they'd grown sophisticated enough to draw fake "Hallmark" stamps on the back of their hand-drawn birthday greetings; the bottle of sand he'd collected on one of their trips to Ivy Bay and had kept on his dresser ever since; and the scrap of lace he'd saved from one of the flower arrangements at their daughter's wedding.

As she flipped through the pages of a scrapbook John had made when he was a boy, with photographs, magazine clippings, feathers, and ancient leaves all pasted to the page with the same school glue, she heard a footfall in the hall. When she looked up, Betty stood in the doorway.

"Mary," she said. "There you are. I came home, and all the lights were out in the living room."

"I decided to go through some things tonight," Mary said simply, looking up from her spot on the floor, where she sat surrounded by the jumble of John's things.

"Oh," Betty said. She understood exactly what this meant, Mary knew. Betty had been incredibly gentle about John. She never brought him up unless Mary mentioned him, which Mary rarely did. And she never opened the closet that held his things. "Well," Betty said, "how are you doing?"

For some reason, this simple question brought the tears to Mary's eyes again. But they also brought a smile. "I'm fine," she told her sister. "I'm good. Thanks."

Betty nodded. "Good," she said. She took a deep breath and let it out again. "Well," she said, "I'll just be in my room, if you need anything."

"Thank you," Mary said.

Betty hesitated for a minute in the doorway. The sisters had always been close—so close that they knew when the other one simply needed space and time alone. Mary knew that Betty was trying to make sure she gave Mary that space right now. But after a moment, Betty stepped into the room, picked through the scattered objects on the floor, and knelt down beside Mary to give her an awkward hug. Mary hugged her back tightly. Then, without a word, Betty rose and padded away back down the hall and downstairs to her bedroom.

Mary sighed, some of the worry that had spurred her on all evening eased by her sister's loving gesture. But she continued to sift through the boxes until the closet was completely empty. By this time, a knot of John's favorite ties were piled in front of the display on her bedside clock, and Mary had lost track of the time in more ways than one. But she felt freer than she had in all the time since John died.

When she pulled the last object from the last box, she leaned back against the ottoman and sighed. As her memories flooded back to her, the images that Addison Hartley's book had conjured in her mind receded and faded until she could barely call them up. They were only dim recollections of a book she had read once. But when she held the physical objects that had anchored her life with John in her hands, Addison Hartley's words couldn't stand against them. This was her life. She had hidden parts of it away, but it was richer and deeper and more complicated and more vivid than any book could ever be.

Thank You, she prayed.

Then she began to pack the boxes again. But this time, she left a few things out. She stuck the valentine John had saved in the corner of her own mirror and also kept the glass doorknob that had always pulled out of the front door of their first apartment. The landlord had finally replaced it the week before they moved out, and John had rescued the knob from the trash heap outside and kept it on his desk at work in the years that followed. Mary laid it on her bedside beside her clock, scooped up the pile of ties, and put them in the box with John's old coat. Maybe someday one of the grand-children would want some of these things. It could give them the same connection with their grandfather that the familiar objects had just given her—make them feel they were part of something, help them realize that everything really did hap-pen in color back then. It was only the film that was black and white.

This time, as she packed everything back up, she labeled the boxes carefully in case she wanted to find something in them again: "Clothes," "Books," "Childhood items." As she packed everything back into each box, she felt very different than she had the last time she packed them. That time, she'd felt like she was putting away things she couldn't bear to look at any longer. This time, she had the same feeling of satisfaction she got from putting her house or the shelves or the store in order, as if everything was where it belonged now, just where it ought to be.

It was as she packed up the boxes, organizing the items and compiling all of John's old papers and files, that she found the bankbook. It was in an odd place. When Mary picked up John's high school yearbook, it fell out from between the pages. At first, the little folder didn't seem unusual. It was the same blue leatherette with the familiar stamp of the bank she and John had always used in Boston. But when she flipped it open to see what part of their life it had recorded—their early years, when they'd dole a single can of orange juice out in tiny sips over the course of a whole week; their middle years, when they'd had a special account to save up for the kids' college—she'd found an unfamiliar account.

Mary had done most of the accounting in the family. It was one of the jokes between them. John was the one who dealt with business clients all day long, and Mary was supposed to be the featherheaded English buff. But she had a knack for numbers. She'd brought more than one library out of the red during her days among the stacks, and she was putting the same acumen to work now with the bookshop business. She had liked keeping track of the household accounts, knowing what they had, paring back when times were lean, and saving up when things were flush. She took special pleasure in being able to eke out enough to take the family on interesting trips, by not spending money the same way the other lawyers' wives did: on fancy cars and expensive furniture and clothes.

This account was totally unfamiliar to her.

Well, Mary thought, *maybe it's a defunct account. Something he started for Christmas and then forgot about.*

But when she opened the bankbook, she gasped. There was a substantial amount of money in it. Tens of thousands of dollars.

TEN

Mary shifted the phone against her shoulder, Monday morning. A tinny ring repeated on the other line, then rang again. A moment later, the line clicked, and the connection came through.

"First Boston Bank," a woman said in a crisp, professional voice.

For some reason, Mary suddenly felt like an awkward teenager, nervous and not sure what to say. "Hello," she said. "I'd like to speak with one of your account managers."

"Do you have an account here with us?" the woman inquired.

That was a good question. Mary hesitated, turning the blue leatherette booklet over in her hands.

"Or are you interested in opening a new account?" the woman prompted.

"No," Mary said finally. "I have one."

"I'll transfer you," the woman said.

The bell over the bookshop door chimed. Rebecca gave a cheery wave as she came in. This morning she was alone. Ashley must be off at one of her day schools or summer events.

Mary managed a smile and pointed at the phone. Rebecca nodded and put her finger to her lips.

"Hello?" a man's voice said. He sounded young, and his tone was warm—a born salesman. Mary and John had always liked the service at First Boston. It was part of why they'd only ever worked with one bank during their whole married life together.

"How can I help you?" the man asked.

"I hope you can," Mary said. "I—" She hesitated again, wondering how to explain her situation and how much to explain. When she'd looked over the account on Saturday night, she'd realized that her husband had been depositing money in a secret account, in relatively large increments, for decades. During some of those decades, she knew, they could have really used the money—not just the deposits he'd made, but the big balance that had been growing all that time.

Ever since, Claire's words from so long ago echoed in her head, reinforced by Addison Hartley's story. "He'll always regret it," she had said. "He'll remember me. He won't be able to forget it." And the searing final promise the John character had made in Addison Hartley's version of the story, even as the John character went off with the Mary character. "I'll find a way for us to be together. I promise."

Mary would never have believed John could say a thing like that to Claire. She believed with all her heart in the bond they shared and their life together. But she also would never have believed that he could have hidden such a large sum of money without ever telling her about it or that he could have kept a secret like this from her without showing any guilt or anxiety about it, for years. But now she had the proof of it, right there in black and white.

What had really happened between John and Claire all those years ago? Had it continued past that summer, as Addison Hartley's book suggested? Had the happiness Mary had felt with John all been based on some kind of a sham? Everything in Mary rose up in resistance to that idea. She *knew* John. He couldn't tell a lie to save his life. And he'd given her every reason to believe that his love was real, for decades.

But then, what could this secret bank account mean?

She felt embarrassed too, to be involving this stranger in a situation she herself didn't really understand yet. But to him, she reminded herself, this was all just numbers. He would have no idea what the numbers might mean.

"I've just found an account book for an account that looks as though it has quite a large sum in it," she said. "I was hoping you could help me verify that."

"Well, that sounds like a good problem to have," the young man said cheerfully. "Can you give me the number?"

Mary flipped the book open and read off the long string of numbers as the young man tapped away in the background on the other end of the line. As she did, her eyes scanned down the list of deposits. This wasn't some account John had started, then forgotten about. The deposits continued steadily right up to a few months before his death. The knot tightened again in the hollow of her stomach.

Lord, she prayed, *You tell us again and again not to fear. But I'm going to need some help with that here.*

"*Mm-hmm,*" the young man said.

Mary's stomach lurched. *What does that mean?* she wondered.

More clicking.

"And your name is...?" the young man asked.

"This is Mary," Mary said. "Mary Fisher."

A few more taps, and then the typing stopped. "I'm sorry," the young man said. "But your name isn't on this account. I'm afraid I won't be able to share any of the information with you right now. But I'll be glad to send you the paperwork so the owner can add you to the account," he added helpfully.

"The account belongs to John Fisher, doesn't it?" Mary asked.

"I'm sorry," the young man said, sounding genuinely sorry. "I'm not at liberty to give out that kind of information. You understand."

Mary did. The kind of privacy and care the bank operated with was one of the reasons she and John had always felt so safe there. She sighed. She hadn't wanted to involve a clerk at the bank in the personal details of her life, but it looked like she'd have to at least share one of them with him. "I have the passbook right here," she said. "So I can see the name of the account owner. It's John Fisher, my husband. And I'm sorry to tell you that he's passed away. So I'm afraid it's my account now."

There was a long silence on the other end. Then the young man recovered himself. "I'm very sorry to hear that," he said. "Could you hold on for just a moment?"

"Yes," Mary said.

A tinny recording of a Beethoven sonata began to leak out through her phone receiver.

"They have you on hold?" Rebecca asked sympathetically.

Mary started. She had been so focused on the conversation that she had lost track of Rebecca, who was standing just behind her behind the counter.

"Sorry!" Rebecca said. "I didn't mean to interrupt. I just came to get these." She held up the sheaf of papers the distributor always left with new deliveries, to match the order to the actual inventory. "I'll get out of your way." She lifted one of the new boxes of books and disappeared down an aisle.

"Hello?" A new voice crackled over the line. Another man, but this one quite a bit older. Even with that one word, he conveyed a strong sense of dignity and competence. "Mrs. Fisher?"

"Yes," Mary said with a feeling of relief. Here was someone, she thought, who would be able to work this out in the right way.

"I understand we have some details to work out with one of our accounts."

"I think so," Mary said. She took a deep breath. It was never easy to say, but she had to explain the situation. "My husband passed away recently. In sorting through his things, I discovered a bankbook for one of his accounts that I hadn't been aware of. I'd just like to get some information about it and have the funds transferred."

"I understand," the man said again. "And you were your husband's heir?"

"Yes," Mary said. With a few sentimental exceptions, an old baseball bat for his brother and a few thousand dollars for his longtime secretary, she had been the sole beneficiary of his will.

"I see." If anything, the new man typed even more furiously than the first man Mary had talked to. When the little burst of keyboarding had ended, he spoke again. "I'm very sorry to hear about Mr. Fisher's passing," he said. "We'd like to make this as easy as possible for you."

"Wonderful," Mary said.

"But, you see, we are bound by certain rules. Since your name isn't on this account, we can't transfer the funds to one which you now control without the paperwork necessary to indicate that you are in fact Mr. Fisher's heir in this case. I know this must seem like quite an inconvenience to you, but you understand that we are bound by federal laws that are designed to protect our clients."

"I understand," Mary said. Her heart sank, but at the same time, she was slightly comforted by the bank's insistence on protecting John's funds. "Can you let me know what exactly you'll need and who I ought to direct it to?"

"I'll handle this for you myself," the man said. "My name is Sullivan Holmes." He rattled off a telephone number, and she scrawled it down, along with an e-mail address. "You worked with a lawyer to settle your husband's estate?"

"Yes," Mary said. Her and John's old friend Al, whom they'd both known since John and Al were struggling first-year law students together, had handled all the details for her. It had been an incredible gift. And Mary knew that for every hour Al had spent with her—and there had been many—he had spent many more on his own, working out all the details of the will and accounts.

"If you'll just put that person in touch with me," Sullivan told her, "I'm sure we can work out all the details for you over the next few days."

"Wonderful," Mary said with a feeling of relief. She knew she could trust Al, even more than she could trust the bank. And whatever the mysterious account might reveal, she was glad to know that she would get the news from a friend, not a stranger. Maybe Al even knew something about the account and what it was for. "I'll call him right away."

"I'll look forward to hearing from him," Sullivan said. "Is there anything else I can do for you today?"

"No, thank you," Mary said. "You've been very helpful."

She set the phone down in the cradle to clear the line, then picked it up again, flipping through her dog-eared address book as she did. A moment later, she heard the first long ring of Al's phone. Her heart jumped with anticipation, but as the phone rang again, and again, the anticipation faded. Finally, the rings died out, and Al's voice-mail message came on, prompting her to speak after the beep.

"Al," she said once the beep had sounded. "This is Mary. Mary Fisher," she added. "I hope you're doing well. I just had a question for you about John's estate." She hesitated. It wasn't really just another detail, she thought. And she needed an answer now. "An important question, actually," she said. "If you could give me a call back as soon as you're able, I'd be grateful. Thanks so much." She left her numbers, both at the shop and on her cell, so Al wouldn't have to go through the trouble of looking them up, then hung up again.

Trying to distract herself from the worry, she sorted the morning's mail, then opened up her e-mail account. There, among advertisements from several suppliers and distributors and a new order, was a reply from Addison Hartley. Mary's heart leapt as she scanned it. In his classic terse correspondence style, he told her no gift was necessary but included an address. In the final line, he told her, not very graciously, that she could send any questions. He didn't add anything about being glad to answer them.

Well, Mary thought, that was better than nothing.

This time, the letter she wrote back almost seemed to type itself. She thanked Hartley for his response and told him that a gift would be waiting for him when he returned from Europe. Then she added a few questions from "local readers." This wasn't a lie, she reminded herself. After all, she was a local reader too.

Some local readers, she told him, had been struck by his grasp of the look and feel of the small Cape town where his book was set. She knew he was a great researcher, but she wondered if he had any deeper personal connection with the Cape or even Ivy Bay itself. Her readers would be so interested to hear about anything along those lines, if he'd be willing to enlighten them.

She read the letter over one more time. It seemed to her to hit the right tone: light but still curious. And if he answered this one, she'd be able to gauge better how much she could press him on her other questions.

Lord, she prayed, *I know I'm in over my head here. But please help me learn everything you want me to.*

Then she hit Send, and her letter swished through the ether, to the famous writer on the other side of the globe.

ELEVEN

❧

For the rest of the morning, Mary jumped each time the phone rang or the e-mail pinged. She fought against her disappointment as she answered questions about shipment dates for new deliveries and a better rate on her store credit card. She also had to give advice to a young mother—if her precocious daughter had already breezed through all the Agatha Christie titles, she might think about introducing her to Dorothy Sayers.

A few times, Rebecca reached for the phone, a job that Mary usually delegated to her, but each time, Mary shooed her away. Around noon, the phone rang again. Rebecca started dutifully to pick it up, but Mary dived for the phone and answered it.

It turned out to be a bookshelf salesman whom Mary had reached out to months before, when she was making the decision about what bookshelves to install in the shop. Apparently he had only just now gotten far enough down his list to return her call. Mary let him know the decision had been made and the shop was already open, and she hung up feeling slightly hopeful. Despite the salesman's disorganization, his call had made her realize how much she'd accomplished in the past few months. Maybe all these things she was worrying about now would look as different with a little time as the bookshop did from when she'd first leased the building—an empty, dusty office that was now a cozy bookshop.

"Waiting for an important call?" Rebecca guessed.

Mary glanced at her. It was hard not to be drawn in by Rebecca's warmth and charm, but she still had her doubts about her. She didn't know if she could trust her, especially not with something this sensitive. She gave a brief nod.

Rebecca took the hint and didn't press further. "Well," she asked, "would you mind if I knocked off for lunch? I was just going to go get a little something."

A little thrill ran through Mary. This was what Rebecca had asked her the other day, before she'd gone off in the opposite direction. What was she up to now? Well, there was only one way to find out.

"Sure," Mary said. "Go ahead."

"Great," Rebecca said. She swung her purse over her shoulder and started for the door. And outside, just as before, she turned toward the docks.

Mary went to the door herself and watched as Rebecca walked way down the street. Her heart pounded. She looked back at the empty shop. She hated to leave it. Consistent business hours were so important, especially for a fledgling business. But so, she decided, were employees she could trust. An instant later, she'd set the lock on the door, flipped the Open/Shut sign, and hurried away, following Rebecca. She waved at Jayne Tucker through the window of Gems & Antiques and walked on.

Mary kept Rebecca in sight as Rebecca walked quickly down the street, then turned left onto 6A again, headed toward the waterfront. At first, she hung back so that Rebecca wouldn't catch sight of her, but as they reached the docks, she hurried to catch up. There were too many side streets and nooks among the docks and shanties. It would be too easy for Rebecca to slip away without Mary being able to figure out where she went.

But when Rebecca did finally swerve off of the main road of broken pavement that ran by the docks into a little row of shanties, Mary almost lost track of her. She actually had to run a few steps to catch a glimpse of Rebecca just before she disappeared into the depths of a small blue clapboard fisherman's shanty.

Mary stopped and stared, puffing both from the exertion and the excitement. A tiny part of her felt a bit ridiculous, trailing her own employee through the wilds of the dockyards as if she were some kind of secret agent. But another part of her was fired up with indignation. This proved she had been right to doubt Rebecca's word. And it was the indignant part of Mary that marched over to the weatherworn door of the fisherman's shanty and gave it a few sharp raps.

She'd thought she heard something rattling inside, but at the sound of her knock, the rattling stopped. Mary tried to glance in the single window, but it was grimy with sea salt and sand dust. She knocked again. Again, no response.

Well, unless Rebecca had disappeared through some secret tunnel, she must still be in there.

"Rebecca?" Mary called. Then she tried the door handle. It turned easily in her hand, and she pushed it open.

Inside, Rebecca sat at a makeshift desk made from a pair of lobster traps and a piece of an old sign advertising the sunny

Cape Cod weather. On the desk sat a manual typewriter, with a half-typed sheet of paper sticking up from it like a sail stiff in the breeze. A sea-glass mobile of light blue and clear green glass hung from the low ceiling and turned gently in the low light from the single window.

Rebecca, who was seated at the typewriter, turned back, shock on her face. "Mary!" she said.

"What are you doing here?" Mary asked. "You told me you were going to get lunch."

It took a minute for Rebecca to collect herself. But when she did, Mary still didn't recognize the expression on her face. It was nothing like the friendly, open one she showed to customers—or to Mary. Instead, she seemed furtive and sullen. "Why should it matter to you what I do with my lunch break?" she asked.

"It matters to me that you tell me the truth," Mary said. "And this isn't the first time you've lied to me."

Now Rebecca's face registered surprise, and was that hurt in her eyes? "What do you mean?" she said.

"Last time you told me you were going to the Tea Shoppe for lunch," Mary said. "But you went somewhere else then too."

"I just came here," Rebecca said. A pleading note had entered her voice. "I'm sorry, Mary," she said. "I should have told you. But a friend of mine told me her husband wasn't using this old shanty anymore, and I could fix it up for a writing retreat. I can't come here with Ashley, because there's nothing for her to do here. And—" she stopped.

"And what?" Mary demanded.

"Well," Rebecca said, "sometimes it's embarrassing to tell people you're going off to write. Especially when you never sell anything or make any money doing it. Then they ask you about it, which is embarrassing, or they don't ask you about it, which is even worse. So I told you a white lie. I shouldn't have. I'm sorry. Please don't fire me. I love working with you, and I love the shop so much. It's like a dream come true to work there."

Her tone was sincere again, and she had the same open expression Mary was used to seeing. Mary's heart started to soften, but she steeled herself. Rebecca still hadn't explained why she'd lied about talking with the woman who looked like Claire at the reading.

"But those aren't the only times you've lied to me," Mary insisted.

"What do you mean?" Rebecca asked, her eyes wide.

"Ashley clearly knows Addison Hartley," Mary said. "But when I asked you, you said you don't know him."

"I don't!" Rebecca cried. "Why would I know a famous writer like that?"

The surprise and alarm in her voice was convincing—but so was Ashley's obvious affection for the renowned author.

"Well, Ashley certainly seems to."

Rebecca shook her head and gave an uneasy laugh. "That's how Ashley talks about authors," she said. "She'll carry on whole conversations with A. A. Milne and Beatrix Potter too. They're friends to her, in her mind. You know how dramatic she is. And she's seen me reading Hartley's books dozens of times. And when she got to meet him at the reading, she was even more sure they must be friends."

Mary pondered this a moment. It lined up with what she knew of Ashley's active imagination. But it didn't fit Rebecca's reaction to her question.

"Then why did *you* act so strange?" she insisted. "When I asked you about it?"

"Because you were so strange when you asked the question!" Rebecca said. "I could tell you were upset about something, but I had no idea what. And I didn't know you well enough to tell if it would be all right to ask. You seemed to be the one who wanted to ask all the questions just then."

Mary felt a small pang of remorse. Rebecca's story was believable—on this point. "You can always ask me whatever you want," she said. "There's no such thing as a bad question."

"Thank you," Rebecca said, still obviously uncomfortable.

She wasn't the only one. Rebecca's connection to Addison wasn't the only thing Mary had on her mind.

"But what about the reading?" Mary said. "The woman I saw you talking to."

The encounter with Claire had been blazed into Mary's mind, but it didn't seem to have made the same impression on Rebecca.

"What woman?" she asked, looking confused.

"You were standing beside her while Addison Hartley read," Mary told her. "She's about my age. Shoulder-length blonde hair. I saw you lean over and make a comment to her during the reading, but when I asked you about her, you said you hadn't met her."

Rebecca's eyes widened in recognition. "Oh," she said. "I remember. I talked to her a bit before the reading began."

Mary nodded in triumph.

"You see?" she said. "And you talked to her once it started."

Rebecca nodded slowly. "Not very much," she said. "I just leaned over and said, didn't she think that Addison Hartley looked a lot like Sean Connery."

Mary had to suppress a smile. Rebecca was right. Now that she mentioned it, Addison Hartley did bear more than a passing resemblance to the famous actor. "But you told me you didn't talk to her," Mary pressed on.

"But this isn't what you asked me!" Rebecca said. Her voice rose and broke, and tears sprang to her eyes. "You asked me about some lady called Candace, or Callie—"

"Claire," Mary corrected her.

Rebecca's eyes, still bright with unshed tears, lit up. "That's right!" she said. "Claire. You asked me if I'd talked to a woman named Claire, and I told you I hadn't. And I didn't," she insisted. "This woman's name was—" She paused, her brow furrowed in concentration. Then it relaxed as the idea came to her. "Verlaine."

Mary sagged against the door frame of the little fishing shanty as all the implications of Rebecca's statement dawned on her.

"It wasn't a lie," Rebecca went on, still eager to prove herself. "I didn't know it was so important. I would never have lied to you about it. I just didn't know we were talking about the same woman."

"It's all right," Mary said, her own head still swimming. She raised her hand to pat Rebecca's shoulder. "I can see it's all been a misunderstanding."

But a misunderstanding that had proved that Claire *was* in her shop the other night, though. So why had she been there? Did she have some kind of connection with Addison

Hartley? She must have recognized Mary, after all, but why had she hurried away when she did? And where was she now? As Mary wrestled through these questions, Rebecca went on, still concerned about her job.

"I should never have told you the white lie about coming here, though," she said. "I'm so sorry. I'll never do anything like that again."

Mary patted her arm. "I know you won't," she said. "And you don't have to make up a story for me. You're right. I don't mind how you spend your lunch break. I love that you have a writing nook. You can always tell me that you're coming down here, and I'll even say some prayers while you're here, that your writing will go well."

Now the tears sprang to Rebecca's eyes again, but not for the same reason. "Thank you," she said.

"Oh, don't thank me too much," Mary said. "I'm a big reader, you know. And you're a good writer. When you write a great story, you're really doing me a favor."

Rebecca shook her head. "Thank you for saying that," she said. "I hope maybe one day it'll be true."

"It's already true," Mary said. "I got suspicious of you after the misunderstanding at the reading, and I did a bit of sleuthing about you on the Internet. So now I've read just about everything you've ever written."

A big smile spread over Rebecca's face. "I'm not sure anyone else has even done that," she said. "You might be my biggest fan, then."

"Well," Mary said, "I'll take that as a compliment." She checked her watch. "According to my watch," she said, "you've still got about forty minutes before you have to be at the shop. You'd better get back to work."

Rebecca scooted her chair back to the desk and smiled over her shoulder. "Okay, boss," she said.

Mary smiled and pulled the door shut. But as she walked back to the shop through the rows of clapboard shanties and alongside the bobbing masts of the boats, her mind raced. It felt strange to know that she'd been in the same room with Claire after all these years. It made her long for the simpler days, before their friendship had become so complicated. But it also stirred up all the questions she'd been struggling with all week. How had Addison Hartley learned about their story? And what had really happened between Claire and John all those years ago? If John were still alive, she knew, she'd simply go to him and ask him. And most of her still believed that the answers he would give her would scatter her fears and worries. But he wasn't here to ask. And the only person who did know the truth anymore was Claire—if Mary could only find her.

TWELVE

—◆◆◆—

"I'm sorry," the young woman who had answered the phone at Al's law office said. "He's out for the day."

Mary toyed with the pages of her address book on her kitchen counter. She'd just tried Al's cell for the second time and gotten no answer, so she'd glanced down the page and found his office number. Maybe he had the cell turned off while he was at work. She didn't expect him to call her back instantly, but they'd had a long friendship, and he'd always been prompt about returning calls from her, usually within the hour. It felt strange not to hear from him for over a day, especially when she'd been clear that the topic was important to her.

"Is there any way to get a message to him?" Mary asked. "It's important."

"I can leave a message on his cell," the girl suggested.

Mary shook her head, even though the girl couldn't see her. "I've got that number," she said. "I've already left two messages."

"Oh," the girl said.

Mary wondered briefly what the change in the girl's tone meant. Was she taking the call more seriously now, since

Mary was obviously friends with Al? Or had she just decided that Mary sounded like someone her boss needed to be insulated from?

"Well, he should be in within the next few days," the girl said after a moment. "I can make sure to give him your message then."

"That would be wonderful," Mary said.

"Mary Fisher?" the girl confirmed.

"That's right," Mary said and gave the girl her phone number.

"Got it! I'll let him know."

"Thank you," Mary told her and hung up the phone.

Then she looked around. Claire's decades-old threats echoed through her mind one more time, amplified by their shadows in the Addison Hartley book, and the hints Bernice had dropped at the prayer group about the mysterious story that had made the rounds in the local gossip. Then her thoughts stuck on the hints Bernice had dropped. Mary had been turning the story over and over in her mind, wishing she could just get a few more facts to work with. But Bernice clearly knew some details Mary didn't—or thought she did. And even if the story that had circulated Ivy Bay wasn't true, learning what it was might help Mary unravel what was true. A jar of blueberry jam stood on the counter, put up the night before by Betty. Mary picked up the bottle and looked at it thoughtfully.

A few minutes later, she rang the doorbell of Bernice's trim Cape Cod home. When Bernice answered, she gave Mary a big smile.

"Well, isn't this a nice surprise?" she said.

Mary held up a small basket filled with a few mysteries and a gleaming jar of blueberry jam.

"Just a little something for you," she said.

"Don't just stand there!" Bernice said. "Come on in!"

She welcomed Mary into a snug front room and then led her quickly into the kitchen, where a pot of coffee was brewing. There, she set the basket down on the counter, picked up the heavy bottle, and turned it over in her hands.

"That's not just *any* blueberry jam," Mary said. "It's spiced blueberry jam."

"Spiced?" Bernice repeated.

Mary nodded. "Betty adds just a dash of cayenne."

Bernice raised her eyebrows.

"That's what my kids thought," Mary told her. "But now they won't have it any other way."

"This is so kind of you," Bernice said. "Really, I should be the one bringing you gifts. You're the one who's new in town."

Mary shifted her purse on her shoulder. "Well, it was so nice to get to talk with you at the prayer group," she said.

"I'm just so grateful to you for starting it," Bernice jumped in. "Prayer's one of those things—it's always so meaningful when I do it, but it's so easy just not to do."

Mary nodded. "I know exactly what you mean," she said.

"And listening to you talk about opening the shop made me remember how much I love a good mystery."

"Well, you should be set here for a while," Mary said. "*Black Iris* is one of my favorites this year. It's the third in a series of mysteries set in eighteenth-century Europe. The sleuth is a woman, the wife of a French diplomat, and she solves mysteries and court intrigues all over the continent, moving from place to place as her husband's assignments are changed and as the political climate in the different countries shifts." Mary could hear the earnestness in her own voice, but she never tried to temper it when talking about great books.

"*Ooh* yes!" Bernice said. "I love that idea. Some mysteries are so hard-boiled these days. I'm excited about a bit of history with this one."

"I think you'll probably love the costumes she describes too," Mary told her. "I keep hoping they'll make some of those into a movie, just so I can see the clothes."

"I can't wait!" Bernice said. "I'll have it read by the next prayer meeting!"

"If you start it tonight, you might have it read by tomorrow morning, actually," Mary said. "It's that good."

"I'd better be careful, then," Bernice said.

I have to ask her again about Claire, Mary told herself. But still, she couldn't think of how to do it. How could she begin to frame a question like that? *"Excuse me? Can you tell me the truth about whether anything ever happened between my husband and my best friend?"*

"I wanted to ask you," Mary began and then stopped, stuck on the problem of how to phrase all the questions that crowded her head—both the ones Bernice might be able to answer and the ones that perhaps no one ever could.

Bernice's smile had vanished, replaced by an awkward expression. She looked like she might already know what Mary was about to ask and that she wished she could be anywhere in the world other than there right now. Her uncomfortable look didn't help Mary to come up with a question, but she bumbled on.

"You mentioned something," she said, her face getting red. "About my husband John and my old friend Claire. I was just curious about it, because a strange thing happened at the shop last week. I actually thought I saw her, and I just wanted—"

Mary was clearly floundering. As she listened, Bernice's expression changed from discomfort to sympathy. Then she dived in herself.

"You know, I felt bad about that," she said. "I really wish I hadn't said anything."

Mary smiled gratefully. "No," she said, "it's actually okay. I've really been wondering about some things recently, and it sounded like you might know something that could help me."

"Oh, I doubt it," Bernice said, waving her hand. "You know, when I talked to you, I realized how silly the whole thing was. Just a small-town story," she said. "It's nothing for you to worry about."

"Well," Mary tried again, "I have been wondering about it. I'd love to hear it, even if you don't think it adds up to much. It might help me understand some other things that have been happening."

Now Bernice's discomfort had returned. "You know what?" she said. "I just really don't think it bears repeating. I should have known better than to say anything in the first place. I try not to tell stories about people I don't really know, and I broke my own rule. I think it's probably best if we both just forget about it. All of this happened so long ago, anyway," she added. "It hardly matters now."

Maybe not to you, Mary thought. The image of Claire standing in her bookshop, just last week, rose up in her mind, along with all the details and characters from Addison Hartley's best seller. *And it sure seems like something about what happened back in those days still matters to someone right now.*

"I'd like to hear it," Mary insisted. "Even if it doesn't seem like much to you, there might be something that could help me."

Now Bernice had actually begun to back away from her, toward the living room. "I really think it's best if we forget all about it," she said. "Forgive me for ever mentioning it. I'm sorry."

"Have you ever met Addison Hartley?" Mary asked, trying another tack. If Bernice wouldn't tell her the story, maybe she could at least explain something about how Hartley had ever heard it in the first place.

Now Bernice looked totally bewildered. She obviously recognized the name, but she didn't seem sure where she'd heard it. "Addison..." she repeated, stalling.

"He's a writer," Mary said.

"Oh, right," Bernice said. Now full recognition dawned in her eyes. "Didn't he just come to your shop?" she asked.

Mary nodded. "Yes," she said. The little leap of pride that she'd always felt when she said that had vanished, she realized, replaced by the stress of the past several days. "But I was actually wondering if you'd ever talked with him before. Did he ever come to town?" she asked. "Maybe while he was doing research?"

Bernice shook her head. "Nope," she said. It seemed like the first time she'd really been certain of anything since Mary started questioning her about the old story. "A big writer like him. I think I'd remember that." She looked behind her and took another few steps toward the living room, clearly trying to give Mary the hint that it might be time to go.

Mary smiled, trying to salvage the visit. The prayer group had only met once, and already she had a member who was literally fleeing the room rather than talking with her.

"All right," she said, trying to return the conversation to a light tone. She picked up the blueberry jam from the counter and gave it an awkward wave. "Well, enjoy the jam," she said, heading for the door herself so that Bernice didn't feel compelled to hustle her out.

"Thanks so much for it," Bernice said, her expression relieved. She made a weak attempt at a smile. "I can't wait to try it."

Then she hurried ahead of Mary to open the door, let her out, and waved.

"Thanks again!" she said. Mary wasn't sure if she was thanking her for the jam or for ending the awkward conversation.

She waved back, went to her car, and drove home, deflated. Part of her had to admire Bernice's reluctance to repeat rumors, but part of her suspected that Bernice's stand on the subject had more to do with not wanting to share an awkward story with Mary than any genuine moral compunctions. The story still mattered to Mary, to Addison Hartley, and perhaps even to Claire herself. And despite Bernice's assurances that the story didn't add up to much, if it was still recalled forty years later, it was a story Mary wanted to hear.

THIRTEEN

A ll the lights were blazing in the kitchen when Mary got home. Betty was at the stove, a bright apron tied around her neck, with pots and pans bubbling and sizzling.

"You must be having a good day," Mary said.

Betty turned around with a smile as bright as the apron. "I am," she said. "I hope you're hungry."

Mary set her purse down on one of the chairs around the kitchen table. Then she put Gus's carrier on the floor and flicked open the catch on the door. It swung open, and Gus scampered out and darted into the back rooms of the house, on his regular evening patrol.

"What's all this?" Mary asked, going to the stove.

"Homemade pasta," Betty said with a hint of pride. "With tomato sauce. I just dropped the gnocchi in now."

Betty had always been a great cook, and on her good days, she often embarked on ambitious meals, often from new recipes she'd clipped from her beloved gourmet magazines; the more steps the better. If her energy didn't hold out, sometimes those meals ended in frustration and a trip to the local diner, but tonight's dinner looked and smelled amazing.

"It smells delicious," Mary told her.

"You're telling me," Betty said. "I've been smelling it all afternoon. I can't wait to try it. And what you see here isn't all," she added. "There's asparagus with parmesan roasting in the oven as we speak. And tiramisu in the fridge."

Mary gave her sister a sideways hug. Then she sighed and sat down at the table, which was already set for two, with Betty's signature style. She'd clipped a handful of zinnias from her garden and fastened a few of them through each napkin ring, adding bursts of pink, yellow, and orange to the otherwise simple place settings.

"How about you?" Betty asked, stirring the bubbling pasta water.

"What about me?" Mary asked.

"You don't seem like you've had a good day yourself," Betty said. "I might even guess you've had a bad one."

"Well," Mary said, loath to sound as if she was complaining, "I couldn't say it was good."

"Is everything all right at the shop?"

Mary thought for a moment. Actually, that was something she had to be thankful for. That morning, she'd gone to work not knowing whether she could trust her new hire or not. Now her fears on that account had vanished. In fact, her budding relationship with Rebecca was stronger than it had been. Rebecca had even given her a hug as she was leaving and thanked Mary for the encouragement on her writing. "Another boss might just have fired me," she said. "But you encouraged me to keep working on my book. That's amazing. And I'm going to make it worth your while. You'll see."

As she wondered this, she realized something else. Bernice wasn't the only person she knew in town. Betty had lived here ever since she was first married, and her husband's family had lived here for generations before he married her. Betty had been a full-fledged member of the Ivy Bay community for decades. If a story had circulated town about Claire and John, was there a chance that she had heard it?

"Everything's fine at the shop," Mary said, leaning forward in her chair. "Listen. Did you ever hear anything around town? About Claire and John?"

Betty turned her back on the bustling stove top to look at Mary. "Well, that was out of the blue," she said. "Why do you ask that? Did somebody say something to you?"

"Bernice," Mary said. "At the prayer meeting. She brought it up like it was something I must know all about, and as soon as she realized I hadn't, she clammed right up. I actually visited her today, too, and I asked her again, but she wouldn't tell me anything."

"What did she say at the prayer meeting?" Betty demanded.

Mary thought for a minute. "Well, nothing, really," she said. "But she acted like she knew something about the story, even though she wasn't really friends with Claire. There was just something I didn't like about the way she said it. I just thought if the story traveled far enough to get to her, maybe you'd heard something?" She didn't know why she felt so nervous when she asked, but she pressed on anyway. "Have you?"

Betty shook her head decisively and with a trace of annoyance. "Small-town stories," she said. "Sometimes I think they get worse the more people pretend not to tell them."

"So you think there was one going around?" Mary asked, a sick feeling in her stomach.

Betty shrugged. "It sounds like it to me."

"But you never heard it," Mary said.

"That doesn't necessarily mean anything," Betty said. "People who tell those kinds of stories aren't stupid. And there are probably a few stories going around town about how I might react to someone telling tales about my sister's husband." She grinned. Betty had a good heart, but something of a fiery temper—especially where people she loved were concerned. She was right; there were probably more than a few stories circulating the Ivy Bay grapevine about how she might react to gossip about Mary and John and Claire.

Mary managed a smile.

"I'm sorry," Betty said, turning back to the stove. "But we both know there's nothing to it. And in my experience, the more you ignore one of these stories, the sooner it dies."

"Well, this one seems to have lasted forty years," Mary said ruefully.

"You'd be surprised," Betty said. "My husband's mother wore an eggshell wedding gown instead of pure white, and some of the old ladies at the nursing home are still talking about it."

Mary toyed with the petals of one of the zinnias at her place. "Well," she said, "did you ever see Claire in town or hear that she was around? Did she come back for visits or holidays or anything like that?"

Betty shook her head. She lifted the small pot of pasta from the stove and carried it over to the sink, where she drained it through the waiting colander. Then she dumped the fresh gnocchi back into the pot and carried it to the stove. "I never saw her after that summer you brought John to visit.

By the time I was dating Edward, her family had moved out of town. They never came back that I know of, not even to visit." She poured the sauce into the gnocchi pot and stirred vigorously. Then she began to spoon large dollops of pasta onto the two plates she'd set out beside her on the counter.

"I'm glad you're here for this," she said.

"You would have had trouble eating all that yourself," Mary agreed.

"No, I wouldn't have," Betty said. "That's what I was afraid of."

"So you never heard anything about her?" Mary asked. "Ever again?"

Betty pulled a pair of oven mitts on, then leaned on the edge of the stove for a moment, thinking. "I think I heard she went out west for school."

Mary nodded. "That sounds right," she said. "I found the school she went to, out west. I just couldn't find anything after that."

Betty glanced at her. "So you're really looking for her, aren't you?" she asked. "Do you really think it's so important? After all these years?"

"I don't know," Mary said. "I wouldn't have said so. But she's the one who came to my shop."

"Are you sure?" Betty asked, turning around to take out the roasted asparagus. She clanked the aluminum tray down on the stove top and deftly scooped a bunch of parmesan-crusted spears onto each of their plates. Then she carried them over to the kitchen table and sat down across from Mary. "You want to say grace?" she asked.

The two sisters bowed their heads. "Lord," Mary said, then hesitated. "Thanks so much for this beautiful day, for such a great meal, and for my sister. Please be with us and lead us on. Amen."

"Amen," Betty added heartily.

Mary took a bite of the gnocchi. It was delicious: hot and tender, with a tangy sauce. "You've outdone yourself," she said.

"Thank you," Betty said proudly. "So it really was Claire?" she asked. "In your shop? How did you find that out?"

"She talked to Rebecca," Mary said. "It took me a minute to figure it out, because she told Rebecca her name was Verlaine. But Verlaine was Claire's middle name. That can't be coincidence."

"Not with a name like that," Betty said. "But you can't come up with anything else?"

Mary shook her head. "There's nothing I can find. I even called her graduate school, but the company she went to work for folded years ago, and she hasn't been in touch with the school since."

"*Hmm*," Betty said, digging into her dinner with gusto. "I just don't—" She was distracted momentarily by the savor of the asparagus. "This *is* delicious," she said.

Mary smiled. Somehow all the mystery surrounding Claire and John didn't seem quite so upsetting when she was seated before a gigantic Italian feast.

"Now, let me think," Betty said. "I'm trying to remember if I ever heard anything else…" She took another bite of gnocchi, her brow furrowed in concentration.

Then her eyebrows shot up. "She was married!" she said and turned to Mary. "Wasn't she?"

Mary shook her head. "I don't know," she said.

"She *was*," Betty said. "I'm pretty sure I heard that. Because she married some fellow from around here. Not Ivy Bay, but on the Cape. I remember someone talking about it, because she always used to say how she couldn't wait to get away from all these little towns."

That sounds like Claire, Mary thought. *And like the kind of small-town gossip that might hold a nugget of truth.*

"Do you remember anything else?" Mary asked.

Betty screwed up her face again. She started to shake her head, then stopped. "Smith!" she exclaimed. Then she frowned. "But not exactly. Smithfield or something. Because they were saying wasn't it funny that Claire had basically married just a regular Smith or Jones, when she always used to think she'd wind up with someone so much more exotic."

"Smithson?" Mary repeated.

"Or something like that," Betty said. "That's all I remember, honey, really. I wish I could remember more."

"Well, a married name is a lot more than I'd found on my own," Mary said. Her fork hung over her plate as possibilities began to unfold in her mind.

"I'm glad I could help," Betty said. "But don't let that gnocchi get cold."

FOURTEEN

◆━◆◆◆━◆

C laire Smithson, Mary typed.

Then she hesitated and glanced around the book-shop. A few customers lingered over the titles, but other than that, everything was quiet. Mary had spent most of the morning searching for Claire Smith-somethings. She'd visited the Facebook pages of almost two hundred Claire Smithfields and another fifty pages of Claire Smithers. Along the way, she'd gotten glimpses into the lives of everyone from a Tennessee cheerleader to a New Mexico retiree who raised Bernese mountain dogs—but none of the Claire she was looking for.

This afternoon, after she'd kept her appointment to help one of the local book clubs choose their next selection for the month, she'd started in on the Smithsons, but so far, she was having similar luck. This new search brought up a police-woman in Boca Raton, a high school science-fair champion, and the owner of a specialty tea shop near Boston. No Claire.

I wonder if Betty got the name right, Mary wondered. *What if it's just Smith, after all?*

She typed Claire Smith into the search box, then leaned back in her chair.

"Only seven million?" she said out loud.

Ashley, who was reading in the bathtub, looked up at her curiously, but when Mary didn't say anything else, she stuck her nose back in her book.

Some of these are duplicates and false results, though, Mary thought. *Let's see what comes up on Facebook.*

Typing Claire Smith into Facebook brought up what seemed like a potentially inexhaustible list of names, reeled out on page after page, each page with ten new names, but no familiar faces. Mary closed the window out and leaned back in her chair again.

The last Claire Smithson search blinked at her on the screen, the tea maker outside Boston. Mary stared at it for a moment. Then she leaned forward again.

Claire had married a local man, Betty had said. Even if they'd moved out of town since then, perhaps there was some mention of her as part of a local family or even the record of her wedding, whenever it had happened.

Her fingers flew across the keys as she typed Claire Smithson, and added, Massachusetts.

This time the list was smaller, but after she spent a good fifteen minutes sifting through it, none of the hits seemed to refer to Claire, although she did learn that Boston boasted a young champion violinist by the same name.

As she closed that search out, Rebecca walked toward the children's nook. She rumpled Ashley's hair.

"How's that book?" she asked.

Ashley looked up reluctantly. "Good," she said with a hint of bemusement, as if she couldn't understand why her mother would interrupt her in the middle of reading to ask her how it was, when it was obviously good, since she was reading it.

"Can I help you with anything?" Rebecca asked. Mary walked back to the counter, and she glanced at Mary's screen. "Oh," she said. "Are you still looking for that lady from the reading?"

Mary felt herself flush, both because the topic of Claire made her nervous and because she still felt a bit sensitive about having chased Rebecca down to the docks over it earlier that week. Of course, she'd been in the right to make sure her new employee was honest, but if it hadn't been for this whole situation with Claire, would she have been so suspicious of Rebecca?

"Oh," she said. "I'm just a little curious. We were good friends once."

"Some of my old friends have looked me up on the Internet," Rebecca said. "It's been nice to get back in touch with them."

Mary nodded, but not very vigorously. Would Claire think it was nice if Mary ever did manage to find her? After all, she'd already been in the shop and fled when she saw Mary coming over to meet her. Maybe Claire had already made it very clear how she felt about being in touch with Mary again. On the other hand, Claire seemed to have done some other things that gave Mary a reason for wanting to be in touch with her, whether Claire wanted to see Mary or not, including telling the story all over town that had evidently reached Addison Hartley.

"Excuse me," one of the customers said from the aisles. He was an older man in a seersucker suit and a pair of white bucks. He looked a little bit like he'd just wandered in off the street from some other century, and he was holding two books aloft. "Could you give me a bit of advice about these titles?"

"I'll go," Rebecca said, speaking low. She gave Mary's arm a little squeeze and went over to look at the books the man held in the air. To the man, louder, she said, "Well, let's see. What have you got there?"

As Rebecca slipped in among the stacks, Mary had a sudden flash of her standing among them as an audience member during Addison Hartley's event. Then she remembered what Rebecca had told her. "She told me her name was Verlaine." Mary's memory of Claire as Claire had been so clear that she couldn't think of her as anything else. If she'd thought about it at all, she'd thought vaguely that Claire must have been somehow trying to hide her identity with Rebecca by using her middle name—an idea reinforced by her hurried exit from the shop when she saw Mary.

But what if Claire hadn't actually been trying to throw Rebecca off the track somehow when Claire said her name was Verlaine? After all, it seemed that Claire had been using that name as early as during her undergraduate years. Both the college and the business school she'd attended had had it prominently associated with her files. And Mary had known her once now, but that had been decades ago.

Mary's fingers flew across the keys: Verlaine Smithfield, Massachusetts.

The resulting search was a mishmash of literary allusions, Massachusetts travel tips, and advertisements for the maker of the highly salted gourmet hams.

Mary shook her head, deflated. But she didn't give up. She typed in Verlaine Smithson, Massachusetts.

This time, the top of the screen came up with a name, address, and phone number: the white-pages entry for the resident of a town about an hour down the Cape from Ivy Bay, Verlaine Smithson.

Mary had been searching for this all day, but when she saw it, her hands turned cold. A mystery was one thing—full of possibilities that provoked all kinds of curiosity. But meeting up face-to-face with her old friend and asking for answers to the questions Mary now had was quite another.

All these details had matched Betty's description: the "Smith-something" name, the local marriage. So apparently those tidbits of small-town gossip had been accurate. Mary just hoped they weren't always so accurate—at least not with whatever stories had been circulating the town about Claire and John.

But there was only one way to find out those answers now.

Mary scrawled down the home address for "Verlaine" on the scratch pad beside the register. Then she checked the clock. It was already around five, and she had scheduled Rebecca to stay until closing time this evening, in hopes that Mary could get some errands done around town before all the shops closed. But now she couldn't even remember what it was she'd planned to do. And if she left now, she could easily make it up the Cape before dark.

She stuffed the paper in her purse, then swung Gus's travel case down to the ground and called him. A moment later, he scampered around the corner. After a moment of consideration, just to maintain his dignity, he slipped into the carrier. Getting him to come in in the evenings was always a little easier than any other time, because he knew the fancy cat food was waiting for him at home for dinner.

Rebecca was just coming down the aisle, followed by the older man, who still had both books in hand. "This young lady's a great saleswoman," he announced. "I'm going to take them both!"

Rebecca hid her surprise at seeing Mary all packed up and ready to go. "You're taking off?" she asked lightly.

Mary nodded. "We talked about you closing the shop . . ." she began.

Rebecca nodded. "Don't even think about it," she said. "We'll take care of everything." She slipped behind the counter as Mary slipped out with Gus.

"Now, let me take these for you," she was saying to the older man as Mary went out the front door.

A few minutes later, Mary had dropped off Gus at home, consoling him with a bowl of his favorite tuna-and-bacon cat food, and was spinning up the coastal highway on the way to Claire's new hometown. It was hard for Mary to believe that Claire might have lived there longer than she had lived in Ivy Bay, and that for all those years, the people she met had been calling her by a different name. But that shouldn't be so hard to believe, Mary reasoned. Both of them had been alive for much longer than they'd known each other before their friendship foundered. But some things didn't seem to have changed, like the stories Claire had told about her and John so long ago. Maybe that was actually the strangest part—that anyone would still be holding on to that old story, after the years had changed everything else about all of them.

The drive up the coast would have been a delightful one if Mary had taken it for any other reason. It was a welcome break in the routine she'd fallen into since she opened the shop, and she was pleasantly surprised by her own spontaneity. The sky was blue with long stripes of thin white clouds, and when Mary caught glimpses of the ocean where the road curved along the coast before diving back into the heart of one of the many small towns that dotted the Cape; the water was deep indigo and sparkling like crystal. All along the way, the Cape's characteristic shops, restaurants, and beaches beckoned her to stop for a moment, get a scoop of ice cream, investigate the nooks and crannies of an old antique shop, take off her shoes and let her bare feet get a treat on the warm sand. Bright banners waved over the doors of shops, and happy families crowded the narrow sidewalks, children balanced on their fathers' shoulders while their mothers pushed strollers beside them, and young couples held hands as they shopped from window to window.

But Mary barely saw any of them. She was too busy trying to decide what to do once she got to the town where Claire now lived and what she would say to her. What to do was an easier question. By the time Mary left Ivy Bay, it had been close to six o'clock. Even if Claire worked some kind of day job, it was likely she'd be home by the time Mary reached the address she had for Claire. But visiting Claire at her house created a whole host of unknowns. Would her family be there? What would they think of Mary? Had Claire told them the stories about John she'd been telling around Ivy Bay when she and Mary were both young? But why would she tell her new family stories about some other man? No matter how Mary turned it over, she couldn't come up with a plan. As she drove past the Welcome sign at the border of Claire's town, she realized that was because she simply didn't have enough information. It had taken her this long just to get an address. She'd simply have to go to it and see what happened.

She'd known her way up the coast to Claire's town, but she had no idea where the address was in it. As she drove into the downtown area, she pulled over into a parking spot and typed the address into her phone. The icon whirred for a moment, then disappeared, showing a map with a few short turns between her and her destination. Mary pulled back into traffic and followed the directions.

They led her through the homey downtown and into a division of very large shingled homes on big wooded lots, all recently built on a well-kept, crushed-shell road. The map insisted that she had arrived at her destination when she reached the mailbox at the bottom of a long drive leading up to a tree-screened home with gray shingles and stone-blue shutters. Mary took a deep breath.

Lord, she prayed, *I know You are with the lowly and foolish. And I feel foolish right now. Please be with me.*

She nosed the car past the mailbox and up the long drive. Past the initial grove of trees, a sunny lawn opened up, spreading on a low hill to the house. The garage was built for three cars, but none of the bays were open. Mary parked in front of the far one and hopped out. There was no point in hesitating now that she was here.

The door was made of thick dark wood, with an imposing brass knocker. Mary lifted it and knocked.

As the seconds ticked by, she cycled through all the things she had to say to Claire. Should she demand answers about the story that had circulated town first? Greet her old friend as if bygones were bygones? Not do anything until she found out whether Claire even recognized her?

But when the door swung open, a dignified, well-dressed man, about Mary's own age, stood inside—not Claire. "Yes?" he said.

Mary shifted from one foot to the other. All her clever introductions and gambits had fled her mind. "I'm looking for Claire," she said simply.

As soon as she said it, she had to steel herself to keep from flinching. After all, everything she'd discovered indicated that Claire went by Verlaine now. She probably sounded to him like some door-to-door salesperson or political activist who went banging on people's front doors and asking for people according to names on a list they'd been given. Thinking that made her realize she hadn't introduced herself either. What would she tell him if he asked who she was? An old friend? Something else? She wasn't sure.

But the man didn't ask her any of those things. Instead, an expression of real sorrow crossed his face. "I'm afraid she's not here," he said.

"Do you know when she might be back?" Mary pressed. Something about the sadness in his face had touched her heart. It made it easier for her to honestly tell him, "I'm an old friend of hers. I was hoping to drop in and visit."

But the man's expression of sadness only deepened. "I'm sorry," he said. "You must not have seen her in quite a while. You see, we're separated."

FIFTEEN

❖

Mary stood frozen before the man at the door, stunned silent by the jolt that passed through her at his announcement. Her certainty that Claire was still living with her husband, and the first sight of him at the door, had allayed her fears about Claire and John. But now they came rushing back.

"I'm so sorry to hear that," Mary managed.

The man nodded without really seeming to hear her and shoved his shock of silver-gray hair back off his forehead. "Thank you."

Mary waited, not sure what else to say. After a minute, he met her eyes. "At first I thought it was only going to be for a few weeks," he said. "But now it's been—" He looked away, as if he were counting in his head. Then he named the exact number of months since John's death.

Another shiver ran down Mary's spine. But the shock also energized her. She might not like what she was hearing, but it sounded like she had come to the right place.

"I'm afraid I actually didn't know anything about this," she told the man. "I actually knew Claire back in Ivy Bay."

Was it her imagination, or did another flash of sadness cross the man's face when she mentioned that name?

"I just thought it would be nice to catch up with her after all these years," she said. "Do you have any idea how I might get in touch with her?"

"I can pass your information on to her," the man said. "I'm not sure how she'd feel about me sharing hers."

Mary nodded. "I understand," she said, handing him a card for the bookshop, which included her own cell number.

He took it, looked at it, and looked back up at her. "Mary," he said.

Mary nodded, watching him closely for any sign of recognition. John had known Claire well; maybe too well. Had Claire told her own husband anything about Mary and John?

If he did recognize her name, he did a good job of hiding it.

"I'm Brad," he said and stuck his hand out.

Mary shook it, not sure how to take the fact that he didn't seem to recognize her. It could mean that Claire had thought their friendship was old news, not important enough to mention. Or it could mean Claire was keeping a secret.

"Nice to meet you," Mary said. "Even though I wish it were under other circumstances." He might never know, she thought, how true this was.

Brad tried to manage a smile. He slipped the card in his pocket. "I'll pass it on to her the next time we talk," he said. Then a thought seemed to cross his mind. "Her mom's been real sick," he said. "We just put her in a nursing home a few months ago. So if you don't hear from her for a little while, she's had a lot going on recently, taking care of her and trying to do her own work. It's been hard."

His voice had turned tender and concerned when he said this. Mary watched him with surprise. Claire was lucky, she thought, to have found a man who still showed this much tenderness for her and her worries even after they'd been separated from each other for almost a year. How many men would say, "We put her in a nursing home," when they'd already been separated from their wives for months? Her heart also tugged a bit at the thought of Claire's mother stuck in a nursing home. She'd always been a vibrant, active woman, and as Mary had aged herself, she'd begun to understand how hard it was for an active person to learn they had to slow down. She also knew how hard this time must be for Claire. Since they'd lost Claire's father when Claire was very young, Claire and her mother had been extremely close. Unlike most girls, Claire had shared everything with her mother, just as if she were another school friend. It must be incredibly difficult for her to watch her mother's health fail.

"I understand how that can be," Mary said. "She's lucky you understand how hard it is."

Brad shrugged. "She doesn't seem to think I understand much of anything these days," he said. "And maybe I don't. I don't know."

"It can be hard in a marriage too," Mary said. "Figuring out how to help each other through a time like that." She felt a tug of sympathy with him over the fact that he was sharing these kinds of details with a complete stranger. But his confidences also gave her an opening to press on. "Have you been married for long?" she asked.

"Thirty-four years," he said. "I met her at her first job out of grad school. I outranked her at the firm then, but not for long." A faint smile played over his lips at the memory.

Then it faded. "I guess her work didn't help us in the long run either."

"Her work?" Mary repeated.

Suddenly, Brad seemed distant again. He tapped the card in his pocket. "You know," he said, "I think it's probably better if you just talk to her about all of this."

"Of course," Mary said.

Brad stuck his hand out again. Mary took it and gave it a warm squeeze. "It's nice to meet you," he said somewhat automatically.

"You too," said Mary.

"I'll pass this on to her, first chance I get," he said.

"I appreciate it," Mary told him.

The heavy door swung shut again, and the weighty brass knocker clunked.

Mary made her way back to the car. When she got in, she sat there for a moment, turning it all over in her mind. She wondered if Brad would pass the card on to Claire and what Claire would do with it if he did, but mostly she was struck by the deep feelings Brad still had for Claire. It was both touching and hard to watch a man who evidently still cared so deeply for his wife, even though the two of them had been separated for so long. What had gone wrong between the two of them?

And did it have anything to do, Mary wondered, with her and John?

SIXTEEN

The bell dinged over the door of the shop. Mary looked up from the counter, where she'd been ineffectively trying to get her mind on a new book order ever since she opened a few minutes before.

Pastor Miles stood in the door, holding it open for Trevor to come through. This time he didn't come full speed ahead, as he usually did. Instead, he stepped inside and glanced around with an expression that mixed eagerness and trepidation. Clearly, he was on the hunt for something, but what? Mary had never seen him seem so interested in anything outside the books in the children's section.

The pastor smiled and nodded.

"Hello!" Mary said.

Rebecca looked up from one of the bookshelves she'd been scanning. In off hours, she'd gotten in the habit of working through the shelved stock, making sure everything was still in the right place after customers had clumsily browsed and replaced titles themselves. She gave a cheery wave and went back to sorting through the spines.

Pastor Miles smiled.

"Nice to see you again!" Mary said. Trevor took a few more steps down the main aisle, obviously looking for something.

"Hi, there, sweetie," Mary said. "Can I help you find something?"

There was a rustle behind her as Ashley, already en-sconced in the bathtub, closed the volume she'd been reading and stuck her head around the corner to investigate.

When her face appeared, Trevor's own face lit up. "Ashley!" he exclaimed.

"I think this may be what we're here for," Pastor Miles said and grinned.

"Hi, Trevor," Ashley said, smiling.

Again, a tiny flash of unease passed through Mary as she wondered how Ashley would react to Trevor's enthusiasm over seeing her. But Ashley seemed perfectly able to handle herself.

"Come to the children's nook," she said. "There's a boat here."

"A boat?" Trevor repeated.

Ashley gestured for him to come, and a moment later he was happily trailing her to the nook.

"That's brilliant," Pastor Miles said, coming over to the counter, where he and Mary both watched as Ashley intro-duced Trevor to the old-fashioned bathtub that Betty had found at one of her endless sales and outfitted with a scrap of blue rug for the kids to sit in. "When I told him it was a bathtub, I couldn't get him to go anywhere near it."

As they gazed down the aisle at the two children, Trevor climbed gamely over the high porcelain lip of the tub, then stood up proudly in the "bow," posing like a great sea captain facing down a northeasterly wind.

"I guess it's all a matter of definitions," Pastor Miles concluded.

"I guess so," Mary said.

"So how are things going around here?" Pastor Miles asked.

Mary's face must have flickered somehow, because the expression on Pastor Miles's face changed from easygoing to concerned. "Oh," she said. "Just fine."

Pastor Miles scanned her features closely. "You sure?" he asked.

Part of Mary just wanted to pour the whole story out to him then and there—the strange visit from Claire at the reading, the weird connection between Addison Hartley's work and her own story, the mysterious bankbook that Al still hadn't called her back about. It would be such a relief just to tell it all to someone else and get their take on it. But as much as she wanted to tell someone, she realized it wasn't really Pastor Miles whom she wanted to tell. It was John. Even a few weeks ago, she wouldn't have allowed herself to feel this way. She would have just powered right on through. But now she couldn't keep the feelings down.

Lord, she prayed, *thank You for friends who care about me, whether or not they understand what's happening.*

She nodded in response to Pastor Miles's question. "Thanks for asking," she said. "I've just got some things on my mind."

"Well," Pastor Miles said, "I don't know if you'd ever like to share them, but you should know I'm always available."

"I do know that," Mary said. It meant a lot to know there were people out there who were willing to help her—even if right now she had no idea what kind of help to ask for. "I just have some things I'm working through."

Pastor Miles nodded. "Yep," he said. "Everybody does that a little different. You just let us know if there's anything we can do."

Rebecca tiptoed up to the counter. "I got too close to the children's nook," she said, talking low. "And you should have seen the look Ashley gave me! She told me she was doing just fine on her own with this customer."

Mary smiled. "We'll have to give her some kind of promotion," she said.

"Well, Trevor sure does enjoy her," said Pastor Miles.

"Oh, we're glad to have him," said Mary.

"She enjoys him too," said Rebecca. "She's down there telling him stories, and he goes right along with them. Sometimes the other kids don't want to sit and listen. They're all excited about their television shows and video games. I think it's good for them both."

"Do you think she's in midstory now?" Pastor Miles asked. "I didn't mean for us to stay here for too long, especially since it's not time for us to make our next purchase yet."

"Oh, don't worry about that," Mary said. "Please."

"I appreciate it," Pastor Miles said. "But I also promised his mother I'd have him home pretty soon. This was really just supposed to be a quick stop along the way, after we got breakfast downtown. I'm just going to meander down there and see if I can find a natural stopping point in whatever yarn she's telling."

He ambled down the aisle, paused a few feet from the children's nook and listened.

"It sounds like maybe you've got more than one writer in the family," Mary said.

"I know," Rebecca said ruefully. "I keep trying to get her interested in being a doctor or a lawyer, but it never sticks. Maybe I should stop buying her books."

"I'm not sure that'll work if she's already hooked," Mary said. "Does she know what a library is?"

Rebecca smiled and nodded.

"It may be too late, then," Mary said with mock seriousness.

"Well," Rebecca said, "it could be worse. She could want to be a bookstore owner."

"Then she'd really be in trouble," Mary said.

Pastor Miles had collected Trevor and came down the aisle now, holding his grandson's hand as the boy walked along beside him obediently but somewhat reluctantly, while casting longing glances back over his shoulder, where Ashley followed them.

"The story is to be continued," Pastor Miles announced when they reached the register. "Can you say thank you to Ms. Mary for letting us visit today?"

"Thank you," Trevor said with a toothy grin.

"You're welcome, honey," Mary said. "You come back anytime."

"Ashley's going to remember where we are in the story," Pastor Miles said. "The next time we come in, she said she'd tell us the rest."

"Or some of it," Ashley said with an author's precision. "There's a lot more. It will depend on how much time we have."

"There's a pirate!" Trevor bellowed. "He has a leg made out of smelly cheese!"

"Well, we'll certainly look forward to that," Pastor Miles said.

Mary smiled as Pastor Miles led Trevor to the door, where Trevor turned back and gave everyone a vigorous wave before they stepped out into the bright Cape morning.

"That sounds like a good story," Rebecca said, mussing Ashley's hair.

Ashley ducked.

"I'd like to hear the rest of it," Rebecca said.

"You can listen when they come back," Ashley said, reclaiming the book she'd discarded when Trevor came in. "I don't really like to tell them more than once. It's not as exciting the second time around."

"That sounds like a rider in an author-appearance contract," Mary said.

"I'll just have our lawyers add it in to the one we've already got," Rebecca joked and went back out to continue working through the stacks.

Mary reshuffled the publishers' catalogs, reviews, and sticky notes she used to stock the store. Usually this was one of her favorite things about running the shop. The first time she placed a big order, for hundreds of books, she'd felt like a kid in a candy shop. When she was little, she'd actually dreamed about going into a bookstore with all the money in the world and coming out with crates and crates of books. In her imagination, she'd needed a whole parade of horses and elephants just to get all the books home. But this was even better. It wasn't just buying a store out; it was buying a whole store. Now ordering hundreds of new books for stock was a regular event in the life of the business, but until today, it had always given her a thrill.

This morning, though, she could barely bring herself to concentrate on the lists of titles, the copies of jackets, and the bright photographs of the cover art. Every time she tried to concentrate on whether this or that title might be a good fit for the shop, her mind wandered to the question of Claire. Mary couldn't get over the timing of Claire's separation from her husband and how close it was to the time of John's death. It was the sort of thing that she might have easily dismissed as coincidence once, but with John's hidden bankbook and Claire's appearance in her shop, it was downright disturbing. Had Claire somehow been in touch with John for all these years? Had his death led her to some kind of final rift with Brad? And how had Addison Hartley heard of any of this? What was the explanation for the weird similarities between Addison Hartley's book and Mary's own story?

She turned the page of one of the publishers' catalogs and stared at it blankly for a long minute before she realized that, not only had she not really read or seen anything on that page, but she also couldn't remember anything about the book that had been described on the previous one.

"This is ridiculous," she muttered to herself and pushed the whole mess aside—sticky notes, catalogs, and all. Then she pulled the keyboard over and began to type.

SEVENTEEN

The first name Mary typed in was Brad's. The initial facts that came up when she searched his name were run-of-the-mill: a mention as part of his Ohio high school class on a Web site dedicated to reunions, a formal picture of him in a suit and tie on the Web site for the financial-planning company where he worked, and a few stray photos of him taken at company barbecues and sporting events. Mary sifted quickly through the text on the pages that mentioned him, but none of it told her anything she wouldn't have already guessed about Brad or anything more about Claire and their estrangement.

This brought her back again, as so many times before, to Addison Hartley himself. Claire might know the truth of her story with John, but it wasn't certain that she was the one who had told Hartley. Perhaps he'd heard the story some other way. And only he knew that answer.

When Mary tried searching Addison Hartley's name again, she quickly found the same standard biography she'd found the last time. But as she sifted down through the search pages, here and there, she found a new nugget of information. Several of his friends from his school days in Kentucky and Texas had posted memories of him on his high school reunion Web site. The tone was one of surprise—apparently Hartley hadn't done much to distinguish himself in the eyes of his classmates while he was in school, although someone had dug up a few articles he had written about the swim team in the school paper and posted them on the site. Several pages into the search results, Mary found his name on a list of rodeo stars in a regional rodeo from the 1980s. At first she dismissed it as a case of mistaken identity, but when she clicked through to see the poster, there he was. His frame was thinner and his face much less lined, but he was still unmistakable. Mary suppressed a smile. His stint as a rodeo cowboy hadn't made it into any of his official biographies.

And it didn't seem to have lasted long. Apparently, he'd been practicing his craft as a writer even as the rodeo went from town to town during that summer in the late 1980s, because his first book appeared just a few years later. After that point, the cowboy hats disappeared, replaced by tweed jackets and a pair of tortoise-shell glasses that he may or may not have really needed. A trace of his cowboy days survived in the denim shirts he sometimes wore under his expensive jackets, but now the horses he'd been photographed with were replaced by a string of dewy starlets and fellow authors, all in their own trademark getups. After a while, Mary realized, she could guess the writer's genre pretty accurately just by what they were wearing—the romance novelists with their ruffled shirts, the literary types with their black turtlenecks, the thriller writers in their bomber jackets. His first half-dozen titles were all blockbusters, but then he seemed to drop off the map for a few years. During the mid-1990s, there were almost no reports or news items about him, except for a handful of notices from his publisher, which seemed to be halfheartedly assuring his public that he would be back soon with a new title. And he did, in fact, burst back on the scene a few years later with another blockbuster, in what was now an unbroken stream of them up to the present day.

As Mary scrolled through the list, her e-mail box dinged. She switched over to it without much hope, the From field read: Addison Hartley. Mary's skin tingled as she opened it, but her heart sank as she read the two-line message, which was almost devoid of punctuation and capitalization, as if he'd typed it out from a mobile device on some European street corner. "No connection with Ivy Bay," it read. "Sorry to disappoint."

Now Mary's dander was up. She knew Addison Hartley was a famous writer. But who had made him famous? Booksellers and librarians like her, and readers like the ones who had crowded her shop to see him. They'd spent hours reading his books and giving themselves up to the worlds he imagined. Couldn't he spare more than a few terse lines for them?

Her eyebrows drawn together, Mary tapped out another letter. The tone was still grateful and polite, but now her questions were pointed. Actually, she wrote that the parallels between Ivy Bay and his book were so plentiful it was hard to believe he didn't have any personal connection. In particular, she added, the romance subplot seemed to mirror the details of events that had happened in Ivy Bay years ago. Was it possible that, even if he hadn't visited Ivy Bay himself, someone from the town had shared the story with him? Her readers would be so interested to know, she said. She then hit Send with a flourish.

She closed her e-mail and frowned, still unsatisfied. If anything, Hartley's dismissive tone had only made her more determined to find the connection between him and her story. She still hadn't discovered any link between Addison Hartley and Claire. She'd already tried and failed to find a link between Hartley and Cape Cod. But now she typed in his name along with both of Claire's alma maters. Hartley had spoken once at California State, but it had been in the past few years, long after Claire had graduated and moved on. He'd never been to her business school in Chicago, at least not as far as Mary could tell. And typing in combinations of Claire, Verlaine, and Smithson along with Hartley's name didn't bring up anything.

Mary paused and looked at the blinking search box. She'd been at it for almost an hour, and she still hadn't found anything. Then she noticed the toggle boxes on the search engine pages. She'd been searching for returns on Web pages, but there were also options for searching solely for images and videos. Claire seemed to have changed her name so many times that it was hard to search for her on text pages. But Mary had recognized her in an instant when she saw Claire in the store. Maybe that was a better way to search for a connection between her and Hartley.

But when she typed in Hartley's name along with Claire and tried an image search, she only came up with pages of Hartley standing with publishing-world doyennes and models. One of them, to Mary's excitement, had been named

Claire, but she was a flaming redhead with a piercing violet gaze that Mary noticed she was always directing at the camera rather than Hartley. All of these were mixed in, to Mary's amusement, with dozens of pictures of a baby named Claire Addison Hartley, posted almost every day by her extremely proud parents.

But even with the addition of the baby photos, that image search returned only a few pages of images. Mary went back to the top of the image search again. This time she erased Claire and tried Verlaine.

Hartley had also dated a starlet named Nicole Verlaine. The first several pages of the search were filled with images from what appeared to be a handful of public appearances the two of them had made. In one, Nicole wore a light blue sequined dress with a skirt of feathers perfectly dyed to match the bodice fabric. In another, she towered over Addison in a pair of sky-high pink heels. On later pages, Hartley was honored at a dinner where he received honorable mention for a literary award dedicated to a French poet. Then the search began to degrade as they often did on later pages, with more and more images that didn't seem to have anything to do with Addison Hartley; some were random pictures taken by photographers named Addison or Verlaine. Mary clicked through a few of these, her enthusiasm waning as she sifted through fuzzy images of the author snapped by superfans at signings or conferences and a series of backyard nature photographs by an Annie Addison.

Then, just as her eyes had begun to glaze over and she was about to click out and begin another search, she had a shock of recognition. The image was the same low quality of most of the pictures around it in the later pages of the search: just a group of people, their faces overexposed by clumsy use of the flash, seated around a round table in some kind of banquet hall. But this time, the faces were familiar. By now, Mary had seen so many images of Addison Hartley, in so many poses, that she would recognize him anywhere. But his wasn't the only face Mary recognized. Claire sat at the table too, not just a part of the same group but right next to him.

She was perhaps twenty-five or thirty in the picture, her face still unlined, her haircut stylish for its time. The event wasn't formal, but the people at the table were well dressed, Addison in one of his tweed jackets and Claire in a business suit. And they were clearly engaged in conversation. Addison's head was inclined toward Claire, and her hand was in the air, gesturing as she told him something.

Mary's heart jumped as she clicked on the Web site, an archive of past events at Valley Financial Services in California. She hadn't been sure what she'd feel if she made a connection between Claire and Addison—anger or betrayal or something else. But she was surprised to discover that what she actually felt was relief. The similarities in Addison Hartley's story and her own seemed undeniable to her, but the idea of trying to explain them to anyone else had made her feel a little nutty. Who would believe that a big-time author had stolen elements of her life story and put them in his most recent novel? But now that she had the proof of the connection in front of her, she felt a sudden calm. She wasn't crazy after all. There was a real mystery here. She didn't know all the answers yet, but at least she hadn't been dreaming it all up. She took a deep breath and let it out.

Beside her on the counter, Gus looked up. She smiled at him and scratched his ears. "I think we're getting somewhere," she told him.

Gus flicked his ears and curled up with an air of satisfaction, as if he'd known all along that they were getting somewhere and was just glad that she knew it now too.

Mary clicked on the link to the picture. It led her to the page of a financial-services company in California, featuring some of their big-name clients. The caption identified the hotel the gathering had happened in. Addison Hartley's name was also in bold letters, along with the names of several other people at the table in smaller type, including Claire, who was listed as C. Verlaine Wilkes.

Mary took her cursor back up to the search box. She typed in C. Verlaine, then hesitated. After a moment, instead of typing in Wilkes, she added Smithson and hit Enter.

The top hit was a financial-services company in the town she had just visited the day before. When Mary clicked on it, the screen revealed a list of the company's associates, each with a professional picture and a brief bio. Claire's was the second picture on the page. At the top of the page was the company's contact information, complete with a street address.

Mary typed the address into the search box, and a map came up, dead in the center of town. Then she switched back to the company page and checked the hours. They were open that night until six thirty. Mary checked her own clock. It was only eleven. Claire hadn't been at her home address, but her husband hadn't said anything about her leaving her job. In fact, he'd complained about the work she had been doing. So it was almost certain that Mary could find Claire at her work address. If Mary left now, she could be there well before the company closed for the day.

EIGHTEEN

R ebecca," Mary said, picking up her purse. "I need to go out for a bit. Are you all right here?"

Rebecca looked up from the book she was reading. When the shop was in shape and quiet, she'd taken to reading new titles, with Mary's prompting—so that she could be up on the books when customers came in asking her opinions on them. "Absolutely," she said. "When should we expect you back?"

Mary looked at the clock. She didn't have a good answer for that. What would she find when she met Claire? Would the conversation last for hours? Would it be over in a moment?

"I'm not sure," she said.

"It's just that I'm scheduled to be off around four," Rebecca said. "And I promised to take Ashley over to a marine biology class at four thirty."

"We're going to catalog a tide pool," Ashley announced seriously.

Mary settled the purse over her shoulder and nodded with a decisiveness she didn't feel. "I'll be back by then," she promised. "You can call me on my cell if you need anything between now and then."

"We'll be fine," Rebecca told her. "Have fun."

Mary wasn't sure if that was in the cards, but she managed a smile anyway. Gus, who had hopped down from the counter when she stood up, threaded through her ankles questioningly. She bent over and ran a hand down one of his soft gray sides. "I'll be back before you know it," she said. If she had to, she could see if Betty was available to give Gus some attention while she was gone.

Gus gave a small meow, unconvinced.

The drive up the coast in the morning was even more spectacular than it had been the evening before. Instead of points of light on the caps of the waves, the entire ocean seemed like a sea of blue glass, with high banks of giant white clouds dotting the pure blue of the sky. There were fewer people out than there had been the evening before, except for the active types. She passed several cyclists, including a couple pedaling along clumsily on a bicycle built for two. Neither of them seemed to know exactly what they were doing, but after she passed them, she could see in her rearview mirror that both of them had giant grins on their faces. When the road curved near the water, she could see a few kayakers, surfers and swimmers, as well as some sailboats tacking their way out toward the horizon.

Somehow, the drive seemed shorter than it had the night before. Then she'd felt unsteady, uncertain, full of questions. She had barely been able to imagine how her conversation with Claire might go. Today, she still had questions, but now she had more answers, and she knew which ones she still wanted to ask.

Her indignation and eagerness to know the truth carried her over the miles between Ivy Bay and Claire's new town so quickly that she was surprised to find herself driving past the little sign welcoming visitors to the business district, familiar to her from yesterday. As she did, she slowed down and ducked her head below the sun visor, so it was easier for her to look at the building numbers and street names. According to the map she'd looked at online, Claire's office was just a few blocks past the edge of town, on a side street, less than a block from the main street.

After passing a bakery, a shell shop, and a boutique selling an array of madras patch dresses, she caught sight of the sign she was looking for: Harbor Court. It wasn't much of a court, she discovered after she turned—just about half a block of charming wood and shingle storefronts that ended at a small cul-de-sac where a metal railing marked the end of the road. The railing overlooked a low drop-off where the fishing shanties and boathouses that stretched down to the water began, and parking spots had been marked off neatly along the railing and down the street.

Mary parked the car and got out. She hadn't caught sight of the address as she drove down the block, but as she walked back down it, she found it easily, sandwiched between a shop selling antique jewelry and a gourmet luncheonette. She could also see why she missed it from the car—the place was nothing more than a narrow door, painted a crisp nautical blue, with the address displayed in bronze letters. A tiny blue-and-white wooden sign, almost illegible from the street, announced Cape Financial Services.

Mary tried the door. The handle turned in her hand, but the door didn't budge. She leaned into it with a good push, but it was no use. The place was locked.

She stepped back and scanned the area again. Was there something she'd missed?

After a moment, she saw it, just to the right of the door—a shiny aluminum box, which clearly housed some kind of intercom. "Cape Financial Services" was printed on it in tasteful letters, beside a small white button.

Mary took a deep breath and pressed the button. A moment later, a woman's friendly voice crackled from the box.

"Welcome to Cape Financial Services," she said. "How can I help you?"

"I'm here to see..." Mary hesitated briefly. She had been about to ask for Claire Wilkes but caught herself just in time. "Verlaine Smithson," she finished, with what she hoped sounded like sufficient dignity. It was strange, she thought as she waited for the other woman's answer, how so much had changed in the past decades.

"Do you have an appointment?" the woman's voice crackled. It was still friendly, but Mary could tell from the slight change in tone that she'd already discovered that Mary didn't.

"I don't," Mary said. "I was hoping she might find some time to squeeze me in."

"May I give her your name?" the woman asked.

Mary's chin came up slightly. Claire wasn't the only one whose name had changed since the last time they met. And despite whatever stories Claire had told Addison Hartley, Mary was the one who had married John in real life. "Mrs. Fisher," she said. As she did, she felt a tug at her heart. She'd always loved referring to herself as Mrs. Fisher throughout her marriage, and it had been one of John's favorite nicknames for her. "Mrs. Fisher," he'd ask sometimes when he came home from work, "could I take you out to dinner tonight?" Or, "Mrs. Fisher, could I interest you in a walk around the block this evening?" Despite the hard times they'd weathered together and the times they'd driven each other completely crazy, the little charge Mary got when she gave her name as Mrs. Fisher had never worn off. It still gave her the same thrill it had the first times she'd practiced writing it as a teenager, in the very first days when she and John had been dating. Some of those times, she realized now, had probably been in all those letters she wrote to Claire.

Since John died, she had avoided using "Mrs. Fisher," afraid of the wave of loss that now came when she said the name. But today, despite the pang, it felt good to announce herself as Mrs. Fisher again. And, she realized, the pang had faded. But the little charge she'd always gotten was just as strong as ever.

The woman on the other end of the intercom still hadn't answered. Mary wondered if Claire could have guessed who this Mrs. Fisher was, or if the common name had confused her into thinking she was a stranger or even an existing client. If Claire did know it was Mary, would she even let her in?

As she was wondering, the intercom crackled again. "Come on in," the woman said, all the warmth returned to her voice. The door chimed, and Mary could hear the lock clank open inside.

Hurriedly, she caught it and pushed her way in before the lock could slide closed again.

She found herself at the foot of a long, narrow staircase. In contrast to most commercial entryways, the vestibule was pristine, with a thick, intricately woven oriental-carpet

runner that led up to a landing one floor above, lit by a sub-
stantiallooking brass light fixture that matched the address on
the door almost too well. Tastefully matted photographs were
hung at intervals as Mary climbed the stairs—well-groomed
families sitting in Adirondack chairs beside gardens of Cape
roses overlooking the water, large boats in full sail, sandy-
haired children arranged around a patient golden retriever
whose coat had been brushed to a high gloss.

On the landing, Mary came to a door marked Cape
Financial Services in equally tasteful brass letters. This time,
when she tried the door, it swung open.

The office inside was dominated by another large orien-
tal rug, with leather wing chairs edged with brass tacks to
one side, and an administrative assistant seated behind an imposing mahogany desk beside a spray of greenhouse lilies and
delphiniums. The woman, middle aged, with curly black hair
and a string of pearls at the collar of her navy blazer, smiled
as Mary came in. A hallway hung with paintings in ornate
frames led away from her on the left.

"Hello," she said. "It'll just be a minute. Ms. Smithson
is on a call right now, but as soon as she finishes up, I'll let
her know you're here." She indicated the wing chairs behind
Mary. "Can I get you anything?" she asked. "Water? Coffee?"

"No, thank you," Mary said and took one of the nearby
chairs. So that explained how she'd gotten in so easily, she
thought. And the assistant's long pause when Mary was out
on the street. She hadn't wanted to interrupt Claire's call, so
she'd had to decide for herself whether to let "Mrs. Fisher" in
or not. Which meant, Mary realized, that Claire still had no
idea that Mary was waiting right here, just outside her office.

A moment later, one of the lights on the assistant's phone flickered, and she scooped the receiver up and pressed a series of buttons.

"Ms. Smithson?" she said. "I have a Mrs. Fisher here to see you. Very good."

She hung the phone up.

"You can go right in," she said.

Mary tried to return the assistant's smile as she passed the desk, but she had no idea whether the expression she gave her wound up looking much like a smile or not. She also had no idea where Claire's office was, so she was relieved to discover that each door seemed to have another brass nameplate attached to it. The first two were for men Mary had never heard of, but the third on the left read: C. Verlaine Smithson.

Mary raised her hand and knocked.

"Come in," Claire called.

At the sound of her voice, Mary had the same reaction she'd had to seeing her at the store. All the years of distance and all the recent questions seemed to melt away. And despite them all, the old excitement she'd always felt at seeing her friend rose up in her. She walked through the door with a genuine smile.

But when Claire caught sight of her, there was no answering smile on her face. She rose from behind an even more imposing mahogany desk than the one Mary had seen outside, her expression changing quickly from surprise to anger.

She crossed her arms over the waist of her expensive power suit. "What are you doing here?" she asked.

NINETEEN

M ary's first question was already answered. It was clear that Claire knew exactly who Mary was and that she wasn't exactly delighted to see her.

But Mary didn't let Claire's chilly welcome throw her. After all, Claire wasn't the only one in the room with questions.

"I saw you at Addison Hartley's reading last week," Mary began. "I was wondering what you were doing there. And then I read his book."

It felt good to finally be talking with Claire face-to-face after all these years and after all the worries and questions of the past week. Despite Claire's scowl, Mary couldn't help but remember all the long conversations they'd had together as girls. It had been so easy to talk to Claire back then, and she looked so familiar now. It was hard to believe that this wasn't all just some kind of misunderstanding that they could patch up easily, now that they were finally in the same room again.

"His new book reminded me a lot of our story," Mary added.

Claire raised her eyes dismissively. "Well, you know what they say," she said. "There are only a handful of stories in the world. Writers just tell the same ones over and over."

"Well, maybe," Mary said. "But if they do, at least they change the details. These were all the same. Everything but the names. And the scenes where the character based on John meets the character based on you."

Claire gave a strange smile. "Are you sure about that?" she said.

"When we were kids, you also told me that nothing happened between you two," Mary said. "But that's not how the book goes. Claire, please. I came to ask you about the truth."

"Don't you know?" Claire asked, her tone still combative. "You were married to him for forty years."

How does Claire know that? Mary wondered. She and John had been married for just forty years when he became sick, and he hadn't lived to see the end of the year. Had she been in touch with John after all? The strange timing of Claire's own separation from her husband rose again in Mary's mind.

"Did something happen between you two?" Mary demanded.

"I told you you'd never understand what John and I meant to each other," Claire said.

"That doesn't answer my question," Mary told her.

Claire shrugged. "I'm afraid I don't know what to tell you about that," she said. "Lots of people see connections between their own lives and the stories they read in books. It's why they keep reading them."

Mary frowned in frustration. For a moment, Claire had seemed to admit that she knew about the similarities between Addison Hartley's book and their own story, but now she'd sidestepped into generalities again. Well, Mary had already discovered too much about her connection with Addison Hartley to believe that.

"I know you know Addison Hartley," she said.

She took a brief moment of satisfaction in the look of surprise that crossed Claire's face at this, but Claire quickly masked it.

"Because you saw me at the reading?" she said. "I'm sorry, I just happen to be a fan of his. I didn't even get to stay till the end."

Mary shook her head decisively. "You've known him a lot longer than that," she said. "I've seen the pictures of the two of you talking at the banquet for Valley Financial Services in California. You've known him for decades. You told him your story. But you forgot that it's my story too. I bet he'd be interested to hear my side of it."

A shadow of fear passed over Claire's face before it turned into a professional mask again. "I'm sorry," she said. "I have another appointment now. I'm afraid you'll have to go."

"Not till I get some answers," Mary said.

"It's time for you to go," Claire said again. "I wouldn't like to have to ask someone to usher you out."

Mary studied her old friend's face. She didn't know this expression, because she and Claire hadn't been prone to fights in their younger days. But she knew Claire well enough to know that she didn't make idle threats. If she brought something up, she was willing to follow through on it.

Mary sighed. "I just want to know the truth," she said. "Whatever it is. John's gone now. Don't you think it's time we got over this?"

"Maybe it's done for you," Claire said. "But I guess I never got over things as easily as you could."

Mary stared back at Claire, but Claire's expression didn't soften. Mary had barely been able to get anything out of her, and it was clear that Claire was done talking now.

After a minute, Mary turned and went out.

In the waiting room, the assistant gave her a clipped professional smile. "All set?" she asked.

"Thank you," Mary said and went to the door. As she went down the ornately carpeted stairs in the narrow hall, the hurt and anger of her encounter with Claire began to set in. By the time she got to the street, her mind was crowded with questions, and her heart was riled up and sore. Part of her wanted to march back up and cause a scene in Claire's office, refusing to quiet down until Claire gave her answers. But another part of her realized this would play right into Claire's hands, making Mary look like an emotional mess while Claire kept her cool as the rational one.

But what else could she do?

She unlocked her car door, sat down inside, and bowed her head. *Lord,* she prayed, *You say all things work for good for those who love You. I do love You. I just don't see how You could call any of this good.* She took a long breath. *I just need some answers, Lord. Please help me find the truth.*

She lifted her head and began to search in her bag for her keys. While she was still digging past her calendar and Tylenol and wallet, her phone began to ring.

It was an unfamiliar number, from Boston.

She answered. "Hello?" she asked.

"Mary," said a familiar voice.

"Al," she said gratefully. She'd been so rattled by Addison Hartley that she'd forgotten all about John's mysterious bankbook. Maybe now she'd finally get some of the answers she couldn't get from Claire. And maybe there was some simple explanation for all of this. *Thank You*, she prayed briefly. Then she asked, "How are you doing?"

"Fine," Al said. "Just fine."

"I'm glad to hear it," Mary said. "Did you get my messages?"

"I did," he said. "I'm sorry it's taken me so long to get back to you. What can I help you with?"

Briefly, Mary explained her discovery of the bankbook. She gave him the number and the name of the man she'd spoken with at the bank.

"Do you know anything about this?" she asked.

"Ah," Al said. She could tell from the discomfort in his voice that he was hesitating.

"Al, you've got to tell me," she said.

"Tell you what," Al said. "Merilee and I are coming to the Cape on Friday. Could we sit down then and work through the papers, and I'll let you know anything I've found out?"

"I wish you'd just tell me now," she said.

"You know I think it's better to talk over anything of importance in person," Al said, his voice still friendly and reasonable but unmistakably firm. "That's always been how we've done it. Can we plan on Friday?"

Mary sighed. "I guess," she said.

"Great," Al said. "I'll let you know when we're on the road."

TWENTY

M rs. Fisher!" Ashley announced when Mary came in the door of the bookshop. "There she is!"

Mary checked her watch. She'd thought she had plenty of time before Rebecca and Ashley needed to go—at least half an hour, in fact. But Ashley had the air of someone who had been waiting with bated breath for her return.

"Am I late?" Mary asked. "I'm sorry, I—"

Behind the counter, Rebecca shook her head. "You're early," she said. "By quite a bit. Ashley is just very, very excited about marine biology."

"I don't want to miss it," Ashley said. "We only have a few hours, and then the tide comes in. And no one can stop it. You can't call it up and ask for just a few more minutes."

"All right, honey," Rebecca said. "We'll leave in just a minute. How are you?" she asked Mary as Mary came behind the counter to put away her purse.

Mary nodded. She didn't really have a good answer to that question yet. She wasn't sure when she would. But she was glad to be back at the shop. "Thanks for asking," she said.

"We had a good afternoon," Rebecca told her. "I think you'll be happy with the sales."

"Great," Mary said. On another day, that might have been her only concern. Today, the question of sales in the shop had been the furthest thing from her mind. She stashed her purse in its usual spot and straightened up.

"You two go on," she said. "I'm all set here."

"You sure?" Rebecca asked. "It's not even four yet."

"I don't want to stand in the way of Ashley's budding career as a marine biologist," Mary said. "Go ahead. Maybe she'll make an important discovery before the rest of the class even gets there."

"Then she'd have to name it after you," Rebecca joked. "The Fisherlopteria."

"I'd be honored," Mary said, smiling.

Rebecca slipped out from behind the counter. "Okay, honey," she said. "I think we're ready to go."

Ashley hopped down from her perch, swung her backpack onto her back, and took the stance of a fearless explorer. "I want to find a sea urchin," she said. "They used to be plentiful, but now they're rare. Not many of them come as far as Cape Cod, but it's been known to happen." Mary smiled at her precociousness.

"Well, if anyone could find one...," Rebecca said.

The bell rang over the door as they opened it. Then it swung shut behind them.

Mary let out a long sigh. She sat for a moment, drinking in the silence and order in the shop. It was easy to take it for granted on any other day, to worry about the bills or the customers or the next delivery or the way the stock was organized. But now the bookshop seemed like a haven from all her other worries. There might always be another task to do at the bookstore, but at least all the tasks here were clear. If a book was out, she ordered another one. If something was out of place, she knew where to put it back. And if someone needed something, she knew just where to find it.

None of those things seemed to be true for her in the rest of the world right now. She'd found Claire, but that still hadn't seemed to make any of the missing pieces fall into place. If anything, seeing Claire had only intensified Mary's questions. If nothing had happened between Claire and John, then why did Claire still seem so angry and hurt after all these years? But something in Mary's mind still resisted the possibility fiercely. She'd known John better than anyone. He'd had his difficult moments and his long silences, but he was a deeply caring man and honest to a fault. He was the kind of man who, if he discovered a cashier had given him too much change, would go back into a store and stand in line again just to return the money. It just didn't seem possible that he could keep a relationship with Claire secret from Mary for all these years.

Mary let her head fall into her hands. In any case, being back in the quiet shop was a welcome respite from the other events of the day. The verse from Thessalonians, *Give thanks in all circumstances*, drifted through her mind. It was one of her favorite verses, but at times like this, it sometimes felt like a thorn in her side. Still, whenever she tried to follow it, she often discovered she had more to be thankful for than she had recognized. *Thank You for this shop*, she prayed. *Thank You for Rebecca and for Ashley.* The thought of Ashley brought a smile to her lips. *Thank You for Betty. Thank You for tide pools and for the beautiful drive. Thank You that I*

*know where I'm going to sleep tonight and that I'm not wor-
ried about where dinner will come from. Thank You for books.
Thank You for Ivy Bay.*

When she raised her head, she didn't have any more
answers than she had had a moment before, but the anxiety
she'd felt all day had faded, and her shoulders felt light, as
if some kind of weight had slipped off of them.

Thank You that You know all these answers, she prayed. *No
matter what happens.*

Her e-mail dinged.

Mary opened it almost instantly. At the top of her in-box
was a message from Addison Hartley.

Were these the answers she'd just been praying about?
Maybe it really was true that the moment you released a thing
was the moment God gave it back to you.

At first her heart leapt when she opened the message. It
had a real heading and was a full paragraph long, complete
with punctuation. But as she read the message, her heart sank.

Mrs. Fisher,

> *The charge you make, that my work resembles the
> lives of actual residents of your town, is a very serious one.
> You may not understand the full implications of your sug-
> gestion, but I ask you to kindly refrain from repeating it
> to others. If you persist in your questions to me or in these
> suggestions to others, I will be forced to take legal action.*

> *Yours,*

> *Addison Hartley*

Mary stared at the screen, stunned. She glanced down at
the friendly note she'd sent to Addison and then at the legal
threat he'd sent back. It was hard to believe anyone who read

her letter would ever dream of replying in the tone Hartley had. But it let her know one thing: She had struck some kind of chord.

The bell over the door rang. Mary looked up, half expecting to see Rebecca or Ashley returning for something, but instead Pastor Miles stood in the door.

Mary's smile of welcome faded quickly when she saw Pastor Miles's expression. His normal open and friendly face was tight with worry, and his eyes darted around the store.

"Pastor Miles," she said. "What's wrong? Can I help you with anything?"

"It's Trevor," Pastor Miles told her. "He's gone!"

Mary rose from the stool behind the counter. "Gone?" she repeated.

Pastor Miles nodded, his anxiety palpable. As he talked, he began to move around the shop, searching through the shelves as if he couldn't take even a moment out of the search in order to explain himself. "I brought him home this afternoon, and everything was just fine. His mom was home, working on some homework for her summer school classes, and he was out playing in the yard. He does that all the time. We've never had any problem with it. He just plays until we call him, and then he comes in. But this time, when she called him—"

His words broke off, and he didn't seem able to go on.

"He didn't come in?" Mary finished for him, gently.

Pastor Miles shook his head. Then he took a deep breath. "He didn't come in, and he wasn't in the yard. We searched the whole place. Then we searched the house. Then we searched them both again. Kayla's going door-to-door in the neighborhood now. And I came downtown to see if he'd come over to any of his favorite spots. He loves this place, and ever since he met Ashley, he hasn't stopped talking about it. So I just thought—"

Mary nodded. "That makes perfect sense," she said. "And I wish he were here, but I haven't seen him since this morning."

"You've been here all day?" Pastor Miles asked.

Mary shook her head. "No, but Rebecca and Ashley were here until a few minutes ago. And I'm sure if Trevor had come in alone, they would have contacted you."

Pastor Miles pushed his hand back through his hair, considering this. Then he nodded. "I'm sure you're right," he said.

He'd wound his way through the entire bookshop now, assuring himself of what Mary already knew—his grandson wasn't there.

"I'm sorry," Mary said.

"Thank you," Pastor Miles said, but he was already moving through the door. "I need to keep checking through town."

"Of course," she said.

But just before he reached the door, Mary had an idea. "Pastor Miles?" she asked.

He stopped and turned.

"I know the prayer group has only met once, but I'd like to alert them about this," she said. "Would you mind that?"

Pastor Miles nodded. "I'd love to know people are praying for us," he said.

Mary's hand was already on the phone. "I'll start calling right now."

TWENTY-ONE

❖

The first number Mary called was Bernice's.

"I'll pray here," Bernice told her. "But I'd really love to pray with the other girls. Would you mind if I just came down to the shop for a few minutes? I think this would be good to do in person."

"That's a great idea," Mary said.

When she was done calling down the list, several of the woman had agreed to meet up in the shop as soon as they were able. Bernice actually walked through the door as Mary was hanging up from speaking with the last one, and a few minutes later, they had a genuine gathering in the back of the store, where the two comfortable chairs anchored the reading nook.

Mary pulled out a few of the folding chairs that they'd last used for seating at Addison Hartley's reading, and their little group gathered together in a clumsy circle. To her surprise, Dorothy Johnson didn't make any comments about how better to arrange the chairs or organize the meeting. She just pitched in, carrying the chairs down the aisle and moving a few books out of the way so that there would be more room. Maybe this was the side of her Pastor Miles saw, Mary thought. If it was, she could see why he might think highly of her.

The women's prayers for Trevor were brief but heartfelt. Mary felt a pang of self-consciousness about the idea of a customer walking into the store and discovering a prayer group in process, but she quickly squashed it. After all, praying for a missing boy was nothing to be embarrassed about. It might actually do someone good to see it.

Once the prayers began, she even lost track of those rationalizations, as the women prayed for Trevor's safety; for comfort for his mother Kayla and for Pastor Miles as they looked for him; for wisdom about where to look; and for Trevor's quick return. Bernice badgered God like an irritated housewife who'd just discovered that her husband had forgotten to take out the trash. She knew He knew better than that, and she couldn't understand why He didn't just set everything right again. Lynn cried as she imagined what it must be like for Kayla to cope with a missing child. Dorothy's prayer was measured and logical, like a woman talking with a shop owner, explaining what she needed down to the last detail. But all of them agreed on the basics: God had the power to help them, and if they asked Him, He'd listen.

The prayers only lasted for a few minutes, and despite Mary's worries, no other customers came into the shop while the group was praying. When they had finished, the women began to drift back to whatever they'd interrupted to join the group. Mary promised each of them that she'd let them know as soon as she had any news, and they all agreed to continue their prayers until they heard something. Bernice was the last to leave.

"Thanks so much for doing this," she said.

Mary glanced up at her, glad to see that Bernice wasn't fleeing the scene. But she didn't want to say anything to bring up the earlier awkwardness. "All I did was stay at my own store," Mary told her. "You're the ones who came from all over the town to pray."

Bernice gave her a little hug. "Yep," she said. "But if nobody had asked us, we wouldn't have known to come."

"Well, I'm glad to do it," Mary said. "It's better than sitting around, worrying."

Bernice nodded. "Yes," she said. "And it feels good to know that if something ever happens to me, I know the kind of people who would drop everything to come and pray for me."

"I hadn't thought of it that way," Mary said. "I guess it's true."

"Well, that's how it is," Bernice said. "Welcome to Ivy Bay."

As the door was still chiming overhead from her exit, it swung open again. Rebecca gave a rueful grin as she and Ashley came in. "Hi," she said. "I hope you don't mind us coming in. Apparently we were so excited about the tide pools we forgot to pack the book we'd been reading. And apparently we won't be able to sleep tonight unless we find out what happens."

Ashley picked up the slight mockery in her mother's tone and looked up at her with exasperation. "She's stuck in a *turret*, Mommy," she said. "And the dragons are coming."

She scampered down the aisle and back around the corner, where she located the book she'd been reading with an unerring homing instinct, then stashed it safely away in her backpack.

"How were the tide pools?" Mary asked.

"Good," Ashley said with an attempt at an expert's nonchalance. "We saw anemones and mussels, and one boy found a sea star." It was clear from her tone of voice that she felt somewhat robbed that this discovery had not been her own, but the fact that someone else had found it couldn't completely dim its wonder.

"Well, I'm glad to hear that," Mary said.

Ashley returned to Rebecca and took her mom's hand. "Okay," she said.

But Rebecca was looking closely at Mary. Something in Mary's expression must have attracted her writer's sharp eye. "Is everything okay?" she asked. "Did anything happen while we were gone?"

Mary hesitated a moment before answering. She didn't want to scare Ashley by talking about the disappearance of another child. But if anything was seriously wrong with Trevor, she'd hear about it soon enough. And the more people who heard he was missing, the more people who could potentially do something.

"Pastor Miles came in here a little while ago," she said. "Looking for Trevor. Apparently he's disappeared."

Rebecca's face went white. "Disappeared?" she repeated. "They don't know—"

"He and Kayla have looked all over the neighborhood. Now he's searching around town."

Rebecca shook her head and reached down to embrace her own daughter, as if to make sure she was still there. Ashley squirmed a bit in her mother's arms.

"Trevor?" she said.

"Yes, honey," Mary said.

"He's going to be a sailor," Ashley said.

Mary nodded again, automatically, in the kindly way she'd respond to any child's nonsense prattle.

But an instant later, a chill went down Mary's spine. A sailor? Until now, it hadn't even occurred to her that Trevor might wander down by the water. But that wasn't impossible, or even unlikely, she realized now. The water was just a short walk from downtown. And with Trevor's attraction to boats, it would be an attraction for him.

"A sailor?" Mary asked carefully. "Of which boat?"

"Mr. Henry's," Ashley said. "He told me this morning."

At the mention of Henry's name, Mary felt a surge of relief. Maybe this explained everything. Was it possible that Henry had agreed to take Trevor out and just not realized that Pastor Miles wasn't aware of the plans?

"Excuse me," Mary said, picking up the phone and flipping through her phone list. "I'm going to call Pastor Miles."

Rebecca nodded and began to pull Ashley toward the door. "We'll get out of your way. Let us know how it goes."

Mary nodded good-bye to them as Pastor Miles's phone began to ring. It didn't even get through the first full peal before Pastor Miles answered.

"Hello?" he said, his voice high and tense.

"Pastor Miles, this is Mary," she said.

"Is he there?" Pastor Miles asked.

"I'm sorry, no," Mary said. "But Rebecca and Ashley came in just after our group finished praying for you, and Ashley remembers Trevor saying that he was going out on the boat with Henry this afternoon. Did you know anything about that?"

"The boat?" Pastor Miles said. Mary could hear the same horror in his voice that she'd first felt when she heard the idea. She hurried to comfort him.

"With Henry," she added again. "I thought maybe they'd made arrangements, and Henry wasn't aware Trevor hadn't told you, or—"

"No, that's impossible," Pastor Miles said. "I just saw Henry at the ice-cream shop. He hadn't seen Trevor all day. He actually went out looking for him himself as soon as I told him what had happened."

Mary's heart sank. "Well, then," she said. "Does Trevor know his way to the water?"

"I'm afraid he does," Pastor Miles said. "I have to shoo him away from it almost every time we come downtown. I can't believe I didn't think of this before. I guess I just didn't want to imagine that—"

"There's no time for imagining," Mary said. "We just need to get down there."

"You're right," Pastor Miles said.

"You tell Henry and Kayla," Mary said. "I'm going to close up the shop, and I'll meet you down there."

Moments later, Mary had turned off all the overhead lights in the shop, except for a small one behind the counter to keep Gus company until she came back. He trailed her to the door, curious as to why she'd be leaving without him.

"I'll be back," she promised him. "Just as soon as I can. You take care of the place, all right?"

Gus gave her a look that let her know he'd at least take care of himself. She set the lock and pulled the door shut, then hurried down to the water.

When she reached the turn down to the docks, two other figures were already hurrying down the way before her in the twilight. She instantly recognized them as Pastor Miles and Henry, who had taken Trevor on the recent boat trip that had so completely captured the young boy's imagination.

"Any luck?" she asked as she caught up to them.

"Not yet," Pastor Miles said, tight-lipped. He was walking so fast that Mary had to half run to catch up with him.

"Trevor!" Pastor Miles bellowed.

"Trevor? Honey?" Mary echoed.

Nothing stirred on the docks or on the sand nearby. They walked along the cramped roads that led along the water, scanning the shapes of the shanties and the bobbing boats for anything that might be out of place. Henry moved away, toward the beach, and the three of them stopped, scanning the sand and the water. Then Henry raised his voice. "Trevor?" he called.

At this, what had seemed to be a lump of net or buoy detached itself from a dinghy overturned nearby on the beach. "Mr. Woodrow?" came a boy's voice, sleepy but excited. Then, suddenly, Trevor was barreling through the night toward them. "I knew you'd come!"

An instant later, Pastor Miles had his grandson in his arms, squeezing him tight and scolding him at the same time.

A moment later, he was fumbling in his pocket for his cell phone.

"Kayla?" he said, with Trevor still clasped tightly to him. "I've got him. Yes. Yes, I'm coming home."

Lost in his own thoughts, he started off down the beach, still carrying his grandson and assuring his daughter.

Henry let out a long breath. "I'm sure glad that turned out the way it did," he said. "I wouldn't have liked to see—"

"I'm glad too," Mary said. Her heart was still beating hard from the excitement, and now that she was left alone on the beach with Henry, she wasn't quite sure what to say.

Henry seemed to be wondering the same thing. "Well," he said, "I guess we'd better get back, then."

Mary nodded as they continued to stroll. She had several longtime acquaintances, of course, but in many ways, Ivy Bay was still new to her, full of people who seemed more like strangers than friends. But Henry really knew her and had really known her for years. That was a gift she couldn't put a price on.

"Something on your mind?" Henry asked.

Henry, even more than anyone else, might understand her worry and upset over the appearance of Mary's teenage story in Addison Hartley's book. He'd been friendly with them all at the time and even given John his stamp of approval after he'd taken John out on the tiny sloop he'd worked three summers to save up for. Part of her strained toward the relief of sharing her worries and confusion with Henry.

But as she began to try to think of how to put them into words, she realized that it was impossible. Henry hadn't known her and John for the last forty years. There was a chance that he might believe the lies Addison Hartley had worked into his fictional tale, and Mary didn't think she could stand that. No, for the time being, this was something she needed to keep to herself. It felt, she realized, like something that was just between her and John—not to be shared with anyone else.

"Not really," she finally answered.

"Not really?" Henry said broadly, raising his eyebrows. "That sounds mysterious."

Mary smiled at him and shook her head.

"I know that look," Henry said. "No point in me asking again. Not until you're ready to tell me about it."

Mary just offered a demure shrug.

"I'm amazed you recognize the look, though," she said. "After forty years."

They'd reached the edge of town now and stepped back from the beach onto the pavement that ran through the fishing shanties.

"Well," Henry said, "some things just stay with you, I guess. You know what I mean?"

Mary watched him for a minute. In the moonlight, some of the lines that had appeared on his face in the years since they'd first become friends faded, and she could almost imagine he was the same joking, familiar boy she'd known all those years ago. "I do know," she said.

Henry grinned. "Well, I've got a charter group tomorrow that wants three kinds of ice cream in their cooler. So I need to get down to the store before they lock everything up."

"Thanks so much for helping us find Trevor," Mary told him.

Henry held his hand up. "Please," he said, "that's not the kind of thing you need to thank a person for. It's just the right thing to do. You want me to walk you back up to the store before I go?"

"Actually, I think I'll stay here for a minute," Mary said.

Henry nodded. "All right," he said. "I'll see you around."

As Mary stood at the edge of the beach, he walked up into the lit streets of downtown Ivy Bay. Mary stared out at the dark water and added another thank-you to the list she'd been making earlier that day. *Thank You that Trevor is home safe.*

Then she stood looking down the coast at the pine bluff. She still felt like it was trying to tell her something. She just didn't know what that was.

TWENTY-TWO

J ohn?" Mary asked.

She was sure she'd heard him calling her name up ahead, as he sometimes did when they went to the pine bluff, but as she pushed through the soft branches of the pines, she couldn't seem to catch sight of him. Then suddenly, the pines disappeared. But they didn't end at the edge of the bluff overlooking the sea. They fell away at the edge of an unfamiliar beach.

This is all wrong, Mary thought and turned back, thinking she'd just slip back among the pines and find her way again. But now the pines had vanished. In their place was the long road she'd driven several times now, on the way up to Claire's new town.

She jolted awake with a start, then sat up.

"Did you sleep all right?" Betty asked her at breakfast.

From the look on Betty's face, Mary could tell her sister already knew the answer.

"Not really," she said.

Betty caught her hand as Mary laid Betty's breakfast down in front of her on the table. "You're not still letting that old gossip bother you, are you?" she asked. "About Claire and John?"

Mary shook her head. "Not exactly," she said. "Or at least not *just* that. It's not just that the story circulated around town. It's that it turned up in Addison Hartley's most recent book."

Before, Mary had been worried that this might sound crazy, but now she was too convinced of the fact herself to worry about how they sounded to someone else. Her tone must have been convincing, despite the unlikeliness of the story. Betty's eyes widened.

"Are you sure?" she asked.

Mary nodded. "If I wasn't before, I am now," she said. "I actually wrote him, thinking there must be some mistake. And he wrote back yesterday and threatened me with legal action."

"Lawyers!" Betty said. "Well, he wouldn't have a leg to stand on if you could prove the story was true."

Mary shook her head. "Actually," she said, "that's what I'm worried about."

But even after the conversation with her sister, she couldn't shake the images from the dream. As Mary dressed and got ready, they continued to swirl through her head. She'd felt, before she went to bed, like some kind of answer lay in the pine bluff, and she hadn't been able to figure out what. That was probably why it had appeared in her dreams now, she told herself. And it was no surprise that something about Claire would show up as well, given the day she'd had. She could also see why the beach might appear, since she'd been there just before going to sleep. But why all three of them? Why at the same time?

As she washed her face and brushed her hair, the image of the beach came back again and again. It hadn't actually been the one she'd been on the night before, she realized. She'd been familiar since she was a girl with the sandy cove where the boats took shelter. But it wasn't totally unfamiliar either. Strangely, it felt like something she might have imagined in another dream. But she didn't have a lot of memories of dreaming about beaches. Could she have dreamed it once before, long ago, and then forgotten it?

It wasn't until she walked through the door of the shop and saw the Addison Hartley display still dominating the entrance that she realized where she'd seen the beach before. It was the bit of shoreline she'd imagined for the scenes where the character based on John had met up with the character based on Mary in Hartley's story. But what had it been doing in her dream? And why had it appeared with the pine bluff?

The answer came to her in a flash of insight. Maybe this was what the pine bluff had seemed to be saying to her last night: Addison Hartley had gotten all the other details of the story right. But he had gotten the pine bluff wrong. So whoever told him the story must not have known about it. Of course, there was a chance that Hartley had changed that detail, but why would he change that one and not any of the others? No, this seemed to be another confirmation of the fact that Claire must have shared her version of the events with him at some point. But Mary had suspected this for a while now. What the dream and the pine bluff helped her to see, though, was new. They made it seem like whoever had told Hartley the story had had to do some imagining of their own to fill in the blanks. So whatever Claire imagined had happened between Mary and John, or whatever had really happened, she'd never learned about John and Mary's secret haven.

The realization helped settle and calm the part of her that had felt exposed and betrayed ever since she finished Hartley's book. The best-selling novel might tell Claire's side of the story, but it seemed that Claire, and Hartley, never really knew the truth of Mary and John's relationship. And that meant that some of Mary's most precious memories were safe from the exposure they might have had if John had really been sharing his secrets with Claire for all these years.

Rebecca came in as Mary was putting her things down. "I was so glad to hear Trevor was all right," she said.

"Thanks to Ashley," Mary told her.

Ashley took this all in stride, giving Mary a polite nod as she made her way back to her nook in the children's corner.

Mary fired up the store computer for the day, musing over the details of the dream. There were so many competing versions of the story out there—her own memories, Addison Hartley's prose, Claire's veiled threats, Brad's uncomfortable hints. Wasn't there anyone out there who could tell her the simple truth? She shook her head slightly as the screen lit up, thinking how much had changed over the years. It was hard to lose friends and loved ones, no matter how you lost them. John, Claire, even Claire's mother. How had the years separated her from all of them?

Then her thoughts came up with a sharp jolt. Claire's mother, she thought again. *Claire's mother.*

For all this time, Mary had been thinking that Claire was the only person still living who could tell her the truth about what happened between Claire and John all those years ago. But Claire's mother was still living. And Claire had always told her mother everything, at least when Mary and Claire were girls. And Mary knew that Claire's mother had tried to get Claire to repair her friendship with Mary. Claire had even said as much during one of their last conversations. "My mother doesn't understand either," she'd told Mary. "She thinks we can just get over it and be friends again."

Instead of bringing up the store accounting system as she usually did, Mary clicked on her Internet browser. As soon as the search engine came up, she realized something else about Claire's mother: Her name likely hadn't changed the way Claire's had over the years. Holding her breath, Mary typed Mrs. Wilkes' name into the blinking box—Olivia Wilkes—and she added the name of Claire's new home in Cape Cod.

The first hit that came up showed an Olivia Wilkes in a town between Ivy Bay and Claire's new home: as the winner of a nursing-home-wide bingo tournament. Mary smiled involuntarily and clicked on the link. There was Claire's mother, older but unmistakable, wearing a cheap tiara and holding up an empty bingo board for the camera. Even if Mary hadn't recognized the face, she would have recognized Olivia Wilkes' verve for life. She'd passed a lot of it to her own daughter, and it had been one of the things Mary had enjoyed most about knowing both of them during the good days of her and Claire's friendship.

Mary scrolled through the rest of the bingo pictures, then closed the page to find the nursing home's location and address. A quick visit to the maps section told her it was less than an hour away.

TWENTY-THREE

◆◆◆

R ebecca," Mary said.
  Rebecca stuck her head out from among the stacks.
"Yep?"

"Listen, I've got to run an errand," Mary said.

"We've got it," Rebecca said. "The store's in good hands.
I've been meaning to tell you, I feel pretty confident here
now. If you even wanted to start scheduling me to take
some mornings or evenings on my own, I'm sure I could
handle it."

Mary nodded, grateful again for Rebecca's quickness—
and kindness. Mary said, "I think we can do that."

Rebecca beamed. "Great," she said.

"I don't think I've ever seen anyone so happy to have to
take a shift by herself," Mary said.

Rebecca's smile grew even brighter. "It might be silly," she
said, "but I already love this place like it was my own. And
getting my own shifts is a far cry from being worried that I'm
going to be fired."

"Oh, I'm not firing you anytime soon," Mary assured her.
"Your problem is going to be that I don't ever want you to
leave."

"Well, that's a good problem to have," said Rebecca.

Mary gave Rebecca a hug.

"You have to go," Rebecca said when she released her.

"That's right," Mary said. "I do."

"Well, you better get going, then," said Rebecca.

A few minutes later, Mary was spinning up the coast road again, but this time, she turned off onto a side road about forty minutes south of Claire's new town. Mary was glad to see that the nursing home that housed Olivia Wilkes was one of the most beautiful on the Cape—just as classic and tasteful as Claire's own imposing home, if not more so. It was set in the woods overlooking one of the Cape's famous inland lakes—a group of beautiful gray wood Cape cottages that spread out in a half moon along the rim of the water, looking out at a pristine pine forest on the other side, which was perfectly reflected in the still water.

Well-kept paved walks, perfect for negotiating with walkers, wheelchairs, or canes, led between the buildings, many of which were also connected by glass breezeways. The center of the complex seemed to be a large Cape mansion, perhaps the original structure on the property, with a long ramp leading up to the front doors.

Mary parked her car in the lot near the main building and went in. Inside, she was greeted by a young woman in a yellow polo shirt and khaki shorts, her hair pulled back in a neat brunette ponytail. "Can I help you?" she asked.

"I hope so," Mary told her. "I'm here to see an old friend of mine. Olivia Wilkes."

The girl's face lit up. "Oh, Mrs. Wilkes," she said. "She's a favorite of ours around here."

REWRITING HISTORY ∼ 199

"I'm not surprised," Mary told her, smiling.

"Let me just tell her you're here," the girl said. She made a quick call, announcing Mary's arrival. This time, Mary could hear Olivia's excitement even from the distant receiver.

"She'll be delighted to see you," the girl told Mary. "You just want to go out these doors and walk along the lake path to the third house. She's waiting for you."

"Thank you," Mary said and went out the doors where the woman had pointed.

The snug cottages along the lake's edge didn't look like any other retirement community Mary had ever seen. If she looked closely, she could tell that they were each built to a similar plan, but that's where the similarities ended. Each one was painted a different color—sienna, red, blue—and each was set back into its own unique cluster of mature trees and tasteful landscaping.

When Mary passed the first house, she caught sight of some motion in the trees beyond. A few steps later, she realized what it was. Olivia Wilkes was standing on the deck of her house, a neat blue cabin with gray shutters, and waving to beat the band.

Mary smiled and began to hurry down. When she reached the house and made her way up the winding walk from the lake path to the deck that led up to the front door, Mrs. Wilkes enveloped her in a giant bear hug. Even after all these years, her hug was unmistakable. Mary had been wrapped in hundreds of them during the course of her girlhood, almost every time she came into the Wilkeses' house—or left it. It gave her the same feeling she'd had just for a few brief seconds when she'd first seen Claire, despite everything that had happened to them: excitement to see a long-absent friend. But this time, Olivia didn't do anything to snuff that feeling out. Instead, she held Mary at arm's length, just the way she had when Mary was only ten or eleven, and beamed at her.

"Well, Mary Nelson," she said, using Mary's maiden name. "You haven't changed a bit. Let me look at you."

Mary smiled at the obvious but kindly falsehood. She could almost say the same thing about Olivia, actually. The years had added wrinkles to her face and stolen some of the color from her hair, but her spirit was unchanged, warm and sparkling.

"How are you doing?" Mary asked, squeezing her hand.

Olivia squeezed it back. "Well, I'm doing great," she said. "Now that you're here. I can't tell you what good it does an old lady to see her old friends. It almost makes me feel young again. But what am I doing? Have you been traveling? Do you need to sit down? Can I get you something to drink?"

Mary decided on answering only the last of these questions. "A drink sounds great," she said.

Olivia turned and bustled into the house, holding the door to welcome Mary into a lovely great room with a vaulted ceiling. To the left was a wide kitchen with an island in the middle. On the island sat a clear pitcher surrounded by halved and squeezed lemons and what looked to be peels from a gingerroot.

"I just made some ginger lemonade," Olivia told her, as if she were confiding a secret. "I always love ginger lemon tea in the winter, and I got to missing it this morning, but it's been too hot for tea. So I thought, why not ginger lemonade? I just boiled the gingerroot in a gallon of water and then used that to make my regular lemonade recipe. Would you like to try some?"

Mary nodded. "I see you're still experimenting in the kitchen," she said. Claire had come by her creativity honestly. Her mother was a wonderful experimenter in the kitchen, and she reserved her boldest departures for nights when she was having guests, so she was famous for putting a dinner on for visitors with the announcement that she had never actually tried the recipe before. But because her flights of fancy in the kitchen always seemed to result in something wonderful, her guests always greeted these announcements with excitement, rather than the dread they might inspire from a less-gifted chef.

Olivia giggled. "I guess some things never change," she said, pouring Mary a large glass of the ginger lemonade. "Now let's see, where do you want to sit?"

"What would you like?" Mary asked.

"Well," Olivia said, "I must admit I'm partial to that deck, especially in the summer. And I won't be able to sit out there for much longer, once fall sets in." She led Mary back through the door, and the two of them took seats on the stuffed chintz and wicker furniture, under the swaying tops of the trees.

The scene was so peaceful that Mary could have believed she really had just come to visit an old friend in her lakeside cottage. But the questions of the last week couldn't remain dormant for long. As she sipped the lemonade, tangy and sweet with just a hint of the ginger's fire, she wondered how to ask the questions she'd come with.

"Well, it's certainly been a long time," Olivia said as the trees rustled overhead and the mirrored surface of the lake trembled under a sudden breeze.

"It has," Mary agreed.

"So tell me what I've missed," Olivia said. "What are you up to these days?"

"Well, I own a little bookstore down in Ivy Bay," Mary said.

"Oh my goodness!" Olivia said. "Have you been there all along? If I'd have known, I bet I'd have been one of your best customers. At least until recently," she said. "It's not so easy to get around now."

"I'm sure you would have," Mary said. "But I just opened it this year."

"Well, that sounds like a dream come true," Olivia said.

Mary paused for a minute. With all the grief of losing John and all the details of opening the store, sometimes it was easy to lose track of that fact. But Olivia was right. Owning the store was a dream come true.

"Yes," she said. "I really enjoy it."

"I'm sure you do," Olivia said. "And what were you doing before that?"

Mary hesitated. How could you sum up a whole life in a few sentences? She struggled for the words, and then, once she found them, she struggled again because the words seemed so simple. Was this all she'd done? she wondered. All she had to show for all those hopes and dreams she'd shared with Claire and Olivia so long ago? "Well, I was married," she said. "We lived in Boston. We had two children, Jack and Elizabeth. Jack's a pediatrician, and Elizabeth is raising her two children. Jack has one of his own, so now that's three: Daisy, Emma, and Luke."

"Oh, I bet they're precious," Olivia said.

Mary smiled and nodded. "I worked as a librarian for years," she continued. "And when my husband passed away, I came back here to live with my sister Betty and opened the bookshop."

"I'm so sorry to hear about your husband," Olivia said. "I know how hard that can be."

Mary nodded. Olivia really did know, she realized. She had lost her husband when she was much, much younger than Mary, and when she still had a young child to raise on her own. Mary still felt John's loss each day, and maybe she always would, but she had had many more years with him than Olivia had with her husband. It had never occurred to her to be thankful for all those years she'd had with John. She'd just taken them as her due. Of course the two of them would share a full life and old age together. But that wasn't promised, she realized. Olivia hadn't gotten it. And Olivia's loss made the life Mary had taken for granted seem like a blessing. The verse she had been trying to follow the day before, about giving thanks in all circumstances, flitted through her mind again. Maybe this was part of what it meant, taking time to recognize all the blessings she so easily took for granted.

"Thank you," she said and set the lemonade glass down on the table beside them. "Actually, that's part of why I'm here."

Olivia nodded and held her gaze expectantly.

"I don't know if Claire ever shared with you about what happened that summer before we went to school."

Olivia nodded, her gaze turning slightly sad. "She did," she said. "I always wished there was some way to patch that up. The two of you were such good friends."

Mary wondered how much to share with Olivia now. She didn't want to add any worry to the sweet older woman's world by explaining about Addison Hartley's book and her miserable encounters with Claire. Maybe she could get the answers she needed just by asking about the past, without dragging in the present.

"Well," Mary said, "I married John."

Olivia's face broke into a wide smile, as if Mary had just brought her the news the day she was engaged. "You did?" she said, clasping her hands. "Oh, honey, that's wonderful."

Mary couldn't help but smile back. And some of her unease over the situation with John and Claire lifted as well. If Claire had confided any really deep secrets about John to her mother, would Olivia be this overjoyed to hear Mary had married him? In fact, if Claire had been confiding secrets about Mary and John to Olivia, wouldn't Olivia already *know* they were married?

"Thank you," Mary said.

"He was such a sweet boy," Olivia said. "*Shy*, my goodness, but so sweet."

"We were very happy," Mary told her. "But I've always wondered..."

Olivia watched her carefully as she trailed off, but she didn't prompt her.

"I wondered about John and Claire," Mary said. "Claire seemed so sure that there was something there..." *Sure enough to tell the story to a best-selling author*, she added silently. Mary trailed off. She couldn't quite bring herself to ask the question outright, but Olivia seemed to understand. She patted Mary's hand.

"Oh, honey," she said. "Have you been worrying about this all these years?"

Mary shook her head. Thankfully, she hadn't. For most of her marriage, the old story had been the furthest thing from her mind. "No," she said. "But sometimes—"

Olivia cut her off with a firm shake of her head. "You know Claire," she said. "Her imagination is a blessing, but it can also be a curse. Sometimes I think it keeps her from seeing the good things she has right here in this world."

"So John—" Mary began.

Olivia shook her head again. "Claire's feelings for him were real," she said. "But she was very young then. So young she could build a story out of just about anything, whether it had any grounding in real life or not. And maybe she needed to learn how to do that, to make up for everything she'd lost."

Mary thought back. She'd never seen the difference in their lives as children, but now she could see how different her life had been from Claire's. Mary had never even imagined the idea of losing her father until she was a grown woman, but Claire had lived with that reality every day and with other realities that Mary hadn't faced as a girl—making do with her mother's small paycheck, balancing all her many hopes and dreams against life's harsher realities.

As all this ran through her mind, Olivia's face broke out in a nonsensical smile. Then, to Mary's surprise, she began to wave at something through the trees.

Mary turned to see. There, at the foot of the path down to the lake, stood Claire.

TWENTY-FOUR

——◆◆◆——

Mary barely recognized her from the day before. Then, Claire had been buttoned into a power suit, her outfit finished by tasteful but pointedly costly jewelry. Today, she wore a simple denim skirt and a light cotton shirt, the kind of thing either of them might have worn for a day on the water forty years ago. Her hair was swept back in a ponytail, and she carried a stack of books in her arms.

But her expression was the same. Mary didn't have any idea how Claire had looked as she came along the lake path, but as soon as she recognized Mary, the same look of shock and fury, now even more intense, had appeared on her face. Mary's mind raced. Running into Claire at her mother's place, especially in the middle of the day, had never occurred to her. Claire's job had seemed much too high-powered for her to light out in the middle of the day to visit her mother, almost an hour away. But here she was.

Either Olivia couldn't see far enough to glimpse the scowl on her daughter's face, or she'd chosen to ignore it. "Hello, honey!" she called cheerily. "It's so good to see you. And look who dropped by! It's Mary Nelson."

"Actually, Mom," Claire said as she came up the walk to the deck, the anger in her voice barely controlled, "I think it's Mary *Fisher* now."

Mary glanced from Claire to Olivia. The palpable anger in Claire's voice as she said John's last name startled her. Everything, including Claire's mother, suggested that nothing had happened between Claire and John all those years ago. But Claire's feelings still seemed as raw as they had back when she and Mary were teenagers.

Claire set the stack of books down on the table and bent to kiss her mother. Mary stiffened on the chair beside her, wondering what she should do. Excuse herself? Try to make polite conversation?

Before she could decide, Olivia rose from the chair beside her. "Well, I'm sure you girls have plenty to catch up on," she said. "I'll just go in the house and fix you up something to drink."

Claire was visibly upset at the prospect of being left alone with Mary again. "Mom," she protested. "You don't really need to—"

Her mother waved her off, already halfway to the house. "I've got some ginger lemonade in here," she said. "You're going to love it."

She disappeared inside.

Claire sat down heavily on one of the chairs. Her expression was perfectly familiar to Mary. She'd learned it well during their teenage years, during Claire's many little skirmishes with her mother—a mixture of rebellion and defeat. Mary suppressed a smile. The last thing she needed to do was make Claire feel that Mary was laughing at her.

"I'm sorry," Mary began and started to rise. "I really had no idea you were going to be here. I just—"

"What?" Claire asked. "Came back to rub your perfect husband and your perfect marriage in my face, just one more time?"

This was so far from the truth that it stopped Mary in her tracks. "I loved John," she said. "But our marriage was hardly perfect."

Claire let out a disbelieving sigh.

"I think you of all people would understand that," Mary added, thinking of the dark take on her story that Claire had somehow passed on to Addison Hartley.

Claire's look became guarded.

"You don't need to pretend with me," Mary said. "I told you. I've seen pictures of you with Hartley that date back to years ago."

"Well, that hardly proves anything," Claire said. "I've worked with a lot of people over the years."

"Yes, but how many of them have written a best-selling story about your life?"

For some reason, when Mary said this, a flicker of contempt seemed to pass over Claire's features. If she was close enough to Hartley to share her story with him, Mary wondered, why the look of contempt?

Then Claire gave another one of her twisted smiles. "None of them," she said and met Mary's eyes. She actually seemed to be suppressing a look of triumph, but Mary wasn't going to be thrown off by her games. There was no denying the fact that Addison Hartley's book mimicked their teenage story.

"I just don't understand," Mary pressed on. "Why would you share our story with Addison Hartley?"

Now Claire gave a short bark of laughter. "I guess that's one way to put it," she said.

Mary was starting to get irritated by Claire's cryptic answers. "There's no denying it," she insisted. "Those descriptive passages are too perfect. They're beautiful, but he doesn't miss a detail."

Claire's eyes lit up. But the glow that sparked in them didn't fade after a moment like the fleeting happiness of a fan sharing details with another fan. It was something different. Mary looked at her in surprise, trying to place it. As she did, Claire dropped her gaze to her lap, as if trying to hide the expression, which still didn't fade from her face.

Then, suddenly, Mary recognized the look: pride. It was just as clear as the similarities between Mary's story and Hartley's book. And Mary had seen it on the face of a hundred other authors during her lifetime. Suddenly, it all fell into place—Claire's girlhood desire to be a writer, the matching details of her story and Hartley's book, her expression of authorial pride.

"You wrote it," Mary said, her heart pounding. "You wrote Hartley's book for him."

Claire tried to resist it, but the smile that spread across her face was uncontrollable. It was the same look Mary remembered from their days as girls, when Claire used to read her each new chapter as she pounded it out.

Mary stared at her old friend, torn between admiration for her talent and the betrayal she still felt over having her story exposed.

"How?" Mary breathed.

"I've always loved books, you know that," Claire told Mary. Without realizing it, Claire seemed to have slipped back into the breathless tone the two of them had spoken in when they shared secrets as girls. "I went to business school because I knew I was going to have to take care of Mom one day, but I took English classes all along the way. Business was my career, but writing was my passion. And I didn't stop writing after school. I wrote all the time—evenings, weekends. Then I met Hartley. He was rich already, but he'd stopped writing. He'd gotten so famous he couldn't stand to think about all the people waiting for his next book. He hadn't written a word since.

"Then one day, I took him a manuscript I'd been working on. I don't even know what I was hoping for it. I think I just wanted him to tell me he liked it, and I shouldn't give up. But the next time I met with him, he told me he wanted to publish it. But he wanted to publish it under his name."

Mary's eyes widened. "Why would you agree to that?" she asked, like she had when they were teenagers.

"I was so young," Claire said. "I hadn't even really dreamed of getting published yet. But here was a big-time writer, offering to share half of what he made with me. He said it was almost impossible for a first-time writer to find an audience, and I knew enough to see that was true. I just couldn't believe my luck. And I didn't have an agent or know anyone in publishing I could ask.

"And then the book did well. Really well. And I knew it was because of Hartley's name, not mine. So when he asked me to write the next one, I did. But then I saw you, and I realized that you'd read the book, or you would read it soon—"

"Didn't you realize that before?" Mary asked. "Or did you think John might find it?"

Claire shook her head. "I knew John was gone," she said. "And I hadn't really thought about you. It was just a story I needed to tell."

Mary's skin prickled at Claire's admission that she'd known about John's death. How had she known? "But the story isn't true," Mary insisted.

Claire's face had become open, almost relieved, as she claimed ownership of the books she'd written under Addison Hartley's name. But now it became guarded again. "You and I have always had different opinions on that subject," she said.

Mary shook her head. This wasn't a matter of opinion. This was about the question of whether her husband had loved another woman or not. And she wasn't going to settle for a vague answer, in her mind, or in anyone else's. "No," she said forcefully. "What you thought just wasn't true. You got the details right in that story, but John never snuck out to meet with you. He never promised to be with you."

"People remember things different ways," Claire said. "And my memories are very clear. You've already admitted that."

"They might be clear," Mary said. "But they're not true." Her mind raced, searching for proof. Claire was right. So many of her scenes were perfectly drawn, with all the details correct, but the feeling wrong. *But she'd gotten the pine bluff wrong*, Mary remembered.

"John and I never met on the beach," she said. "We went somewhere else." Even now, she didn't want to share those memories with anyone. They were hers and John's alone.

Claire stared at her. Mary waited, expecting another angry denial, but to her surprise, after a moment, Claire's eyes began to fill with tears. "I know," she said and dropped her head. She wiped at her eyes. "Or actually," she said, "I didn't know. I knew you two went off somewhere, but I never knew where. I always hated that."

Mary reached out and touched Claire's hand. Claire caught it and held it. "I just felt so lonely without you," she said, her voice breaking. "I missed you so much."

She hadn't said anything about John, Mary realized. Maybe this had never really been about him, after all.

"But you went on to get married, didn't you?" Mary asked gently.

Claire nodded and looked up, her eyes wide. "Brad," she said.

"Weren't you happy with him?" Mary asked.

"I was," Claire said. Her eyes began to fill, and she dropped her head again.

"But did you really carry this torch for John all these years?" Mary asked. "Even while you were married?"

Claire shook her head and looked up again. "No," she said. "Not at first. When I first met Brad, all of that seemed just like a teenage dream. I told myself Brad was the real thing, the man I'd really been meant to be with. And for a while I believed it."

"So what changed?" Mary asked.

Claire shook her head. "Mom got sick," she said. "She's been sick for a while, but a few years ago, it got really bad. She seems fine now, but she goes through these ups and downs, and the downs are really scary. And Brad just doesn't understand."

Mary thought back to the concern she'd seen in Brad's eyes when she'd spoken to him. "He doesn't?" she asked.

Claire's voice broke. "Nobody does!" she said. "It's just so hard. I was supposed to go to work, be there with Mom all the time, be there with Brad all the time, and—I just couldn't do it. Brad started out trying to help me, but then he started complaining about how I was never home."

"He wanted to see you," Mary suggested.

"Well, I couldn't do it," Claire said vehemently. "I just couldn't do it all. So we started to fight all the time. And then we just stopped talking. And I started to remember—" She paused and took a shuddering breath.

"I just remembered how happy we'd been when we were kids," she said. "And I remembered John and how sweet he always was. Anything we wanted—"

"He'd try to get it for us," Mary finished.

Claire smiled. "And he was such a good listener. Brad was always interrupting me, trying to tell me how to do everything. I just"—she paused—"I just started to think about John more and more. And the more I did, the more it seemed like maybe that's where things went wrong. I was just so jealous of you, that you got to be married to him, and I had to be married to Brad. I know John was the perfect husband."

Mary raised her eyebrows. "I loved John," she said. "I still do. But he was never perfect."

"That's easy for you to say," Claire said.

"He wasn't," Mary said. "In fact, it sounds like Brad does a lot of the same things John did. John hated it when I was gone, no matter what I was doing. And he was a good listener, but he was always trying to solve my problems too. Even when I didn't want him to. It used to drive me crazy. But you know what?"

Claire shook her head warily.

Now it was Mary's voice that broke. "I'd give anything to have him back again," she said.

Claire squeezed Mary's hand.

"You don't have any idea how much you'll miss them until you can't ever get them back," Mary said. "You don't know what I'd do to hear John complain that I was coming home too late. Or to have him interrupt me and tell me how to fix something, when I'm only trying to tell him how I feel. I'd give pretty much anything in the world for that," she said.

"Oh, Mary," Claire said. "I'm sorry."

"Whatever's gone wrong with you and Brad," Mary said, "at least he's still here."

Claire shook her head. "I don't know," she said. "I think it's too late now. We've been separated for almost a year."

"But do you miss him?" Mary asked.

Claire nodded. "But I don't think he'd even want me back."

"I don't know about that," Mary said. "I talked to him when I was trying to find you."

"I know," Claire said softly.

"I think he still cares for you," she said. "He told me how hard this time has been for you."

"He did?" Claire said. "You couldn't have told me he noticed that. He was always so busy complaining and interrupting me."

"Well, he does," Mary said. "And he seemed like he wished he knew how to help."

"Sometimes I don't even know the answer to that myself," Claire said. "It's so hard to know what to ask for when you're going through something like this."

Mary knew exactly how Claire felt. After John's death, she'd been surrounded by friends and relatives, all eager to do something, anything to help her. It wasn't that she didn't think she needed any help either. In fact, she knew she did. She just didn't know how to ask for it. "I know," Mary said.

Claire met her gaze and held it. "You do, don't you?" she said.

Mary nodded.

"All right, girls," Olivia called from the door to the deck. "I think you're going to like this."

Just as they had when they were girls, Mary and Claire swung eagerly to see what treats Olivia had in store for them. The older woman gave them a bright smile over a tray loaded with the lemonade pitcher and a fresh glass, along with a heaping plate of caramel-colored brownies.

"Are those—?" Mary asked.

"Butterscotch brownies?" Claire finished.

"Well, you'll have to find out for yourselves," Olivia said, setting the tray down on the table. "Go ahead." Both Claire and Mary dived for the plate. When the first bite hit Mary's tongue, sweet and gooey, with just a hint of salt, and still warm, she gave a delighted *mmm*.

"These are absolutely delicious," she said. "I'd forgotten all about them."

"Forgotten?" Claire said. "How could you?"

"That's not what I meant," Mary said. "You're right. I should say, I'd forgotten that I could never forget them."

Claire grinned, and Mary smiled back at her for the first time since they were girls.

Then Claire dropped her gaze, almost shy, and turned to her mom. "You haven't made these in years," she said. "Why today?"

"Well," Olivia said, "I'd like to say I ran in and whipped them up once you arrived, but the fact is, I started them before either of you got here. You see, I'd been reading this wonderful book."

She pulled out Addison Hartley's most recent best seller and winked. "And there's a character in it who bakes butterscotch brownies for her daughter and her friend. Maybe it was a coincidence, but the descriptions were so eloquent that I couldn't resist searching out my own butterscotch brownie recipe."

"That Addison Hartley," Mary teased. "No one writes descriptions like him." But as she repeated Addison's name, her smile clouded with the memory of his most recent e-mail to her.

"What?" Claire asked.

Mary shook her head. "I'm afraid I might have burned my bridges with Addison Hartley, in any case," she said. "When I was trying to figure this all out, I wrote to him and said I'd seen similarities between his book and a story that happened in Ivy Bay. He wrote back and threatened me with legal action. It wasn't exactly the reception I'd been hoping for."

Claire giggled.

Mary gave her a quick look. It had been so easy to slip back into their old friendship, even after all these years. But had Claire changed, after all? What was there to laugh at in Addison Hartley's threats?

"I'm sorry," Claire said through her giggles. She waved her hand. "You don't need to worry about that."

"Well, I suppose he'll never bring a suit," Mary said. "But still, I'd hoped we might build a relationship between him and the shop." She frowned, still put out that Claire continued to think this was all a joke.

Claire finally brought herself under control. "No," she said. "I mean you *really* don't need to worry. Addison Hartley never saw your e-mails. He's never actually answered an e-mail for himself. At least not to his public account."

Mary's mind quickly put together the last pieces. "You write his e-mails," she said.

Claire nodded. "I'm sorry," she said. "I shot off that e-mail after you came up to the office. I was scared, so I thought I'd try to scare you."

"Well," Mary said, "you do a great job of it, I have to say. I was sure I was talking to a famous writer."

"My daughter is a famous writer," Olivia said with a proud smile. "It's just that nobody else knows it."

"But..." Mary was still confused about one thing. She looked at Claire. "Why would you come to the bookstore at all, if you knew I was running the event?"

Claire grew solemn again. "Part of me hoped that the Mary Fisher in the e-mail was really you, and part of me feared it. Either way, Janine can never turn down a press opportunity, and I was curious to see you. I had just sincerely hoped you wouldn't notice me. It was a pretty dumb gamble, I know." Her smile was rueful, but Mary noted a hint of gladness at the results of Claire's bet. Claire now gave a pleading look to Mary. "I know I don't have any right," she said. "Especially not after what I wrote in the last book. But can I trust you to keep the secret of who really writes Addison Hartley's stories?"

Mary smiled. For some reason, she had the exact same feeling she had as a kid, when she and Claire had stayed up all night swapping secrets. "I've kept a lot of secrets for you over the years," Mary said. "And I've never told any of them."

Claire let out a breath, visibly relieved. "Thank you," she said.

"But this one is a doozy," Mary said, joking now. "Do you think either of us would have believed forty years ago that I'd ever have to keep a secret like this for you?"

"Sometimes it's hard for me to believe, still," Claire said. "And I've been doing it for years."

"It's no surprise to me," Olivia said, nibbling on a brownie. "I always knew she'd be a big-time writer. The only thing that surprises me is that nobody knows her name."

"Mom, I've explained all that to you," Claire said. "If I put these books out under my name, nobody would read them. They read them because they think they're by the great Addison Hartley."

Olivia shook her head tartly. "Nope," she said. "They read them because they're good, my dear. And they'd be just as good with your own name on them. Even better, maybe," she added.

"Mary," Claire said. "You tell her."

Mary couldn't believe how easily they'd fallen back into the patterns of their old friendship and how comforting and familiar it felt. "Well," Mary said, "I think you're both right."

"And you," Olivia said, "I'm surprised you didn't turn out to be a politician."

"Well, my story's not over *yet*," Mary joked.

"You really think these books would sell as well if Addison Hartley's name weren't on them?" Claire asked.

"Now, I didn't say that," Mary said. "I'm not denying the power of a big-name writer's brand. But on the other hand, a big name can only take you so far if you don't have anything to offer. It sounds like Addison Hartley almost found that out for himself the hard way, before you stepped in and started writing for him. In my experience, readers don't care as much about who wrote the book as they care about whether the book is any good. And your books, my dear, are good."

"You really think so?" Claire said.

"I know it," Mary said. "I may not be an expert in much, but I'm an expert in books. Addison Hartley is one of my favorite authors. Or, I should say, you are."

Claire watched Mary as if she couldn't quite believe what she was hearing. "You're not just saying that?" she said.

"I don't tell white lies about books," Mary told her. "They're too important. I think Addison Hartley's work is much better now than it was when he began. The titles you've written for him are much stronger than anything he did on his own. And you're right, Claire. They might not have found a wide audience right away under your own name. But your writing is so good, I can only believe it would find an audience eventually, whatever name you put it out under."

"I've been telling her that for years," Olivia said.

"Well, it's nice of you to say that," Claire said.

"I'm not just saying it," Mary insisted. "I own a bookshop, remember?"

"How could I forget?" Claire laughed ruefully. She reached for another brownie. "Well, I'll tell you one thing," she said. "Whether anyone would buy my books if they knew it was me or not, it means a lot to hear that you like them, Mary. You were my first reader, you know."

"Besides me!" Olivia said.

"Besides my mom," Claire amended.

"Well, you were my favorite writer back in those days," Mary said with an impish grin. "And it turns out, you still are."

TWENTY-FIVE

———◆◆◆———

"Oh, Mary," Merilee said, turning around so she could take in the whole shop. "You've outdone yourself."

Mary smiled. "Well, you know I couldn't have made all these arrangements without Al's help."

Al smiled at Mary and his wife and shook his head. "I hardly did anything," he said. "Just a bit of advice here and there."

"He told me all about it," Merilee said. "He loved working with you to get this store going. He'd come home every day and say, 'Guess what Mary's doing now?'"

Mary smiled. "Well, we're still open," she said. "So I guess we must be doing something right."

Merilee picked up one of the books on the front table. "Oh, this looks good," she said, turning over the newest in a series of mysteries set among a colorful cast of recurring characters on the bayou in Louisiana. She settled it into the crook of her arm and glanced at Al. "I think we need to get this one," she said.

"Whatever you think, honey," Al said, nodding.

Another title caught Merilee's attention, farther down the table. "But this one looks good too," she said. "I just wish you'd opened this place in Boston," she added, smiling back at Mary. "I'd be in here every day."

Mary tried to smile back. She was glad to see her old friends. Al had worked with her for months, laying the groundwork to open the business, but he'd never seen it before. It was good to get to show him what all their calculations and spreadsheets had added up to—the books on the shelves, the light pouring through the windows, the receipts adding up in the drawer. And she was gratified by Merilee's unfeigned enthusiasm for the store. But Al and Merilee weren't here just to see the store. They had stopped by on their way from Boston so that Al could share whatever he knew about John's mysterious bankbook with Mary.

"Well," Mary said, "I know you need to get on your way later today."

"That's right," Merilee said. "Don't you two have something you needed to talk about?"

Al shifted a thick folder under his arm. Mary glanced at it nervously.

"Is there a place where we could sit down?" he asked.

Mary looked around the shop. Merilee and Al weren't her only customers. Several other people dotted the store, reading, browsing, carrying small stacks of titles over to Rebecca at the register. She and Al could retreat to the sitting area at the back, but their conversation would still be audible to customers, and this was a private matter.

"Let's head over to Bailey's Ice Cream Shop," Mary said. Mary knew it wasn't busy this time of day.

Merilee gave a happy little shrug of her shoulders. "You see, it worked," she said. She smiled at Mary's quizzical look.

"This was all part of my plan," she said. "If you two go over to the ice-cream parlor, I can stay here and find some more books."

"I like that plan," Mary said.

"You'd be amazed the lengths Merilee will go to, to get a stack of new books," Al told Mary.

"It really is a problem," Merilee said and moved off down the aisle.

The bell over the door clanged lightly behind them as Mary and Al stepped outside.

"Thanks for coming all the way here," Mary said.

"Oh, we're glad to see you," Al said. "Merilee would have taken any excuse. She misses being able to have you over for our weekend dinners."

"Is this all right?" Mary asked. She indicated one of the outdoor tables made of white filigree iron, which Tess Bailey painted bright white every year.

"Sure, fine," Al said.

"Do you want anything from inside?" Mary asked. Part of her couldn't wait to hear what Al had to say, but another part of her wanted to put it off as long as she could. As long as she didn't know for sure why John had saved such a large chunk of money without telling her, she could make up all kinds of excuses or tell herself it didn't really amount to anything. The past week had made her realize how much she'd missed him, but it had also made her realize how much a person could hide from someone else. She wanted to trust John, so much that even now she was tempted just to tell Al that whatever he had to say didn't matter; he should just transfer the money to the proper accounts, and they'd forget about it.

But that wouldn't really be trusting John, she realized. Choosing to ignore the truth because she was afraid of what it might turn out to be was actually a way of saying she didn't trust him.

The truth will set you free, Jesus had said. But sometimes the truth hurt, and sometimes freedom was frightening.

Al shook his head. "I'm fine," he said. "Unless you want anything."

Mary shook her head. She wasn't hungry. And she knew Tess well, of course, and that she wouldn't mind if Mary hung out on her tables outside without making a purchase. Plus, there was no way to put it off any longer. She took a deep breath and sat down.

Al sat down across from her and laid the thick folder on the table between them. He looked slightly uncomfortable, and he didn't seem to know where to begin. Mary's heart began to beat a little faster. Was it some kind of bad news, after all this?

"I want to start out by saying how sorry I am I didn't tell you about this earlier," Al said.

Mary tried to steel herself against the pang that shot through her at this. So it wasn't just John? Al had been keeping secrets from her too? She'd trusted him implicitly to advise her, not just about John's estate but about starting the new shop. Had he been keeping anything else from her? And why would John tell Al about the money, but not her?

Al looked at Mary with uncertainty, as if he were seeking some kind of absolution or reassurance, but Mary was doing all she could just to keep her features calm. He cleared his throat and went on.

"I just couldn't find it, to be honest," he said. "John had been talking with me about it for years. But he'd done just an excellent job of hiding it. When we were working through the estate, I always expected it to surface, but it never did. And of course, I didn't want to get your hopes up if I didn't know where it was. You never know what people do with these kinds of big sums. It was possible he had already folded it back into some kind of retirement or investment fund. So when I couldn't locate it among his papers, I assumed that must have been what he'd done."

Hopes up? Mary thought. Why should she be hopeful about her husband hiding money from her? If he'd wanted her to have it, why didn't he just put it in one of their joint accounts, where she couldn't miss it?

Al smiled. "So I'm really happy," he said, "to get to give you this. I've been waiting to do it for years, actually."

He pushed the folder across the lacy ironwork of the table toward her.

Mary looked down at it with a sense of foreboding. Her hands sat frozen in her lap.

"You can open it," Al said. "Go ahead."

Somehow, Mary lifted a hand and flipped the front of the crumpled manila folder open.

Inside was a brochure, showing a sailboat with red-and-white striped sails navigating the sparkling water beside a mountainous island.

"A boat?" Mary said and looked up at Al. "Did he buy a boat without telling me?"

Al laughed and shook his head. He lifted that brochure up to reveal the one below it, which showed a white stone house perched on a cliff massed with flowers above a dark blue sea.

"He bought a *house*?" Mary yelped.

"No, no," Al said and spread the stack, which seemed to be full of bright pictures, out on the table between them. In a single glance, Mary took in glimpses of a hillside crowded with homes painted pink and teal and pale green, a set of what seemed to be ancient stone ruins, the painted interior dome of some kind of sacred building. "He wanted to take you to Italy."

"Italy?" Mary repeated.

Al nodded. "He'd been saving for years, putting a bit away here and there. That's how I knew about it. He needed my help to keep it off the books, so it didn't show up when you looked over everything before you signed off on your taxes."

Mary shook her head. "But it's so much," she said. "Just for one trip."

"Well," Al said, "he knew you'd always wanted to go there. And he wanted nothing but the best. His plan was to take you there for six months, as soon as he retired. Or even a year, if he could swing it."

Mary rifled through the huge stack of brochures for Naples, Florence, Venice, Rome, and little towns she'd never heard of. Some locations were deep in the gorgeous countryside, and others were quaint seaside villages.

"But then he died before—" Mary said, and stopped, her heart full.

"Before he could retire," Al finished for her. He nodded, his eyes sympathetic.

Mary gazed down at a brochure someone had sent John about Venice. All the copy was in Italian. All she could understand were the beautiful pictures of the canals and the high bridges linking the age-old apartments that overlooked them.

"I was looking forward to finding this when we executed the estate," Al told her. "I'd given him advice about how to legally structure the money so it was properly taxed but not evident to you. I just didn't know where he'd actually gone and put it. I thought it might be a bright spot for you, in everything else we were doing, to know that he'd been planning this for you for so long. I actually thought it might be a good thing for you to go after all."

Now Mary had reached the bottom of the stack. Under all the brochures was a stack of hand-drawn calendars on the yellow legal paper John had used for everything, not just his work as a lawyer. The pages were crossed out and filled in and covered with notes, as John penciled in his plans of where he'd like to take her, found something else to add to the calendar, shortened one stay, lengthened another, and started over.

"But then we never found it," Al said. "I actually thought maybe he'd told you about it and you'd had to use it for medical expenses, or for something else, maybe for the kids."

"No," Mary said.

Al nodded. "Well, I know that now," he said. "But I didn't want to bring it up if it was a sore point at all. Or if he'd decided it would be better to invest it in something else."

Mary turned over a page of the itinerary John had made. It had them leaving Venice after about a week for another week in the Tuscan countryside. "No," she said again.

"If you don't mind me asking," Al said, "how did you find it?"

"It wasn't with his papers," Mary said. "It was in his high school yearbook."

Al laughed. "Well," he said, "that's one place your wife probably isn't likely to look."

Mary shook her head. "I never did," she said.

Al tapped the iron table with satisfaction. It gave a shuddery rattle. "Like I said, I'm glad to be able to give this to you now. I pulled it out from among his things when we did our first pass through his papers, thinking I'd give it to you when we found the account. When we didn't find it, I just kind of held on to it. I kept telling myself I should give it back to you someday, but it kept slipping my mind. I think it's better this way. I hope you agree."

Mary looked up at him. "I'm still stunned," she said.

Al grinned. "I can understand that," he said. "But in a good way, I hope."

Mary nodded. "Yes," she said slowly.

"Well," Al said, "I know you've got a shop to get back to, and I want to get Merilee out of there before she buys out your whole store. I've been in touch with the bank manager, and he can either add your name to the original account or simply transfer the funds into one of your other accounts. Do you have a preference?"

Mary thought for a minute. Then she fumbled in her purse and pulled out the bankbook. "It can stay in this account?" she asked.

Al took it from her and flipped briefly through the pages. "This is his original book?" he asked.

"I think so," Mary said.

Al let out a low whistle. "Look at how many years he saved for this trip. Your husband loved you, Mary," he said. "You know that?"

Mary couldn't quite get the words out just at that instant, so she simply nodded.

"You want to keep it in here, then?" Al asked.

Mary nodded again.

"Done," Al said and handed the slim blue book back to her. Even though it was no different than any other run-of-the-mill bankbook, the little book felt to Mary as if it had changed right there in her hands. Before, it had filled her with confusion and worry. Now it felt like a beautiful valentine, and she felt like a schoolgirl who just couldn't keep from opening it up and reading it again and again.

"Do you have any other questions?" Al asked.

Mary shook her head.

Al rose. "Can I walk you back to the store?" he asked.

"I think," Mary said, and stopped for a minute, not sure she could trust her own voice. "I'll just stay here for a minute," she finished.

Al nodded, his own eyes suspiciously bright. "All right," he said.

"Please tell Merilee good-bye for me," Mary said. "It was so nice to see her."

"I will," Al promised. "And you let me know if you ever need anything else."

Mary nodded.

"Anything else at all," Al said.

Mary smiled up at him. "Thanks, Al," she said.

"Anytime," Al said. He took her hand and squeezed it. Mary squeezed her old friend's hand back tightly. Then Al started off, back down the street.

Mary watched him go. When he disappeared into the shop, she looked back down at the folder. For a while, she simply opened each brochure that John had collected for her over the years. She couldn't believe their number and variety. He'd planned to take her to see collections of royal jewels, hidden grottoes, the private chapels of Italian royalty, and had tracked down an incredible array of places to stay and eat, everything from a country farmhouse where they could milk their own goats to a suite in a castle where servants filled the ancient tubs with heated water each morning. Some of the brochures dated back into other decades, with travelers wearing styles that seemed outdated even across the cultural divide. Some were in English, and others in Italian. All of them were evidence of the amount of time and energy John had spent on her, without her ever knowing it.

When she'd finished with the final brochure, she turned to the itinerary and began to read it, not just in the few glimpses she'd gotten while Al watched her, but from the beginning, as John had planned it. He'd come up with so many ideas and options that sorting through them was almost like taking several trips at once. In the first week, for instance, he'd penciled in half a dozen plans—an arrival in Rome, with a tour of the art treasures of the Vatican; or beginning the visit with a trip to Capri and then working their way north along the coast. As she read through his plans, she couldn't believe the thoughtfulness and detail in them. He hadn't meant for them to rush. His plans called for stays of a week at most destinations, and sometimes even more. And he hadn't just penciled in an approximate destination; he'd researched exactly which town to visit in Tuscany and then searched and searched until he found exactly the right villa. One of the homes he'd planned for them to stay in was at one tip of the moon on a half-moon bay, overlooking the small fishing village that sent boats out from the opposite tip. One was hidden in the Italian countryside, complete with a garden where hardy Italian roses grew on a stone arbor that dated back centuries. He'd planned a trip to the famous Blue Grotto and found a farm where the two of them would have eaten every meal with the family, who were famed in the region for both their exquisite sauces and their excellent cheese. He'd even looked into a private tour for her of the home of one of her favorite composers and made a note to make sure that he got tickets for the intimate concerts that occurred in the music room of the home whenever they established the dates when they'd actually visit.

But no matter how he tinkered with the plans for the rest of the visit, he'd always had the same vision for their final days in Italy—they'd be spent in the chambers of a former noblewoman in Venice, where the ceilings and walls had been painted with exquisite art treasures by one of the best-known artists in Italy at the time. Their last night would be spent on a gondola ride that ended with a four-course dinner at one of Venice's best restaurants. And under it all, he'd written the corny symbol that the two of them had used back in their high school days to sign the endless notes they'd passed to each other in the halls—a clumsy heart drawn around a cross, with their four initials drawn in the resulting boxes.

Mary's mind was so crowded with images of Italy that when she looked up, her eyes bright with tears, she was almost surprised to find herself on her familiar Cape street. A little clumsily, she shuffled the brochures and the itinerary all back together in the old folder and closed the manila cover. Then she turned and walked away from her store, and turned left on 6A. She continued to the place where the quiet Ivy Bay streets forked. One side ked down to the beach where they'd found Trevor the night before. The other rose up to the pine bluff. She walked up into the dappled shade of the trees, clutching the folder across her waist.

When she reached the spot where she and John used to stand to watch the water through the pine needles, she stopped. This time, when the tears came, she didn't fight them. They rolled down her face like rain on a window-pane, and she had the feeling that, like rain on glass, the tears were washing away something that had made it hard for her to see. The last few weeks had made her question what she thought she knew about John, to dig up memories she'd hidden away to protect herself from the sting of losing him. Ironically, the secret John had been keeping from her wasn't a betrayal but a gift. But even more important than the sheaf of brochures for Italian villas were the memories of her life with John that now crowded into her mind—the feel of his high school varsity jacket numbers on her cheek as she leaned against his shoulder, the moments they'd been able to steal when the kids were young and they'd dropped them off with Mary's parents and then come up here for a bit of time alone, the day they'd come up here and just stood together in silence after they dropped Elizabeth off at college, leaving them with an empty nest. All those memories jumbled together and blended now, along with glimpses and images of John: his smile; his serious, listening expression; the goofy jokes he liked to make when his shyness wore off and he really felt he knew someone.

Mary wasn't sure how she'd describe it. It wasn't as if John was right there in the pine bluff with her. His loss was still real, and she knew the difference between having him there and missing him. But now the memories of him were a comfort to her rather than a pain. And even though she knew he wasn't there, she didn't feel like he was completely gone.

She smiled to herself and shook her head, looking out through the familiar branches at the distant horizon.

Thank You, she thought. The words were small, but they carried a lot—both a prayer to God and a last message for her husband, whom she'd spoken with here so many times before.

TWENTY-SIX

◆◆◆

"M rs. Fisher!" Ashley crowed as she burst through the door of the shop. Her normal self-possession had been completely replaced by an expression of transfiguration.

Mary glanced around for some clue as to the source of her delight and settled almost immediately on the ice-cream cone dripping in her hand. It looked suspiciously familiar, with the dark chocolate swirl and the telltale white chips of pretzel in the chocolate-covered pretzel flavor Mary had dreamed up for Bailey's that month.

"This is absolutely delicious," Ashley said. "Fantastic."

Mary smiled at the little girl's precocious use of her formidable vocabulary as Trevor came barreling in the door behind her. He didn't make any comments on the matching ice-cream cone he also clutched tightly in his own small fingers, but he took decisive action, dispatching a large bite of it immediately after walking in the door.

Rebecca and Pastor Miles came through the door hot on the heels of the two youngsters.

"Ashley," she said. "Didn't I say we were going to finish those outside?"

"Trevor," Pastor Miles tried, reaching for his grandson's arm.

"I was just complimenting Mrs. Fisher on her flavor," Ashley said. She turned back to Mary. "Chocolate-covered pretzels are my favorite. And this is even better than that."

"Well, thank you," Mary said.

"We went to an ice-cream store in Boston once that was supposed to have new flavors," Ashley went on. "But all their new flavors were things like green tea or vanilla with extra flecks. But this has chocolate in it. And real pretzels."

"I helped mix those in myself," Mary said. "We did it at the last minute, so they'd stay nice and crispy."

"They're crispy!" Ashley confirmed happily.

"I'm really sorry about this," Rebecca said. "I told her no food in the shop. We were going to finish it on the way down, before we came to work. Weren't we?" she asked Ashley.

"It was just so delicious," Ashley said. "I had to tell her."

"They're right," Pastor Miles said. For the first time, Mary realized that he was working busily away at his own scoop of her new flavor, atop an old-fashioned sugar cone. She smiled. "I'm glad to hear that," she said.

"Honey," Rebecca said firmly. "Outside."

Reluctantly, Ashley followed her mother out the door. "We'll be back in a few minutes," Rebecca said over her shoulder.

"Take your time," Mary called.

Pastor Miles and Trevor filed out behind them.

Mary looked down at the catalog she had been flipping through, choosing new titles and reorders for the coming week.

The bell over the door dinged again. She looked up, expecting to see one of the children, fresh off a new escape from Rebecca and Pastor Miles. But the new visitor was full-sized. Mary was struck with the same sense of instant recognition and strangeness that she'd had when she first saw her at the bookstore a few weeks ago.

"Claire," she said, a smile stealing over her face. When she'd left Olivia's lakeside bungalow, she and Claire had promised to keep in touch, and Mary had told Claire she would be welcome at the store anytime, but that had been weeks ago, and she hadn't heard from Claire since. She'd thought about calling her several times since then, but she hadn't wanted to push herself on her old friend. "I'm so glad to see you."

Claire gave a smile that was almost shy and shifted a thick manila envelope in her arms. "You must think I'm terrible," she said. "I wanted to call earlier, but I was caught up with a few things."

"Well, it's only been a few weeks since we last talked," Mary said. "So I guess that's better than forty years."

Claire smiled. Mary's joke seemed to give her courage. "I talked with Brad," she said.

"Did you?" Mary asked. "How did that go?"

"We're still talking," she said. "It's nice. It had been so long since we really did that."

"I'm glad," Mary said.

"Me too," Claire said. She laid the envelope down on the counter between them. "Anyway, I brought you something. I thought you might like to see the new Addison Hartley book before anyone else does. Including Addison Hartley."

Mary looked down at the manuscript. She had a brief thrill of the anticipation she always felt at the mention of

Addison Hartley's name, but she also felt hesitation. Reading his last book had been a painful experience for her, and she wasn't sure she wanted to repeat it.

Some of this must have shown on her face. "It's nothing like the last one," Claire said quickly.

"Are there new characters?" Mary asked. That was the only way she could imagine wanting to pick up again where the other book had left off.

Claire shook her head. "No," she said. "But there are a few surprises. The detective's next story takes him to Boston, where he meets the character who was based on you. It turns out that she holds a big piece to the puzzle he was trying to solve in the last book. And while they work together, he learns about things from her point of view and realizes how much John actually loves her."

Claire had slipped from talking about the characters in the book to talking about Mary and John in real life, but Mary didn't correct her. "I'd like to read that," she said. "But what happens to the other woman?"

Claire smiled. "The two of them patch things up late in the book, and you find out that she's met another man in the meantime. It's a real relationship for her, not just the dreams she had made up about John."

She looked down. "Sometimes that's harder than the dream," she said. "But the man she's met is a really good man, and he sticks with her through it."

"I'm glad," Mary said.

Claire looked up again. "I ran the idea past Addison before I started," she said. "He hasn't seen the pages yet, but he loves the idea. He thinks it'll add a whole new layer to the books: introducing a new point of view on the last book each time we write a new one."

"We?" Mary asked.

Claire raised her eyebrows and gave a wry smile. "Well, that's how I talk about it with him, anyway," she said.

"You want to know what I think?" Mary asked.

"Do I have a choice?" Claire said.

They both smiled. This had been a standard joke between the two of them, and they both remembered their part, even decades later.

"Well," Mary said, "I've always wanted to share great books with the world. But now that I know what a good writer you are, I don't feel like I'll have done my job until people know your name, instead of Addison Hartley's."

Claire sighed. "Do you really think anyone would be interested in me, if they didn't think my name was Addison Hartley?"

"I know I would," Mary said. "And I'm not just anyone off the street. I don't know if you realize this or not, but I happen to own a bookstore."

Claire laughed. "Well, I guess that's one down," she said.

"The first one," Mary said. "I want the first copies shipped."

"All right," Claire said. "We'll make that a deal. You'll get the first copies if I ever come out with something under my own name."

"*When* you come out with something under your own name," Mary insisted.

Claire shrugged, but she smiled. "We'll see," she said.

"Yes, we will," Mary said. She picked up the envelope from the counter between them and laid it on the desk beside her. "Thank you for this," she said. "It means a lot."

"See what you think," Claire said, gesturing for Mary to open the bag.

Mary hesitated. Did Claire really mean for her to read it right there, in front of her? From the weight of it, the manuscript was several hundred pages long.

"Right now?" she asked.

"Just a page or two," Claire said.

Mary slid the thick stack of papers from her bag and set the manuscript on top of it. Then she began to flip through the pages: the word count and identifying information, the title, the author page.

When she saw her own name, she froze. Then her eyes focused, and she was able to read clearly: *For Mary, my oldest fan and friend.*

"You dedicated the book to me?" Mary asked.

Claire nodded. "I've never asked Addison for anything before," she said. "But I told him he had to agree to this, or I wouldn't give him the manuscript."

Mary circled the counter and enveloped her old friend in a bear hug. "Thank you so much," she said. "But I'm even happier to have my old friend back."

"Me too," Claire said, her voice muffled by the hug.

The bell over the door dinged. The two of them looked up to see a family of summer visitors come in: a mom, a dad, and two teenage daughters.

"Do you have any books on nautical history?" the father asked, as his wife and daughters scattered among the other shelves.

"I should let you go," Claire said.

Mary nodded. "But not for long," she said.

Claire smiled. "No," she said and started for the door.

"Hello," Mary greeted the father of the group. "I do have some nautical history here, if you don't mind a bit of mystery too."

"Well, let's see what you've got," the man said.

As Mary led the customer through the stacks, she glanced over at the door. Claire was moving toward it just like she had a few weeks before, at Addison Hartley's reading where Mary had first caught sight of her. But this time, instead of slipping out alone into the night, Claire turned back as she put her hand on the knob.

She caught Mary's eye, and both of them smiled.

ABOUT THE AUTHOR

Vera Dodge is a lover of books and the Cape and is delighted to blend both her passions in the series Secrets of Mary's Bookshop. She grew up in small towns in the Midwest.

A CONVERSATION WITH VERA DODGE

◦———◦◆◦———◦

Q: *What draws you to Mary's Bookshop as a writer?*

A: I love books, and I love Cape Cod. It's not so much a question of what draws me, as "what could keep me away?" There's not much I like better than curling up with a good book on a windy beach, or in a snug vacation cottage. And when I write a Mary's Bookshop mystery, I don't just get to while away a pleasant afternoon on vacation—I get to live and think and solve a mystery in the world of Mary's bookshop and Ivy Bay.

Q: *If you could open a bookshop anywhere, where would it be? And what kind of bookshop would it be?*

A: I'd love to open a bookshop in Detroit, near where I grew up in Michigan. Instead of selling the big books of the moment that everyone knows about, I'd like to connect readers to two other kinds. First, I'd like to reintroduce them to great classics that they may have forgotten about, or even been intimidated to start. Second, I'd like to help them find hidden treasures among all the great books that are out today—titles that are just a little bit off the beaten path, but offer something really special.

Q: *What do you hope readers will gain from the books you write in this series?*

A: We might not all be dealing with missing persons cases, but we all have mysteries we need to solve and truths we need to work to find out. I hope readers of Mary's Bookshop will gain the courage to solve the mysteries in their own lives. I also hope they'll be inspired by Mary's ongoing conversation with God to start or continue conversations of their own with Him. In some ways, faith is the biggest mystery of all, and in others, it provides the answers to all our other mysteries.

Q: *Who do you think would win in a mystery-solving contest: Miss Marple or Sherlock Holmes?*

A: With two of the best detectives of all time, I'm not sure that's a mystery anyone has the answer to. But I'd love to read a story where the two of them work together. I think it'd be hilarious to watch Sherlock Holmes have to navigate Miss Marple's old-fashioned manners and see how she'd whip him into shape. And I know that if they teamed up, nobody could beat them!

Q: *What is your favorite mystery book/author?*

A: I'm fond of Dorothy Sayers. She writes very smart, taut mysteries, but was a woman of deep faith. It's hard to pick a favorite of among her stories, because she couldn't seem to write a bad one, so I always like to tell people they can pick up any book of hers they find and expect to be delighted. I also love Wilkie Collins, who wrote some of the first mysteries ever in the English language. His books are full of seaside caves and mistaken identity, and compelling, delightful characters.

Q: *Have you ever had to solve a mystery? Tell us about it!*

A: One of the places I feel like a detective is when I'm doing research on the history of my own family. I comb through old documents and pictures, search the Internet, and even occasionally call up strangers. In some ways, learning the whole story of your family is a big mystery that'll never be fully solved. But each new piece I learn teaches me a little bit more about the struggles and the ingenuity of the people who came before me and gives me encouragement and strength to live my own life.

Q: *Mary loves to make new ice-cream flavors and enjoys reading mystery novels. What are some of your hobbies?*

A: Eating ice cream could actually be described as a "hobby" for me. My great-grandfather actually made his living as an ice-cream maker, and perhaps as a result, my family celebrates just about everything with ice cream. Last Christmas, we even bought six different kinds of peppermint stick ice cream to establish, once and for all, which one was the best. And of course, it doesn't have to be Christmas for us to get ice cream. We'll take just about any excuse.

CHOCOLATE-COVERED PRETZEL ICE CREAM

---◆◆---

1½ cups chocolate-covered pretzels
(store-bought is fine!)
1 cup whole milk
¾ cup granulated sugar
2 cups heavy cream
1 tablespoon pure vanilla extract

Chop the pretzels into small chunks. Set aside. In a medium-sized bowl, use a hand-held mixer to combine the milk and granulated sugar until the sugar is dissolved. This will take from one to two minutes. Stir in the heavy cream and vanilla. Carefully add the pretzel pieces. Pour mixture into the bowl of an ice-cream mixer and churn according to manufacturer's directions. Transfer the ice cream to an airtight container and place in freezer for about two hours.

FROM THE GUIDEPOSTS ARCHIVES

———◆◆◆———

Twice a year Gary and I took the kids and made the 1,200-mile trip up from Alabama to my native New England to visit my folks, crowding into their cozy little house on Cape Cod. I loved those trips. One year my daughter, Michelle, gave me a ceramic cottage that looked like one of the saltboxes on the Cape, with cedar trees on either side and a quaint old rowboat out front. "So you can feel close even when you're in Alabama," she said. I gave Michelle a big kiss and a hug in return.

We all got older. I worried about Mom's worsening diabetes. Dad had a heart attack. Suddenly, they were facing a move to the nursing home.

"I can't let that happen," I told Gary. "Let's move up north and take care of your parents," he said. Our kids were grown by then. It was possible.

We put our things in storage and moved into my parents' basement on Cape Cod, but it wasn't quite the same. The vacation cottage was way too small for the four of us to live full-time.

Gary and I had to find a place of our own. The houses we saw were too expensive or too far from my parents. I tried to take comfort in my favorite Scripture, from Jeremiah: "For I know the plans I have for you, plans for well-being and not for trouble, to give you a future and a hope." But the longer we looked, the more I wondered what lay ahead for us. For my parents.

One summer day the Realtor showed us a saltbox house down the road from Mom and Dad's. It was lovely. Even better, I had a tremendously warm feeling about it, like those old vacations. I couldn't explain it.

What a relief to finally unpack our things! They'd been in storage so long, it was like seeing them for the very first time. Except when I unwrapped the ceramic cottage my daughter gave me. I turned it over in my hands. The sloping roof, the shutters...it was an exact replica of our new house, right down to the cedars and the quaint rowboat the previous owners had left on the lawn. A future and a hope. It had been there all along.

Ann-Marie Walker
Mashpee, Massachusetts

SECRETS *of* MARY'S BOOKSHOP
Reading the Clues
by CHARLOTTE CARTER

From Mary Fisher's perspective, there was nothing more exciting than opening a carton of new books, one like the UPS man had just delivered to her bookshop. She loved the scent and texture of the paper as she rifled through the pages. She supposed that was why she'd spent much of her working life as a librarian and now owned Mary's Mystery Bookshop in Ivy Bay on Cape Cod.

It was August, and the height of tourist season in Ivy Bay. During the summer, she'd become inspired by how history and mystery often collided, so she'd established a theme for the month of August at her store. Across her front window she had displayed a banner: IVY BAY—HISTORY, ROMANCE, INTRIGUE…MYSTERY. Ever since she put up the sign, sales had been so brisk that she just this morning had to order more books.

The sweet scent of freshly baked cupcakes hung in the air. Susan must be baking again. Mary tried not to sample treats from Sweet Susan's Bakery next door too often, but after smelling them all day, it was sometimes all she could do to resist. She distracted herself by shelving the books she'd received in their respective sections, leaving some for the display table in the front, and stepped back to admire her work.

"What do you think, Gus?" she asked her gray cat, who was snoozing near the front counter. He briefly opened one eye, then closed it again.

She decided that was a sign of approval.

The chime over the front door tinkled, and Mary's sister Betty rushed into the shop as though she was being chased by a rabid dog. Her cheeks were bright with exertion, she was breathing hard, and her lightweight cardigan flapped open. Even her blonde hair, the same shade it had been when she was a young woman, looked disheveled.

"What is it? What's wrong, Bets?" A trickle of fear sped down Mary's spine. Had someone been hurt? Was the house on fire?

Even Gus stood, arched his back and stretched, his nap disrupted by Betty's arrival.

Betty scanned the shop as if making sure the coast was clear. There were no customers in the shop, so Betty began. "It's terrible. I don't know what to do!" Betty's words spilled out in a staccato voice, which was very uncharacteristic of her typically calm, even dignified demeanor. "I called Evan at his office but he was out in the field with a client looking over a building site."

"*Sh*, now, take it easy. I'm sure your son will call you back as soon as he can." Mary's sister, who was two years older, wasn't usually so excitable and rarely called her son in a panic.

And given her rheumatoid arthritis, she seldom ran anywhere, but she'd obviously hurried to the shop. She clutched a large brown mailing envelope in her hand. "Come sit down and catch your breath. Then tell me what has happened."

Mary led her sister to the pair of overstuffed chairs in the back of the shop where customers could browse through books at their leisure. Once she had Betty seated, Mary dashed into the back room to get her a glass of water and put on some water for tea.

"Now then..." Mary sat in the chair next to her sister. "Take a little drink and tell me what happened."

Betty's hand shook as she took a sip. She swallowed and exhaled. "I'm being sued," she said, her voice calmer but no less anxious.

Mary sat back and blinked. "Sued? By whom? And why?"

"A process server came to the door no more than an hour ago. He served me these papers." She handed Mary the envelope. "Daniel Hopkins is the one suing me. He claims the Hopkins family owns—" She put her hand over her heart. "He says the gristmill belongs to the Hopkins family."

"The *Emerson* gristmill?" Mary tried to imagine why anyone would say such a thing about the mill that had stood on the edge of town since sometime in the 1600s. She and Betty had played there as children during summer visits to their grandparents, even before Betty had married Edward Emerson, a member of one of the founding families of Ivy Bay. Now the only Emersons left in town were Betty and Edward's sister, Eleanor Blakely, the self-proclaimed family matriarch. Betty's son Evan still lived in town, but all the other Emersons had moved away.

"I couldn't make sense out of those papers the court sent me." She shook an arthritic finger at the envelope. "Edward always told me the Emersons had owned the gristmill since the day it was built. They were among the earliest residents of Ivy Bay. Since Edward passed away, I've faithfully paid the property tax every year. And Evan has even been talking to a contractor about restoring the old place. A considerable expense, but we both think it's the right thing to do. Why would Daniel say it isn't ours?"

Mary recalled a passage in Leviticus 6 where the Lord warned Moses about people stealing or extorting others for their property and how they must make restitution in full plus a fifth more. Betty had certainly not stolen the gristmill from the Hopkins family, and she didn't believe Betty's late husband Edward had either.

Hearing the pot whistle, Mary returned to the back room, filled the teapot, put milk in a pitcher and carried these and cups out front to Betty.

While the tea was steeping, Mary pulled the thick sheaf of paper from the envelope, adjusted her glasses, and skimmed the contents. The suit claimed that, in 1792, Isaac Emerson sold the gristmill to James Hopkins for the price of five British pounds.

She lifted her head. 1792! Gracious but that was going a long way back in history. Why was the sale and ownership of the mill just now being disputed?

"Do you have any idea what five British pounds in 1792 would be worth today?"

Betty shook her head. Her breathing had slowed to normal, and she had regained control of herself. "Probably a lot more than it was then. Evan thinks the property itself is worth quite a lot even though the mill is in disrepair." Still agitated, Betty ran a fingertip along the fabric seam on the arm of the chair.

"Sounds like there may be greed at the bottom of this suit." Mary leaned back in her chair to read the legal papers more thoroughly. "Do you have the original deed for the property?"

"I suppose it's possible, but I don't know that there ever was a deed, per se. Edward's ancestors built the mill so long ago, the area was part of the royal charter given to the Massachusetts Bay Company."

Mary appreciated her sister's depth of knowledge about the history of Ivy Bay, but for the moment she was more worried about Betty's very contemporary problem. "I'm trying to think how to counter this suit. Surely there must be some sort of a record *if* the mill was sold as Hopkins apparently claims."

"All I know is that what I do have is records of paying property taxes for years and years. The town certainly believes we own the mill. As far as I know, there's nothing in the file Edward kept that gives any suggestion the mill was ever sold." She sounded offended by even the mere suggestion that the mill didn't belong to the Emersons. That was understandable. So what evidence was the suit based on?

From the paperwork, it looked like Marc Dougher, an attorney here on the Cape, had filed the suit for Hopkins. Mary wondered what sort of a man he was.

The chime over the door announced the arrival of a customer, a youngish woman dressed in shorts, halter top, and flip-flops.

"Hello," Mary said. "Is there anything I can help you find?"

"No, I'll just browse, if that's okay."

"Of course. Let me know if I can help in any way."

Mary turned back to Betty and lowered her voice. "Tell you what, after dinner tonight let's go through what records you do have. I'm sure there's a way to put this suit to rest in a hurry."

Betty squeezed Mary's hand. "I'm sure, too. Being served with papers caught me totally by surprise."

"I can sure understand that. Speaking of which, what do you know about Daniel Hopkins?" Although Jill Sanderson was in her prayer group, Mary hadn't ever met the man who was her grandfather-in-law. Jill had expressed concern about Daniel's temperament since he'd moved in with her and her husband.

"Not much. I see him occasionally around town, but the Emersons have never been friends with the Hopkins. I do know that they're a family of commercial fishermen and they live on the other side of town." She pursed her lips together and her brows lowered. "I don't want to speak unkindly of anyone, but from what I've seen, Daniel Hopkins is an angry man. I've always avoided him."

Mary nodded, encouraging Betty to go on.

"Edward didn't have anything to do with the Hopkinses, either. I do remember he mentioned a couple of times something about a feud between the two families."

"What was the feud about?"

"He didn't know or wouldn't say. And you know how these stories start up and get distorted over time. Edward believed in live and let live. He had no interest in pursuing whatever it was that had come between the two families generations ago."

As Mary slipped the papers back into the envelope, she wondered if Betty's sister-in-law Eleanor knew more about the feud than Edward had. "Apparently Daniel Hopkins isn't into live and let live."

"I really can't let him take the mill away from us, Mar. It's such a big part of the Emerson family history. Edward was so proud—"

"Bets, try not to worry. I'm sure we'll find a way to stop this ridiculous suit."

Forcing a brave smile, Betty nodded.

Taking a sip of tea, Mary considered the situation. She realized in order to defend against the suit, someone would have to prove Isaac Emerson did not sell the gristmill to James Hopkins or anyone else. No easy task considering the sale was supposed to have taken place two hundred and twenty-five years ago.

And proving something didn't happen was far harder than proving it did.

The young woman who had been browsing waved good-bye and went out the door.

"Maybe we should go talk with Mr. Hopkins. At least to find out what he bases his claim of ownership on," Mary suggested, her voice filled with caring. Betty's face still looked troubled, but Mary could tell her sister was comforted to have Mary by her side.

Betty shook her head. "I'm so upset, I'm not sure I could even be civil to the man. My late husband and his family were honorable people. How dare Hopkins accuse them of being anything but? As much as I want to know what's going on, I don't think I'd have anything productive to say to him. I'm sure Evan will hire an attorney to represent us. Let's wait to see what the attorney advises."

That might be wise, Mary mused. But she had learned that it was often possible to solve a problem by having an honest, open conversation in order to get to the crux of the matter.

"You know what?" She stood and put the tea things back on the tray. "It's a lovely day, and I could use some exercise. Let's take a walk. Maybe it will clear our heads."

"Take a walk?" Betty's forehead wrinkled. "I suppose that's a good idea. I could definitely use a breather."

Mary carried the tray into the back room and retrieved a light jacket. Despite the heat of the day, there was always a breeze blowing off the ocean.

"I haven't been out to see that old mill since I moved back to town," Mary said. "Maybe we'll see something that triggers an idea about how to prove you own the mill."

Betty stood. "That's a good idea. But I should warn you, it's really run-down. Evan thinks it's unsafe."

Even though Rebecca Mason, Mary's one employee, was off for the day, she wasn't worried about closing the shop for a bit. That was the beauty of owning your own business anyway. She flipped the sign on the door to Shut. Letting Betty out first, she locked up behind them.

As they walked, a light breeze coming off the ocean fluttered Mary's gray curls. She reflected not for the first time on how much she loved the little town of Ivy Bay. On the north side of the Cape, it was separated from the mainland

by a channel. Two bridges provided access to Ivy Bay with
its charming stores and shops and Victorian homes, some of
which were on the historical registry.

"Evan was looking at the mill recently. He wants to either
restore the mill or tear it down because of its poor condition.
In fact, the town may insist on us doing something soon.
But you see…" Betty's voice caught. "This is all my fault. In
one of my last conversations with Edward before he passed
away he told me he was sorry he hadn't done something with
the mill. Made it something more that all of his descendants
could be proud of. You remember that we were at the mill
when he proposed to me."

"Yes, I remember. I thought it was very romantic of him."

"And then when he was dying, I promised—"

She rubbed her sister's back to soothe her. "It's all right,
Bets. We'll make it all right."

They walked past Meeting House Grocers, which had
recently become one of Mary's favorite places in town, and up
Meeting House Road. Cars passed by on the street, and
pedestrians were strolling along, peeking in shop windows.

"Evan was going to get something started, and then
he got so busy. I couldn't ask him to drop everything to take
care of the gristmill. But I should have done something before
now. Evan has asked a contractor to take a look at the mill
and give him some cost estimates."

Evan, an architect, lived nearby and had a busy life with a
wife and two daughters. Even so, he had taken over some of
Edward's business interests after his father's death.

"Evan is doing the right thing and so are you." Betty's
emotional response to the lawsuit had surprised Mary until

she'd learned of Edward's final comments about the mill, her nostalgic memories, and the promise Betty had made. No wonder her sister didn't want to lose the mill and fail her late husband.

Betty exhaled and pulled herself together.

Once out of the business district, houses appeared, many of them separated by white picket fences. When the road crossed over a marsh, Mary stopped and held up a finger to get Betty's attention. "Do you hear that? Sounds like we have some saltmarsh sparrows." One of the stocky gray birds flitted so fast from one low-growing plant to another that it was hard to see the yellow markings on his face.

"They are the busiest little birds. They wear me out just watching them flit around."

As they turned the corner, the mill came into sight. Water for the gristmill ran from a pretty pond down a raceway past the mill to turn the waterwheel. Unfortunately, the aging wheel was now tilted at an odd angle, which prevented it from turning on its axis.

Sturdy gray rocks quarried from the mainland formed the mill's foundation. Someone had chiseled "1667" into the keystone block.

Wood siding on the building, weathered gray by two hundred years of sun and rain, showed signs of decay and the shutters for the windows were missing.

The mill had been used for hundreds of years, but it had stopped operating in the 1930s. Edward's father moved the grain production to the new commercial baking facility he opened in New Bedford after the worst of the Depression was over. From there, he began delivering bread daily to grocery stores on the Cape. The company eventually expanded to a broader market, distributing specialty breads and rolls throughout much of New England.

Edward had followed in his father's footsteps, becoming the CEO of the company when his father retired, but the family had always made their home in Ivy Bay, and the mill had always been a part of their family history.

They approached the mill slowly. Years ago, someone had placed two water-worn logs across the raceway for a bridge. Mary scurried across, and Betty followed more slowly.

"Seems to me there was an easier way to get here when we were children," Betty commented.

"Or maybe we were both more agile back then."

"Speak for yourself, little sister."

"I fear age is going to creep up on us whether we want it to or not." Mary laughed and slipped her arm around Betty's waist, hugging her.

"You remember when we were kids and came back to stay with Grandma during the summer?" Betty asked. "The older boys would try to scare us about a ghost that haunted the old place. One time a boy made such a scary noise, you went running out of there screaming."

Mary twisted her lips into a wry smile. She had all but forgotten that embarrassing incident. She couldn't have been more than seven or eight. "It was months after that before I built up enough courage to go back up to the mill."

"The boys swore there were snakes inside the mill, and a buried treasure left there by pirates. And there was something about colonial soldiers hiding there while a whole regiment of redcoats marched by."

"What grand imaginations we all had as children," Mary said with a laugh. "I remember one time some of us used the mill as a fort. We piled up grass-and-dirt clods. When anyone approached, we'd bombard them through the windows."

Although the mill door was still in place, it hung crookedly from old metal hinges. They eased their way into the dim interior, the small windows admitting little light even on a sunny day. The huge four-thousand-pound buhrstone—Mary recalled hearing it was originally from France—looked just as it always had, ready for a load of corn to be brought in.

Mary remembered learning as a child that to make cornmeal, the miller would haul the corn up to the second level and pour it down a shoot. The two matching stones, driven by the waterwheel in the race, would grind it into a gritty product, probably accompanied by a great deal of noise.

During the early years of America, almost every town had a gristmill. Local villagers would bring their corn to the mill to be ground for a fee. If the person didn't raise his own corn, he'd buy cornmeal from the miller. Everyone needed cornmeal, so the miller did business with just about everyone in town. The Emerson who had built this mill had been wise. It had provided the foundation for the family's later wealth.

"I should have brought a flashlight." Mary walked gingerly across the dusty wooden floor. "Be careful. Some of the floorboards look rotten to me."

Betty stepped slowly back toward the door. "I don't think it's safe to walk around in here, Mary. We've seen the place, now let's—"

Mary let out a cry as her foot broke through an aged floorboard.

"Mary!"

"I'm all right." The end of the rotten wood next to the foundation had given way and scratched her leg, but she hadn't fallen more than six inches. Thank the good Lord.

Feeling foolish, since she was the one who had warned Betty to be careful, she shook her head. Hoping to release her foot from the grasp of the rotting wood, she grabbed hold of the end of the plank that had snared her and lifted. The board squeaked and groaned. Then the rotten wood snapped about three feet from where she was standing.

"This place really is rotting," she said. "No wonder Evan wants to either restore the mill or tear it down. It's a lawsuit waiting to happen." Which made Mary wonder why anyone would want to sue for the right to own a piece a property that would be a money pit.

"I hate the thought that some children might be playing in here and get hurt," Betty said.

"If that happened, you and Evan might want to agree that it's owned by Hopkins and let it be his problem."

Betty giggled. "Sometimes you can be very devious, Mary."

Maybe so, but right now Mary's shoe was caught by something under the floorboards. A rock, or perhaps some leftover construction material.

With one leg in the hole, she knelt on the other knee and reached down to feel for whatever was pressing on her ankle and foot. Her fingers brushed something slick.

She tensed. On second thought, she might not actually want to know what was under the floorboards. But her innate curiosity—

"Really, Mary, I think we ought to get out of here before one of us is seriously injured. Those overhead beams don't look all that sturdy to me."

Mary chose to ignore her sister as her hand closed around the slick object. It was not all that big. She felt what she believed was the spine of a slender book. Interesting...

Carefully, she pulled the package out of the hole.

"What's that?" Betty asked.

"Some kind of book, wrapped in oilskin." She set it down next to her and reached her hand back into the hole. "Give me a minute to see if there's anything else down here."

"You'd better hope it's not a bed of snakes."

Mary shuddered. Her sister would have to mention snakes. Worst case, she might find a hognose snake under the mill. It was an ugly creature, but it was harmless, as were all the snakes on Cape Cod. Or so Mary had been told as a child.

Her hand closed around something hard and cold. Smooth like a bone. Oh dear...

Grimacing, she pulled her find out of the hole.

Not a snake, she thought gratefully. But whatever it was, it was covered in dirt and grime. She rubbed her finger over one end of the object. A white spot appeared.

Not a bone either, she realized, rubbing more dirt away.

"What have you got?"

"I'm not sure." Holding the white object, she struggled out of the hole and found more secure footing. Then she picked up the book. Interesting. As far as Mary knew, oilskin hadn't been used as a wrapping in many years. Her heart rate picked up. "These items are old."

"Old? Antique? Show me." Betty took a few more tentative steps farther into the mill.

"Let's go outside where we can see better."

"Good idea," Betty said with a relieved laugh.

Glad to be out of the gloom of the mill, Mary studied the unfamiliar object that she thought might be a bone. Maybe six inches long, it weighed no more than six or eight ounces.

Betty peered at Mary's find, and Mary could see her anticipation rising at the possibility of having found an antique. "Let's wash all that dirt off in the pond. It's probably a piece of some old pottery."

It didn't feel like pottery to Mary—not quite heavy enough—but she agreed they needed to get rid of the dirt.

At the pond, she knelt and swished the thing in the water. Layers of dirt melted away, revealing a porcelain doll standing on a chipped porcelain base. Around the base were the words *Only the Very Best* painted in a bright blue script.

"What a pretty little girl," Betty said. "A sweet face and a charming bonnet. It must be a child's doll."

"Maybe." Looking for the maker's mark, Mary turned the doll upside down. The base and doll were hollow. But she couldn't see an indication of who had made the doll.

Handing the doll to Betty, Mary carefully unwrapped the oilskin package. It wasn't a book, exactly, but rather some sort of bookkeeping ledger with page after page filled with odd markings.

Standing, Mary said, "What do you make of this?"

"*Hmm*, it looks a lot like the record book Edward used to keep track of our expenses. Of course, he changed to using his computer years ago."

The oilskin had kept the binding and pages in good condition, but the notations were indecipherable as far as Mary could tell. Just from the florid handwriting on the title page, she thought the ledger must be old. On each page, there were rows and columns, symbols of some sort. On the left, there were tally marks and what looked to be box-shaped markings across the rows.

She had no idea what it meant. She would have to spend some time studying it to try and learn more about it.

But why had the ledger and the doll been left under the floorboards? Had they been hidden for some reason? Or simply tossed away?

Could they possibly lead to answers about the ownership of the mill?

A Note from the Editors

◆◆◆

We hope you enjoy Secrets of Mary's Bookshop, created by Guideposts Books and Inspirational Media. In all of our books, magazines and outreach efforts, we aim to deliver inspiration and encouragement, help you grow in your faith, and celebrate God's love in every aspect of your daily life.

Thank you for making a difference with your purchase of this book, which helps fund our many outreach programs to the military, prisons, hospitals, nursing homes and schools. To learn more, visit GuidepostsFoundation.org.

We also maintain many useful and uplifting online resources. Visit Guideposts.org to read true stories of hope and inspiration, access OurPrayer network, sign up for free newsletters, join our Facebook community, and follow our stimulating blogs.

To order your favorite Guideposts publications, go to ShopGuideposts.org, call (800) 932-2145 or write to Guideposts, PO Box 5815, Harlan, Iowa 51593.